ALSO BY JESSICA LEE SHEPPARD

Titles available in The Darkness and Light Saga

(in reading order)

Descending Into Darkness

Bound By Darkness

THE ADVENTURES OF

2

IZZY ADAMS

BOUND BY DARKNESS

JESSICA LEE SHEPPARD

SHEPLEN
PRESS
PUBLISHING COMPANY

Book Two of The Darkness and Light Saga

Second Edition July 2025

Sheplen Press Publishing Company

ISBN (ebook): 978-1-0695151-2-4
ISBN (print, paperback): 978-1-7380280-6-1
ISBN (print, hardcover): 978-1-0695151-1-7
ISBN (audio): 978-1-7380280-6-1

Book Cover Design by ebooklaunch.com

To my parents, for always believing in me
and encouraging my love of writing.
Thank you.

Contents

Author's Note

Please note, as I am a Canadian author, the spelling throughout this book adheres to Canadian English conventions, which may differ slightly from American or British English.

PROLOGUE

Flames engulfed the Kingdom of Hellfire. Towering bonfires reached skyward, blanketing the castle in suffocating heat. Chained to the gates, Orbistian souls howled in agony. The fire's roar swallowed their cries. Within the castle's cool stone walls, the searing air mattered little, especially to those shielded from the dark magic's touch.

Inside, a waif-like woman with wispy hair moved down the shadowy hall. She carried a heavy tray, the goblets on it filled to the brim with molten lava. Despite the surrounding chaos, not a single muscle in her face twitched. Her gaze remained distant.

She weaved through the crowd of dancing creatures. They writhed like shadows under a flickering flame, and the air was thick with the heat from their bodies. Scaly, damp skin brushed against her as she passed through the room.

Luminescent spirits thrashed in shackles along the stone walls. They cast a faint light on her path as she moved toward a cluster of squat, puffy-lipped men.

"It's a game-changer," one squeaked.

Another man, eyes glinting with zeal, grabbed a drink from her tray. "A spell to torture souls! I never dreamed we'd be this fortunate," he said. He gulped the boiling liquid, smoke curling from his ears. "A toast to the brilliant King of Midas," he continued, lifting his goblet in tribute.

The squeaky demon spat at the ground near his companion's feet. "Brilliant? Explain the fiasco at the Siege of Sparklafex then," he said, his voice thick with mockery. "Your king fled the scene, tail tucked between his legs."

The goblet-holder hissed and then tilted his drink, splattering his friend's clothes. "My king is no coward," he replied as his companion screamed.

With a swift pivot on her heels, the server distanced herself from the brawling demons.

Ahead of her, a trident shimmered through the drifting clouds of smoke circulating in the room. As she drew closer, the haze dispersed, revealing a tall, curvaceous woman.

The waitress halted, her shoulders tightening as she spotted her. A wicked grin unfurled across the other woman's face, its cruel demeanour marring her beauty. She hoisted the weapon, flaunting it above her head. The venomous serpents sprouting from her scalp were far more unsettling than the weapon she held. They slithered down her pale back, hissing and coiling.

As the server turned to leave, she nearly stumbled into a man. He was dressed as if he had stepped straight out from the pages of an eighteenth-century novel. He stood out in his bowler hat and open trench coat, which revealed a lace-accented Regency shirt. High-waisted trousers and mid-calf leather boots completed the outfit. "Another Bloody Mary," he said, pushing his empty glass toward her. "And make it quick!"

Surprised, she fumbled her tray, sending drinks splattering across the floor. A cluster of nearby women laughed, flecks of foam shooting out of their mouths.

The server hurried away, lowering her head. The man directed his attention to the woman wielding the trident, a smirk curling on his lips. "These dark souls coming to us lately are a bunch of imbeciles. Wouldn't you agree, Medusa?" He moved toward her, and the circle of men surrounding her parted, making way for him.

His fingers brushed the trident's shaft. "Where did you find this magnificent weapon?" he asked. His kohl-lined eyes lit up with a hungry glint. "The Trident of Poseidon, am I correct?"

Medusa's smile was cool as she shifted it out of his reach. "I didn't 'find' it, Mammon. I took it from Poseidon himself."

"Did you now? How marvellous," Mammon said, shifting his weight onto his cane. "Does it truly possess the power to rip apart the earth?"

"I wielded it off the Chilean coast just this morning."

A collective gasp rippled through her companions, quickly giving way to laughter.

"Five thousand souls claimed," she added.

As Medusa continued to regale the crowd, a thin man with raven-black hair cut through the throng toward the King of Midas. The man stopped before him and offered a deep bow. "It's been done, Your Majesty," he said, his voice devoid of emotion.

Turning away from Medusa, Mammon placed a hand on the man's shoulder. "Dead Ringer! You arrived just in time for the festivities!"

The man stiffened at his touch.

A chuckle rumbled low in Mammon's throat. "Still not fond of your nickname, Adrian?"

Adrian's lips pressed into a thin line. "That name was the press's doing, not mine."

"Nicknames are rarely of our own making."

"It should have died with my corpse."

Mammon offered a dismissive wave, drawing Adrian away from the others. "Let us find somewhere a little quieter to discuss business, shall we?"

Adrian cast a scathing look at the hand on his shoulder but complied, allowing Mammon to lead him toward a secluded alcove.

As they navigated through the hall, they passed a group of men covered in thorns. They were tossing around a sentient tomato plant. It flew through the air, shouting obscenities and pelting the men with ripe tomatoes.

"Hey, thornhead," it screeched, whipping another tomato at one of the taller fellows. "Did your mommy confuse a cactus with her date?"

The fruit arced high, and missing its mark, splattered against the face of a passing demigod. Her eyes narrowed into slits as she wiped the dripping juice from her cheek. Gathering a storm of energy in her palm, she murmured, "*Excrucador.*"

The air crackled as she thrust a radiant sphere of electricity at the thorny men. The room's corner became illuminated with a spectacular lattice of electric tendrils. As the glow subsided, several figures lay strewn across the floor, groaning. The faint, acrid scent of charred tomatoes lingered behind.

"It appears your spell works on dark creatures too," Adrian said as the demons struggled to rise.

"Yes. Marvellous, isn't it?" Mammon replied, stepping into the alcove's shadows. Lowering his voice, he asked, "Did the plan go over well? Are there loose ends that need tying up?"

"It went as expected, Your Majesty. I collected Rebekka before the Guard showed up. The power outage at the Department of Spiritual Guidance and Support was well planned."

"And what of the potion? Was it effective on her too?"

"Yes, her dark aura is concealed."

"Excellent. Send her into Orbistia at once. Medusa will surely join me now. Her support is vital to my plan." Mammon's expression darkened, and a sneer distorted his otherwise handsome face. "Soon Orbistia will finally be under my control."

"As it should be, Your Majesty."

"Splendid work, my boy," Mammon said, leading Adrian back toward the party.

The gathering had grown even livelier during their brief absence. It was now teeming with a myriad of creatures. A resonant gong rang out, halting them in their tracks. At the front of the room, Medusa stood before an extravagant red curtain draped across the wall.

A second clang resounded, silencing the music. The dance of the surrounding creatures persisted, their forms contorting grotesquely. Medusa's serpentine hair rose into the air, the forked tongues of the snakes darting out.

"*Excrucador.*" A piercing hiss accompanied her whisper through the chamber. Those with ears clutched at their heads, gritting their teeth. After several excruciating moments, the sound faded away. The snakes settled back onto her shoulders, coiling around her neck.

Medusa fixed a menacing stare at the crowd. She regained her composure, her hand caressing a serpent as her voice echoed throughout the hall. "Much better! Welcome to the Kingdom of Hellstone! Whether you are worthy enough to attend in person or celebrate in your own private hells across our demonic realm, tonight's event will provide some horrifying excitement for everyone!" She beamed at the floating cameras bobbing around her.

Medusa continued, "We gather several times a year in Satan's Kingdom of Hellstone to revel in the chaos we unleash upon one of the universe's planets! Tonight, we celebrate a catastrophe that I hope will be unlike any we've ever seen before. The planet we all dream of destroying —Earth!"

Cheers erupted within the hall but died as Medusa raised her hand for silence. She reached out and grasped a golden cord that hung beside her. "Behold," she announced with theatrical flair, "the Catastraclock!"

With a forceful tug, she pulled the rope. The heavy velvet curtain fell to the floor, revealing a sinister-looking grandfather clock. Its mahogany frame featured intricate carvings, including gnarled vines and anguished expressions frozen in torment. The clock's pendulum cut through the air, its arc casting shadows that stretched and twisted on the ground.

A thin, elegant hand hovered on the brink of touching a miniature replica of Earth that occupied the position where the number six should have been.

"Twenty seconds," Medusa sang out. She flashed a fanged smile at the cameras. "What devastation will the Catastraclock unleash on the hapless Earthlings this year, I wonder?"

Mammon elbowed his way forward, using his cane to nudge others aside. In unison, the assembly began a haunting chant: "Five, four, three, two, one!" As the clock hand clicked into position alongside the Earth replica, a gong reverberated through the chamber. Adrian moved to the edge of the hall, sidestepping an assortment of dancing devils. Red and black confetti rained down upon them as they screamed along to the music.

Shimmering gas filled the clock's face, obscuring the tiny planets and ticking hands. It dissipated, revealing a screen that flickered to life. An aerial view of a small landmass appeared, prompting Medusa to shout, "Vancouver Island!" Before she could say more, a thunderous roar overpowered her voice. The island quaked and shuddered. Chunks of earth gave way, engulfing entire buildings as they collapsed.

The crowd applauded as the camera zoomed in. Cars careened off roads, plunging into yawning chasms opened by the fractured ground. People staggered about, clinging to each other. Amid the havoc, fires blazed through the rubble, flames devouring what life remained.

The celebration within the room reached a fever pitch. The camera panned out to reveal Tofino's shores, a wall of water surging toward them. The tsunami marked the eve of the demonic realm's most sacred holiday with one final, devastating spectacle.

Adrian exited the hall as the screen dimmed. Much like the countdown on the Catastraclock, a new timer had started, its ominous implications unknown even to its key players. The true horror was beginning, and darker days were yet to come.

CHAPTER ONE

A Chilly Christmas Eve

Light snow swirled down from the dark sky, dusting the marketplace below. In the square's centre, a massive tree blinked with festive colours and shiny bulbs, its pine needles trembling in the brisk wind. Last-minute shoppers filled the market despite the chilly weather. Children, bundled in puffy jackets and snug boots, scampered toward Santa's village, their laughter ringing through the air. Behind them, parents shuffled along, sipping on steaming cups of apple cider to warm their hands.

Twinkling white lights adorned the quaint wooden stalls lining the square, casting an inviting glow. Each booth offered unique wares—warm beverages, beautifully knitted scarves, an assortment of baked goods, and homemade Christmas decorations.

A young woman stood at one stall, her tousled blond hair escaping from beneath a snug, blue woollen hat. Snowflakes drifted down, settling on her tweed coat like a soft white veil. She leaned against the stall, cradling a giant snow globe. Captivated, she watched the specks dance inside the glass sphere. Two figures emerged through the shimmering cloud of sparkles. They were locked in an embrace, sharing a kiss under the mistletoe.

Izzy Adams' gaze lingered on the miniature couple as memories of her last kiss with her soulmate washed over her. The silver bracelet on her left wrist caught the soft glow of the lights, drawing her attention away from the ornament. The bangle was a parting gift from Dax—a way to keep her safe when he couldn't be there himself. Izzy wasn't sure exactly how it worked, but Dax had assured her that it would protect her from harm.

She would have scoffed at the idea of needing protection in the past. She was a strong woman. Besides, she didn't engage in risk-taking behaviour—not anymore, not since her father's death . . .

Dax hadn't been worried about physical threats on Earth though. There were other evil entities that the human eye couldn't see. Izzy had experienced them firsthand: demonic bats that dragged your soul into a realm of darkness, ferocious hellhounds out for blood, and psychic vampires that latched onto your essence and drained your energy. The spiritual realm was fraught with danger, yet she longed to return there to reunite with her soulmate.

Izzy sighed. What was Dax doing at that very moment? *Probably planning his reincarnation*, she mused, a sharp ache growing in her chest. It might be ages before they met again.

"Izzy!" A loud voice boomed from behind her. The snow globe slipped through her fingers, and she fumbled to catch it before it hit the ground. She quickly set it on the wooden counter, shooting an apologetic glance at the frowning vendor. Turning, she met the gaze of a tall woman.

"Are you all right, chère?" The woman shifted her shopping bags, her hand coming to rest gently on Izzy's shoulder.

"I'm fine, Lys." Izzy managed a smile, her voice soft. "Just lost in thought."

"You seem to be doing that a lot lately."

"I'm thinking about my exams," Izzy mumbled, moving to pick up a finely crafted nutcracker ornament. "Check this out," she said, her tone brightening as she pulled the string, animating its wooden figure.

Lyssa squealed in delight, snatching the nutcracker from her hands. Obsessed with Christmas trinkets, Lyssa moved past Izzy to the stall, her wallet in hand. She quickly struck up a cheerful exchange with the vendor.

Izzy sighed. Perhaps Lyssa had a point. Izzy's mind was often adrift in memories of the spirit realm. She yearned for one more glimpse of Sparklafex, with its vibrant tapestry of life and the pulsing buzz of the Skyscuttle games filling the air. Above all, she missed Dax. But no matter how hard Izzy had tried, she had not been able to astral project back to that world. Now, instead of basking in the festive warmth of Christmas Eve, Izzy felt as if part of her were missing.

Her shoulders slumping, Izzy turned to her friend. Lyssa was happily tucking the nutcracker into one of her bulging shopping bags.

"Let's get a mocha before we head back," Izzy suggested, stamping her feet on the cold ground for warmth.

Lyssa nodded, slipping her wallet into her purse. "Sounds good, hun. My hands are feelin' like icicles. I still can't get used to these Canadian winters!"

"You haven't even been to Alberta yet." Izzy reached over to take a bag from her friend. "Besides, it's only December. Save the complaints for February."

A laugh burst from Lyssa, bright and clear as a bell. She nudged Izzy playfully with her hip. "Your brother's thinkin' we should honeymoon in Alberta," she drawled, crossing the market square.

Izzy quickened her pace to match Lyssa's long strides. "You should go," Izzy said, veering around a woman laden with packages. "The hot springs are amazing."

The scent of pine grew sharper as they neared the giant Christmas tree at the market's centre.

"So, when are we going shopping for your dre—" Izzy halted mid-stride, narrowly avoiding a collision with Lyssa, who had stopped to look at the tree.

"We're not," Lyssa replied.

"You're not?"

"I've already picked out my dress," she said, eyes twinkling with mischief. "And darlin', it ain't white."

Izzy fought back a smirk. "My mom's going to lose it."

"I know," Lyssa replied, her gaze meeting Izzy's. "But honey, last I checked, it wasn't her walkin' down the aisle."

Continuing their walk, Lyssa shared an amusing story about Izzy's mother's overzealous involvement in the wedding preparations. As she spoke, a strange, prickly sensation crawled up Izzy's spine. Out of the corner of her eye, she glimpsed a shadowy movement next to her.

Startled, she knocked into Lyssa, eliciting a sharp hiss of pain from her friend. "Sorry, Lys," Izzy mumbled, scanning the shadows around the large tree. "I thought someone was following us."

"I don't see anyone, chère," Lyssa said as she stooped to retrieve a dropped bag. "It's just the Christmas lights casting shadows," she added, flashing Izzy a comforting smile.

Izzy's frown deepened as she surveyed the area, yet nothing was out of place. Around them, people were hustling about, wrapping up last-minute holiday shopping or bringing their children for one final visit with Santa. No one was paying them any attention.

"You're probably right . . ." Izzy mumbled, her gaze drifting to a nearby wooden pop-up booth decorated with garlands and cranberries. In the dim light, she caught sight of the shadow of a man cast against the building. As she watched, it raised its hand to wave at her. Izzy glanced around, searching for the source of the silhouette, but found no one. As she focused back on the shadow, it shifted and then dissolved into the darkness. Startled, she stepped closer to the building, squinting to make sense of what she'd seen.

Was he really even there? Izzy rubbed at her eyes and shook her head. *No, I'm not second-guessing myself this time. He was real. I'm sure of it.*

She glanced down at the bracelet encircling her wrist. Dax had told her it would heat up if she were in danger. At that moment, it remained cool against her skin. Whatever she'd seen posed no threat to her. For now, at least.

Lyssa linked her arm through Izzy's, steering them away from the tree. "Let's grab that mocha and go home." Her dark locs brushed Izzy's shoulder as she leaned in against the cold. "I've got a mountain of gifts to wrap," she added, giving her shopping bags a playful shake.

As they drew closer to the beverage stand, the rich aroma of freshly brewed coffee drifted toward them. A cheerful man whistled a holiday tune, artfully topping a hot chocolate with whipped cream and a sprinkle of crushed peppermint. Izzy took her place in line, falling in behind a man gripping a German Shepherd's leash. The dog stood close to its owner, ears perked up, silently scanning its surroundings.

"What a beautiful dog!" Lyssa gushed, her smile widening as she extended her hand toward the animal.

"I've had Biscuit for only two months," the man said quickly, "and she's just started letting me get close. She's a rescue from an abusive home."

Lyssa's hand paused midair. "How anyone could hurt an animal . . ."

As they continued to chat, Izzy's attention drifted. She glanced around, searching for another glimpse of the shadow man. The bracelet on her wrist began to heat up as if reading her mind. Frowning, she gingerly touched it. Her gaze darted through the throng of shoppers until it settled on a sight that sent a chill down her spine. A large raven perched atop a nearby stall, staring straight at her.

Priscilla? Why would her spirit guide want to harm her? Her eyes swept over the crowd. There had to be another explanation. Maybe Priscilla was there to warn her. She stiffened as a group of teenagers walked by, laughing and playfully shoving one another. One of them, deeply engrossed in her cell phone, veered dangerously close to Izzy. Only after the group had moved on did Izzy release her breath.

I'm overreacting, Izzy thought. There was no sign of panic—the crowd around her was composed, each person seemingly wrapped in their own cheerful bubble.

"Oh, look!" Lyssa squealed, pointing down the line. A blond woman clad in an elf costume complete with bells approached them. She was handing out decorated gingerbread cookies, her heart-shaped face lit up with a smile.

Lyssa accepted a cookie from the tray. "Your outfit is darlin'."

"Thanks," the woman replied, her hat bells jingling. "The cookies are homemade." She gestured toward the beverage stall. "A free treat since it's Christmas Eve." She looked at Izzy expectantly, compelling her to reach out and accept one.

"Thanks," Izzy mumbled as the woman walked away.

"These are downright delicious," Lyssa said, her mouth full of cookie. "Aren't you gonna give it a try?"

Izzy examined the gingerbread man's icing before lifting it to her lips. She hesitated, glancing once more at the elf. Positioned beside a nearby stall, she watched Izzy intently. There was a flicker of movement behind the woman, and there he was, the shadowy man. He moved with wild abandon, arms flailing, gesturing frantically toward the elf.

Izzy narrowed her eyes, studying the other woman. The glamour that had veiled her had faded, revealing a tall figure with fuzzy pink skin and tusks curving from beneath her nostrils. Izzy inhaled sharply, the cookie slipping from her grasp. It bounced off her boot and landed in the snow.

"Biscuit, no!"

The German Shepherd devoured the cookie, her long tongue lapping up any crumbs. The owner's jaw twitched as he glared at Izzy. "Sweets aren't good for her belly!"

"Sorry," Izzy mumbled, her cheeks colouring. She glanced at the tusked creature, who now wore an exasperated expression. Nearby, a loud caw erupted from the raven before it took to the air. A piercing whine broke through the clamour of the market. Izzy glanced back at the dog, who was now turning in disoriented circles.

"What's wrong, girl?" her owner asked, bending down to soothe her. She growled and backed away from him.

"Biscuit, it's me," the man said as the dog kept whining and shrinking away. He turned to Lyssa. "She's acting like she did when I first brought her home. It's like she's forgotten the last few months with me!"

Around them, the crowd turned, drawn to the animal's soft growls. Biscuit's owner tried again to calm her, recoiling as she snapped at his hand. Izzy lifted her head and caught the elf staring at her. A spark of understanding flashed in her eyes.

She knows I can see through her glamour, Izzy thought, her pulse speeding up.

Acting on pure instinct, Izzy thrust a finger upward. "There was something in the cookie that lady gave me!" Her arm swung in the direction of the elf.

The other woman's eyes widened as the crowd started murmuring and pointing at her. With calls for the police echoing around them, Izzy gripped Lyssa's arm, pulling her away from the growing throng of people.

"What are you doing, chère? We should stay. The police will want to talk to us."

"I . . ." Izzy paused, the words stuck on her tongue. What could she tell Lyssa? That the elf was really a demon in disguise intent on harming her? *She'd never believe me.* Lyssa might be open about her beliefs in spirituality, but Izzy seriously doubted her friend would accept the idea that other supernatural beings coexisted on Earth with them.

No one would believe me, Izzy thought. The demonic threats, her soulmate, the magical realm of Orbistia . . . She could never tell anyone about her time in the spirit world. They would either laugh at her or have her committed. *A psychotic break*, they'd call it. She had uncovered something incredible but couldn't share it with anyone. She had never felt so alone. Her throat tightened, and a tear threatened to escape her eye.

"I don't feel well," Izzy finally murmured, rubbing at her face. "Whatever was on that cookie must have gotten on my skin."

"Are you okay?"

"I'm fine."

"Darlin', maybe we should head on over to the hospital, just to be sure."

"It's all right, Lyssa. Just take me home."

"Are you sure? What if—"

"I just need to lay down for a bit," Izzy said, pulling ahead of her friend. The snow crunched beneath her feet as she hurried toward the exit, eager to be far away from the demon. It was ironic, really—despite her struggles connecting with the spirit world, it had found its way to reach back to her.

CHAPTER TWO

The Tangled Web of Fear

The window stood open a crack, allowing a cold breeze to flow through the bedroom. Dim streetlights threw a dull light across the floor, faintly illuminating the bed, which was tucked in the far corner. Underneath a mound of blankets, Izzy tossed and turned, her mind lost to a twisted nightmare of a different realm. A muffled cry erupted as her bare foot wriggled free from the snarled blankets, toes clenching tightly.

Darkness crept over the edge of Izzy's subconscious, pulling her deeper into the dream. She found herself in a barren landscape. A biting wind danced around her, kicking up a cloud of dust. Izzy lifted her arm as a shield. Her eyes narrowed against the swirling grit, scanning for any signs of life. But there was only emptiness. She was alone, the only company being the mournful howl of the wind.

Wrapping her arms around herself for warmth, Izzy took a hesitant step forward. Déjà vu washed over her as she peered into the dark void. The vast emptiness, the piercing cold, and the absence of stars in the night sky—it was all too familiar. The pounding in Izzy's ears grew, and her shoulders tightened. She was back in the Kingdom of Nachtmahr.

Dax had dubbed it the Realm of Nightmares—a sinister place where demonic entities lurked in the dark, feasting on fear. The last time she was here, an angel had rescued her. It seemed unlikely that she would be that lucky twice.

I'm on my own, she thought as the air around her filled with an ominous clicking noise.

Wrapping her arms tightly around herself, she found comfort in the pressure. The pale glow of her skin illuminated the ground below, where scattered rocks mingled with loose soil and dead weeds. As the clicking grew louder, Izzy's muscles tensed. Around her, the noise intensified, speeding up and then slowing unexpectedly, creating a disconcerting rhythm in the quiet night.

Izzy's body broke out in a cold sweat, and she fell to her knees. Her eyes clenched shut. Abruptly, the chittering ceased, and a stillness swept through the air. Slowly, she opened her eyes.

Something's out there . . . watching me.

A rock clattered across the dirt and came to rest next to Izzy's bare foot. She stilled as a spindly leg covered in coarse, matted fur stepped out of the shadows. Its claws scraped against the earth as more limbs emerged from the darkness until, finally, all eight legs came into view.

Scrambling backward, she dug her foot into the ground, rocks biting into her skin. She peeked up, taking in the demon's bloated body. It was thick with black hairs that quivered as it released a low, threatening growl.

A small squeak escaped Izzy's lips. The mangled head of a wolf lowered toward her. Foam dripped from its snarling mouth and sizzled as it hit the dirt. Eight red eyes blinked down at her, as its face stopped inches from hers. The creature's hot breath wafted over Izzy's skin, reeking of rotten meat.

Move! Her own voice screamed in her head.

She struggled to her feet. One of the creature's legs slammed her back down. Its claws sank into her body, pinning her against the rocky ground.

A raw scream tore from her throat, but it was cut short as something wet and sticky slammed into her face. Her body heaved as she tried to suck in air, and she tore at the slimy substance covering her mouth.

A claw ensnarled her waist and whirled her around. Izzy's skull struck the ground with a thud, the impact jolting her brain. A tight thread swiftly wrapped around her, trapping her hands against her mouth. The cocoon of silken threads constricted until she was completely immobilized.

Izzy's pulse thundered in her ears, her body flush with a sudden warmth. The demon's snarling grew muffled underneath the layers of web covering her head. Her lungs, starved for air, strained against the pressure in her chest. *I can't move*, she thought, her mouth going dry. Helplessness consumed her, and her body succumbed to the weight of the darkness.

The next moment, everything vanished as she was jolted awake. Izzy found herself staring at the familiar white ceiling of her bedroom. Although she was now conscious, the burning sensation in her chest intensified as she continued to gasp for air. *What's happening?* She struggled to sit up, but like in her dream, she couldn't move. A soft glow filled the room as morning light streamed through the curtains. *I-I can't breathe!* Her throat seared as if engulfed by hot coals, and a guttural noise escaped her mouth.

A gaunt frame was settled on her chest. Deep-set and gleaming with malice, its eyes bore into hers, trying to consume Izzy's soul. Her body broke out into a cold sweat as she frantically willed it to move.

Leaning forward, the demon opened its mouth, revealing broken teeth. Cackling, it let an elongated tongue flop down on Izzy's face. A slimy black trail of saliva smeared across her skin as it licked her.

"It's a shame Queen Mara wants you dead," the creature croaked, extracting its tongue. "You taste delicious . . . like fear and sweat."

Gnarled hands reached out, and nails scraped against the soft skin of Izzy's throat. She shuddered, tears leaking from her eyes as the room continued to dim. A faint sensation stirred near her wrist—a warm, pulsating throb—as the demon's fingers wrapped around Izzy's neck.

"My queen sends her regards. You will see her soon, Orbistian trash," the creature hissed. Bright spots danced before Izzy's vision.

The throbbing on her wrist grew stronger. Moments later, a brilliant white light erupted around them. A loud bang followed, and a high-pitched scream filled the space. The creature exploded in a cloud of shimmering black smoke. It quickly dissipated, leaving Izzy alone in her room once more.

She managed to sit up, the covers falling away from her body. Her lungs burned, and she fumbled for the water on her nightstand. Despite her efforts, most of it spilled down her nightshirt as she brought the bottle to her lips.

She gathered a sip of water in her mouth, then let it slowly slide down her throat, each swallow a painful reminder of the ordeal she had just endured. She set the bottle back down and rubbed at her neck.

The first attack had been a nightmare, she was sure of it. But the creature sitting on her—that had been real. *I almost died*, she thought, cradling her knees to her chest. *I-I don't understand. Dax said demons could only drain our energy . . .* Izzy glanced down at her bracelet, which had begun to cool down. It had saved her life. If Dax hadn't given it to her . . .

Reaching up, Izzy twisted a lock of blond hair around her finger and yanked hard. The demon had said that Queen Mara wanted her dead. Unlike the other demons she had encountered before, it had tried to kill her. A wave of dizziness hit her.

A demonic queen wants me dead. Why?

Before Izzy could contemplate it any further, the door to her bedroom burst open, crashing into the wall. Her older sister, Kate, clung to the doorframe, her eyes wide and face pale. Her breath caught as she saw Izzy.

"I heard a loud noise. I thought it was a gun going off. What happened to your neck?" Kate rushed toward Izzy. She stumbled over a pile of books in her haste, sending them tumbling to the ground.

"I . . . uh . . ." Kate's question echoed in her mind as she struggled to find a rational answer.

Kate retrieved Izzy's hand mirror from the dresser and passed it to her. "It looks like a burn," she said, brushing aside Izzy's hair.

Izzy held the antique silver mirror in her hand, her blue eyes staring back at her. Tilting her chin up, she examined her neck. Her mouth dropped open as she traced the angry patch of red skin. Tiny clusters of blisters were scattered around the edge of the burn.

"I'll be right back," Kate said, letting go of Izzy's hair. She leaped off the bed and ran out of the room.

The handle of the mirror was slippery in Izzy's clammy grasp. She winced as the blisters burst, releasing fluid that streamed down her neck. Transfixed, Izzy watched the burn slowly fade away. Heavy footsteps thudded on the floorboards outside her door. Quickly, she used her comforter to wipe off her skin.

Kate rushed in, her face flushed. She crossed the room and placed the medical kit on the dresser, rummaging through it for the necessary supplies. "Polysporin, gauze, Advil . . ." Kate muttered before turning toward Izzy. "You should put cool water on it first."

"I'm fine."

"No, you're not! Just let me treat it."

"I'm serious, Kate. I'm fine," Izzy said, pulling her tangled hair aside. "See!"

Kate reached over and gently touched Izzy's neck." But . . . I don't understand. You had a terrible burn a few moments ago."

Izzy flinched away from Kate's touch, her skin still sensitive from where she had been injured. "Must have been the lighting."

Kate shook her head and peered out the window. "The lighting," she mumbled. Her eyebrows furrowed as she turned to stare at Izzy, trying to make sense of what had happened. "There was a loud bang . . ."

"Oh, yeah. I must have knocked some books to the floor."

"I knocked those books over, Izzy. Just a few minutes ago."

"No, you knocked *those* books over," Izzy said, gesturing to the pile of meditation books by the door. "I fell asleep with some on my bed. I must have kicked them off."

Kate pursed her lips, glancing at the books scattered near the bed. She paused, leaning forward to lift a slender, sheen-covered volume from the pile. "*The Art of Astral Projection.*" She arched an eyebrow and passed it to Izzy.

Warmth crept up Izzy's cheeks, and she avoided her sister's gaze. "Book club," she lied, slipping out of bed and reaching for the housecoat on the floor. Kate opened her mouth to respond, but Izzy cut her off. "We should get downstairs. Eddie and Lyssa will be here to open gifts soon."

When her sister hesitated, Izzy added, "Honestly, I'm fine, Kate!" She wasn't fine, not really. Someone wanted her dead, her lungs still burned, and it took everything to mask the trembling in her hands. But she couldn't share any of that with Kate.

As Izzy descended the staircase and walked through the family room, the strong scent of freshly ground coffee beans filled the air. She paused to stare at the family portrait hanging on the wall. Her father stood at the back, his wide grin captured in the photograph. Izzy stared into his blue eyes, which were so much like her own. Her eyelids fluttered closed, and she imagined he was staring back at her. A tear rolled down her cheek, followed by another one. It was their second Christmas without him, and the pain of his absence continued to weigh heavily upon the family.

A gentle hand on her shoulder brought Izzy back to the present moment. Kate slipped her arm around Izzy's waist and hugged her. "Sometimes, it feels like he's still here," Kate said, her voice soft.

"Maybe he is."

"It's a nice thought." Kate smiled at Izzy and then dropped her arm from her waist. She moved past her into the kitchen.

Izzy's shoulders drooped. If Kate didn't even believe in spirits, there was no way she'd believe in demons. She could never share her experience with her family. They wouldn't believe her. She imagined her brother laughing at her and Kate looking at her with sympathetic eyes. And her mother . . . No—she wouldn't tell them.

Izzy forced a smile and followed her sister into the kitchen. Sunlight streamed in through the sliding glass doors. Outside, the snow fell heavily, covering the ground in a thick white blanket. As she walked over to the counter, Izzy passed by her mother, who sat hunched over a cup of coffee. She was reading through a stack of paperwork.

"Mornin' Mom," Izzy said, accepting a steaming mug from her sister.

Michelle Adams acknowledged her youngest daughter with a nod, her blond hair falling across her eyes with the movement. She picked up her coffee and took a sip as she continued reading.

Izzy took a seat next to the sliding doors. Her fingers absently drummed against the polished tabletop as she gazed outside. Behind her, Kate busied herself with breakfast, the soft click of the toaster echoing across the quiet kitchen. Soon, the comforting aromas of warm coffee and toast flooded the room.

Sunlight glinted off Izzy's bracelet, and she closed her eyes, her mind drifting back to her last moments with Dax. She could still feel his smooth hands trailing across her skin as he slipped the jewellery onto her wrist. His forehead pressed against hers, their lips brushing together. Izzy's mouth curved into a slow smile, and she sank deeper into the memory. Her nails clicked faster against the table as she became caught up in the moment.

Across from her, a throat cleared—a sharp, deliberate sound. Izzy's eyes flickered open, coming to rest on her mother. Michelle's gaze lingered on Izzy's tapping hand, her eyes narrowing. Heat flushed Izzy's cheeks. She quickly dropped her hands to her lap and looked away.

Michelle's eyes remained fixed on Izzy for a moment longer, her stare boring into Izzy's face. "I'm told you and Kyler are no longer in a relationship," she finally said.

"Who told you that?"

"Your brother."

Izzy silently cursed Eddie and his blabbering mouth. The last thing she wanted was to discuss her romantic life with her mother. She should have known better than to confide in Lyssa with her brother nearby.

"So it's true then?" Michelle continued.

"Yeah."

"What a shame. He comes from a good family."

"He's a racist womanizer, Mom."

"Don't be so dramatic, Isabelle," Michelle said, her eyes rolling upward. "He's a lovely young man. Very respectable."

"You met him once."

"Yes, well, he made a good impression."

"Clearly," Izzy mumbled into her coffee mug.

"Tristan Shear is home from university," Michelle continued, ignoring Izzy. "His mother said he was asking about you."

Izzy's scowl deepened as she stared down at the table. "I'm not interested."

"He would be a good match for you. He's—"

"Wealthy and well connected. I get it, Mom."

"Your father liked him," Michelle said, her voice chilling. She paused to sip her coffee, then added nonchalantly, "His mother mentioned he's free on New Year's Eve. I told her you were as well."

A roaring noise filled Izzy's ears as she stared at her mother. *Is she actually setting me up on a date? On New Year's Eve?* Under the table, her hand clenched into a tight fist. She closed her eyes, willing herself to calm down. *Breathe in, breathe out.* Focusing on the tension in her shoulders and chest, she tuned out her mother's voice as it droned on about Tristan Shear. After a moment, she opened her eyes, her gaze sharpening on Michelle.

"*I said* I'm not interested, Mother."

"But I already told—"

"I'm dating someone else," Izzy said, her pulse quickening as thoughts of Dax flooded her mind.

"Who?" Michelle demanded.

"Someone at college. He's kind and compassionate. We have a lot in common. I . . . I really like him."

"What about his parents?"

"What about them?"

"Where do they work? What clubs do they belong to? Are they from Canada?"

"I don't see how any of that matters, Mom."

Sighing loudly, Michelle leaned across the table. "*Of course* it matters, Isabelle. You want to date a respectable—"

"Is he handsome?" Kate asked, sliding into the seat next to Izzy. She pushed a plate of peanut butter toast in front of her. Izzy's stomach grumbled as the nutty smell wafted up to her nose.

"Thanks, Kate," Izzy said, picking up a slice. "And yeah, he is," she added, biting into the crisp bread. She groaned inwardly as her mouth flooded with the creamy richness of the peanut butter.

"Well, we can't wait to meet him," Kate said, ignoring their mother's tight expression.

A weight settled in Izzy's stomach. *Meet Dax?* That would never happen. At least not while they were all living . . . Izzy licked her lips, her mouth suddenly dry. She would never bring her boyfriend home to meet her family. There would be no embarrassing stories told over competitive games of Monopoly, which she supposed was probably a good thing. But other experiences, like having a date for her brother's wedding, were moments she would never get to share. A cold, lonely feeling gripped Izzy's body, and she stared glumly at her plate, her appetite gone.

"It's Christmas Day, Mother," Kate said, her voice slicing through Izzy's dark thoughts. "Eddie and Lyssa will be here soon." She nodded toward the paperwork stacked in front of Michelle. It's a government holiday. Take the day off from work."

Michelle, who had resumed reading, kept her eyes glued to the resume before her. "Business owners don't take days off."

"You mean *you* don't take a day off," Izzy interjected.

Michelle sighed and removed her reading glasses. She set them on the table and rubbed her temples. Ignoring Izzy, she turned to Kate and pointed to the resume. "Another one that I can't pronounce! Can't Lyssa find us ones with English-sounding names?"

Caught off guard, Izzy nearly let her coffee slosh out of her mug. "Mom! You can't say things like that!"

"What's wrong with what I said, Isabelle?"

"It's disrespectful."

"Oh, not this again."

"Seriously, Mom. You have to watch what you say."

"There's nothing wrong with what I said."

"How would you like it if someone said your name was too hard to bother pronouncing?" Izzy clenched her mug tighter and stared at her mom.

"My name is easy to pronounce."

"To you, it is . . . You can't just dismiss someone's name because it sounds different."

"I wasn't being dismissive."

"Um, yeah, you were," Izzy said, pointing to the stack of resumes. "You said that Lyssa should find you ones with English names. You rejected that person because of their identity."

Michelle stood up, tucking the paperwork under her arm. "Honestly, Isabelle. You are making something out of nothing. It was just a comment. You'll understand where I'm coming from when you take over the business."

Izzy sat rigidly in her seat, her jaw clenching. "Actually," she said, "I'm not."

She shifted closer to Kate, her foot knocking against her sister's under the table. An awkward moment ensued with Michelle staring down coolly at Izzy, her expression unreadable.

"Care to elaborate," her mother finally said, breaking the silence.

Izzy tilted her head up at her mother. The drumming in her ears grew louder, and her tongue stuck to the roof of her mouth. This was not how this conversation was supposed to go. Kate was going to warm their mother up to the idea first. She was closer to their mom. Michelle respected her opinions. Izzy kicked herself inwardly. *Why couldn't I keep my mouth shut?*

Kate's gentle touch on her knee snapped Izzy back to the moment. Taking a deep breath, she met Michelle's gaze. "I'm not going to take over management of the funeral home, Mom. You're great at what you do . . . but I would hate it. The thought of having to work there after school . . . well, I just . . . I feel . . ."

Heat flushed her cheeks as a tremble started deep in her chest. She pressed her lips together, holding back the urge to cry. Izzy's hand snaked up to her hair and began pulling on it, twisting it around her fingers as they slowly grew numb.

Kate reached over and hugged Izzy, smoothing down her hair. Hidden from her mother's view, Izzy let the tears come, dampening her sister's flannel top. The lavender scent of Kate's shampoo was comforting, and after a few minutes, her breathing slowed down. She reluctantly pulled away from her sister.

Michelle's jaw twitched as she quietly studied Izzy. Looking into her brown eyes, Izzy tried to guess what she was thinking. Was she mad? Shocked? Izzy couldn't tell. Her mother was a hard person to read.

"We've already started development at the Belleville site," Michelle finally said, her voice trembling.

"I know. I'm sorry, Mom. Maybe Kate—"

"Your sister is needed here."

"Then have Eddie run it."

"I meant for you to run the Belleville location, Isabelle. It's why we expanded there. You're connected to the community—a familiar face. We *need* you. You can't just change the plan now!"

Izzy flinched as Michelle's voice rose in pitch. Her mother's mouth twisted into a scowl, transforming her face into an ugly mask of contempt. Izzy could practically feel the negative energy pouring from her mom, suffocating the room with tension.

"But I don't want it."

"How can you not want it? I'm handing you a business! You won't have to worry about job security. You would be financially secure. Why would you turn your back on that?"

"Because I would hate it!" Fat tears leaked from Izzy's eyes, streaking down her reddened cheeks.

"Nobody loves their job, Isabelle," Michelle said coolly. She tilted her head toward Kate, her gaze shifting to her oldest daughter. "You knew about this?"

"I was going to talk to you about it, Mother," Kate said, handing Izzy a napkin. "She's not happy. Dad wouldn't have wanted this for her, not if he knew how she felt. She wants to go to university, and I think we should be supportive."

Michelle turned to Izzy again, her face paling. "University?"

"Yes," Izzy said, dabbing at her eyes with the tissue. "For social work."

"A social worker?"

"I want to help people, Mom."

"You can help people at the funeral home. You could become more involved in funeral planning. We could even offer follow-up support. We can switch your role. You—"

"I want to be an advocate. I thought I could do a placement with Amnesty International and get some overseas experience."

"You want to leave the country," Michelle said hoarsely. "You can't leave. You're needed here. I-I can't—"

A loud bang erupted from the front of the house, followed by a soft click as the front door closed. Familiar footsteps echoed in the hallway, and a moment later, Eddie strode into the room, accompanied by Lyssa. Izzy turned away from Michelle and busied herself with her coffee. Hopefully, Eddie wouldn't comment on her tear-stained face.

Her brother glanced around the kitchen, his usually cheerful expression grim as he stared at his family. He took in Izzy's red-rimmed eyes and said, "You heard the news already?" Without waiting for a response, he walked into the family room, heading toward the television. A moment later, the hum of the newscast floated into the room.

Lyssa clasped Izzy's hand in her own. "It's horrible, chère. We listened to it on the radio on the way over. I can't believe it!"

"Can't believe what?" Izzy got up and followed her friend as she moved to stand next to Eddie. Turning to stare at the television, her mouth gaped open. An aerial image of a coastal shoreline was coming into view. Homes and buildings lay in ruins, fragments scattered like broken shells across the sand. The screen flickered back to the newscaster, a young woman with tendrils of black hair whose composure was teetering on the edge of tears.

"The country is mourning the loss of thousands of Canadians today, as a devastating earthquake with a magnitude of 9.0 occurred along the Cascadia Subduction Zone. The earthquake triggered a massive tsunami that swept through Tofino, British Columbia, leaving a trail of destruction in its wake. Rescue teams are searching through the debris, with many people still unaccounted for. The tsunami, which followed shortly after the quake, flooded the coastline, overwhelming local defences."

The camera cut away from the newscaster to show the oceanside town. Buildings stood gutted, with windows shattered and brickwork crumbling. Debris—overturned cars, boats, and fragments of furniture—littered the streets, floating in the murky waters left by the tsunami.

"The prime minister has declared a state of emergency," the newscaster announced, her voice trembling. "Residents in affected areas are urged to follow evacuation orders and safety instructions." She paused, taking a second to compose herself. "This is one of the worst natural disasters in Canadian history. The impact will be felt for years to come."

A hush fell over the family room as the television cycled through one harrowing scene after another. Izzy stared briefly at her mother, who was nestled on the couch with Kate. Clinging to her eldest child, Michelle wept, tears silently streaming down her face.

CHAPTER THREE

Flu-B-Gone

Snow swirled against Izzy's Honda Civic as she pulled up in front of her great-aunt's apartment building. She parked and lingered in the vehicle's fading warmth, glad to finally be off the road. In the car's silence, her mind raced with the events of earlier that week.

The argument with her mom and the news broadcast had sucked all the joy out of the holiday. Reports flooded in by the hour, keeping Eddie absorbed in the television's glow. In contrast, the kitchen hummed with activity as Michelle and Kate prepared Christmas dinner. Izzy, who had never been interested in cooking, found her presence in the kitchen unnecessary. She spent the rest of the afternoon curled up on the couch, talking quietly with Lyssa.

Lyssa had advised Izzy to be patient with her mom. Despite her lack of motherly affection, Michelle still loved her children, and Lyssa was sure she'd come around.

Izzy was not as optimistic. Her mother had never compromised before, and it was unlikely to happen now. Her carefully laid-out plans had been tossed out the window. Michelle would never forgive her.

Since college was not resuming for a few more weeks, Izzy had stayed in Toronto to help at the funeral school. Michelle had maintained a cold distance, tasking her with sorting through a pile of resumes. These were for candidates to staff the new Belleville site. The construction was on track, set to open by spring's end. Izzy frowned as Michelle handed her the resumes. Dealing with them was a managerial task, a role that her mother wanted her to eventually take on. Clearly, Michelle still expected Izzy to follow in her footsteps.

The week had dragged on painfully slowly. The combination of her mother's extensive to-do list and the frosty home environment had Izzy yearning for the arrival of New Year's Eve. As she prepared for the end of the year, it dawned on Izzy that there was one person that she could confide in about the demonic attack—Rhylynn Rivers.

Izzy had met Rhylynn years ago through her great-aunt Audrey, and despite their two-year age difference, they had grown close. Rhylynn was a witch—a fact Izzy had discovered while in the spiritual realm. The problem now was that the younger girl was unaware that her secret was out, and Izzy didn't know how to confront her about it. They were planning to spend New Year's Eve together, and Izzy hoped to find the right moment to discuss the topic.

Her grip tightened on the steering wheel. *Tonight, I'll tell Rhylynn about the demon attack. She'll know what to do!* Hopefully, her friend had connections to a psychic or a medium. Izzy needed to get in touch with Dax. The demon queen that wanted her dead was still out there. Dax could find out why.

The car's interior had grown colder. Izzy shivered and quickly grabbed her gloves from the passenger seat, sliding them on. As she exited the car, a flurry of snowflakes hit her in the face. She winced at the cold and picked up her pace as the wind bit into her cheeks.

Izzy walked into the apartment building and headed toward the panel of buttons near the inner door. She punched in her great-aunt's number, and a jarring ringing filled the small entranceway. "Hello?" Audrey's voice sang out through the intercom.

"It's me, Auntie A."

"Izzy, darling! Come on up."

The door clicked as it unlocked. Grabbing the handle, Izzy stepped inside the building. The lobby was empty, but as she walked past the community room on her way to the elevator, she was spotted by Mr. Smith. Excusing himself from his poker game, he poked his head out the door and called out to her. "Izzy! Back from the big city already?"

A smile tugged at her lips as she took in Mr. Smith's tweed hat, which was sitting crookedly on his thinning hair. He reminded her so much of her late grandfather. She moved closer to him, leaning against the doorframe as she responded, "Hi, Mr. Smith. Did you have a good Christmas?"

"Yes. Mrs. Rivers was so kind to invite me over for a turkey dinner. Your aunt joined us, of course."

"I bet she did," Izzy said, grinning. Her aunt was in a friendly competition with Lila Rivers for Mr. Smith's affection. She had likely invited herself over for the dinner. *I'm glad she wasn't alone over the holidays.*

"And how was your Christmas, Izzy."

"It was . . . it was nice."

"Terrible news, that Tofino business, wasn't it?"

Izzy's face fell at the mention of the natural disaster. "Yes, it really put a damper on Christmas Day. All those people gone . . ."

Seeing her sombre expression, Mr. Smith patted her shoulder gently. "Sorry, my dear. I didn't mean to upset you." He took a step back from Izzy. "I won't keep you from your aunt any longer. Tell her we missed her at the lunch today!"

"It's okay, I'm fine. I'll tell her. Happy New Year!"

Izzy hurried to the elevator, and a few minutes later, she was walking down the hallway toward her great-aunt's apartment. As she drew closer to Mrs. River's door, a bitter smell, like burnt garlic, filled the air. The scent grew stronger with each step Izzy took. She paused, only slightly taken back by the green eyeball affixed to the door. It stared right at her, blinking slowly before disappearing. Izzy's glanced around uneasily. Was Rhylynn cooking up some spell with her grandmother? A shiver ran down her spine. *I can't believe that I know witches!* It made her wonder what else there was out there.

As Izzy continued down the hallway, she stopped before her aunt's door and gently rapped her knuckles against the polished wood. Before she could pull back her hand, the door swung open. The pungent scent lingering in the hallway paled compared to the overwhelming stench pouring out of the apartment.

"Ugg! What is that smell?" Izzy wrinkled her nose as she stepped through the doorway.

"Flu-B-Gone," Audrey said, holding up her hand to keep Izzy back. "Don't hug me now, I'm sick."

"Flu-B-Gone?"

"Some home remedy Lila cooked up for me."

Izzy sidestepped her aunt and moved into the kitchen, where a pot was simmering on the stove. As she peered into it, her stomach clenched at the sight of puke-green liquid. The surface of the soup was littered with chunky bits, and Izzy had to swallow hard to fight the rising bile at the back of her throat.

"You actually drank this? It looks like vomit!"

Audrey laughed softly and moved toward the sink to fill her glass with water. "It's not as bad as it looks, and it's working. I feel better than I did this morning!"

"I believe it," Izzy said as she backed out of the kitchen and into the living room. She removed her coat and hung it on the back of a chair before settling into it. "I wish I'd known that you were sick," she told Audrey, her eyebrows drawing together. "I would have come back sooner."

"And done what?" her aunt said, each step a slow shuffle as she moved toward the recliner across the room. She sank into the plush cushions with a long sigh, closing her eyes. "You would have gotten sick too."

"I don't care."

Audrey's eye popped open, and she fixed Izzy with a measured look. "While I appreciate the concern, dear, I'm not incapable of caring for myself."

Heat crept up Izzy's cheeks, and she glanced away. "I know," she mumbled.

"I'm on the mend, darling girl. Don't you worry about me." Audrey took a sip of her water and continued. "So, tell me, how was your Christmas?"

"It was . . . okay. Eddie and Lyssa came over as they were broadcasting the disaster . . ."

Her aunt leaned back in her recliner, lifting her slippered feet onto the footrest. "Awful, isn't it? Lila and I watched the whole thing."

They sat in a moment of silence. Izzy picked up the crocheted doily from the table and ran her fingers along its intricate details. Images of the broadcast filtered through her mind—skeletal frames of buildings, overturned boats, and, worst of all, bodies. The death toll for both humans and animals was staggering.

Audrey cleared her throat sharply. "Enough about that," she said, her voice cracking. "Tell me about Lyssa. What are her plans for the wedding? You're her maid of honour, aren't you?"

The atmosphere in the room changed instantly, as if a heavy load had been lifted off the air. Izzy smiled as she placed the doily back on the table. "Yeah, I am. We went dress shopping. You are going to love the dress she picked out for me. It's beautiful!"

"I'm sure I will. That girl has good taste."

"Tell that to mom. She's starting to drive Lyssa nuts."

"Oh?" Audrey said, arching a grey eyebrow.

"She's just been a bit demanding. Wants things done a certain way. You know how my mom is," Izzy said, shrugging her shoulders.

"Controlling and pushy."

"Auntie A!"

"Well, she is!" Audrey shook her head. "It isn't right," she continued, "trying to take over that girl's wedding. Your brother shouldn't put up with it."

Izzy rolled her eyes. "He isn't exactly the confrontational type."

"Well, he should be! Your mother is something else . . . Why my nephew had to go and marry that—"

"I applied to university."

Izzy's distraction worked. Her aunt fumbled her cup, and water droplets soaked into her pink housecoat. "You did?"

"Yup. York, Toronto Metropolitan, and Trent. I applied for social work programs."

Audrey placed her cup down and started to rise from her seat. She hesitated and then sat back down, tears shining in her blue eyes. "Oh, Izzy, I am so happy for you. Jamie . . . your father would have been so proud."

Izzy turned away from Audrey to hide the pain she knew was on her face. Her father would have been boasting to anyone who would listen— neighbours, the mail carrier, even the lifeless bodies as he prepared them for embalming.

A lump rose in her throat. He was the kind of dad who would have been proud of anything his children achieved as long as they were happy. Izzy was sure that wherever he was, he was thrilled for her. But what she wouldn't give to hear him say it aloud . . .

"I suppose this means you are moving away then," Audrey continued.

"Yeah . . . as soon as I graduate from Loyalist in April. If I get accepted, I'll work at the funeral home for extra cash over the summer and start university in the fall.

"You'll get accepted," her aunt said, her chin jutting upward.

"Hopefully. I'll miss Belleville, though—my friends, the volunteers at the food bank, and you! I have a lot of good memories here . . ."

"The people and places we love, they stay with us," Audrey said, her voice growing soft. "It's the memories and feelings they give us that keep them close, no matter how far we are from them."

"I know," Izzy replied, her gaze drifting toward the window. The snow had finally stopped. "I feel Dad around sometimes. Yesterday, I could have sworn I smelled him."

Audrey smiled wistfully. "Cloves."

"Eddie wears Dad's aftershave now."

"I noticed," Audrey said as she reached down and pulled her shawl from the depths of her chair. Shivering, she wrapped it around her frail frame. "So, tell me more about the applications," she said, bringing the conversation back on topic.

They spent the next hour catching up and laughing at Lyssa's passive-aggressive attempts to keep Michelle from meddling in the wedding plans.

After another round of laughter, Izzy glanced at the wall clock.

"I have to meet up with Rhy Rhy now," she said, slipping on her coat. She walked toward Audrey, leaning down to kiss her on the head.

"Here," her aunt said, reaching into the side of the recliner and pulling out an envelope. She handed it to Izzy and leaned back into the chair. "It's a hundred dollars. Put it toward your application fees."

"Auntie A! That's a lot of money. I can't take it from you," Izzy said, attempting to give it back.

"Yes, you can," Audrey said, pushing away Izzy's outstretched arm. "Now get going. Don't keep Rhylynn waiting."

Ignoring her aunt's protests, Izzy leaned down and hugged her. "Thank you," she said before turning to leave. "I love you."

"Love you too, sweet girl."

"Call me if you need anything, okay?"

"I will. Go on now."

Bidding her aunt goodbye, Izzy stepped out into the hall and approached Mrs. River's apartment. There was no eyeball studying her from the door this time. Instead, the faint strains of a piano escaped into the hallway, the melody slow and haunting. A soft voice sang out:

"She used to fly on a broomstick high.
A witch with powers to make you sigh.
But something changed fast, and she fell down.
Her magic gone, she hit the ground."

Izzy hesitated as the music increased in volume.

"She's just a human now, no spells to cast.
Forbidden from her love, a love that can't last.
Her heart is breaking, her soul in pain.
A witch turned human, her life never the same."

Lost in the lyrics, Izzy was startled by loud crashing from inside the apartment. A string of curses followed Rhylynn's voice. Izzy chuckled as she imagined the chaos: Rhylynn knocking over a cauldron full of Flu-Be-Gone soup, the vile green liquid splattering everywhere. Mrs. Rivers would be smelling the foul stench of wet dog for weeks! Wrinkling her nose, Izzy knocked sharply on the door.

The apartment grew quiet as the music abruptly cut off. Moments later, the door opened, revealing her friend's flushed cheeks. "Hi, Izzy," Rhylynn said, stepping out into the hall. She closed the door behind her, blocking Izzy's view.

"Hey, Rhy Rhy." Izzy greeted her friend with a hug. The sweet scent of rosemary filled her senses as Rhylynn's curly hair brushed against her face. "Knock something over?" Izzy asked, trying to suppress a smile. She knew that her friend wouldn't give her a straight answer. But, after tonight, that would all change.

The girls left the building and walked over to Rhylynn's truck. The moon shone brightly above them, illuminating the parking lot. Izzy moved around to the passenger side, reaching for the door handle. Before she could touch it, a harsh, croaking noise came from above her. She recoiled from the truck. A raven sat perched on the roof, staring down at her.

Izzy's body tensed, and her hands curled into fists at her sides. *Priscilla.* It had to be her spirit guide. She was mad that Izzy still had memories of the spirit world. But was Priscilla behind the recent attacks?

Izzy refused to let Priscilla ruin her night. She stepped back toward the truck, her eyes still locked with the raven's. The bird let out another croak but didn't leave. Izzy's arm shook as she reached over and yanked open the door. She leaped into the truck, slamming the door shut behind her.

"Everything okay, Iz?" Rhylynn asked, already in the driver's seat with the key in the ignition.

"Yeah. I just got startled by a bird outside. Are you going to start this junk heap or what? It's freezing in here!"

Rhylynn's mouth twisted into a smirk. "Squirtle is not a junk heap."

Izzy burst into a fit of giggles, which quickly turned into a coughing fit as she struggled to catch her breath. "You named your truck . . . after a Pokémon?"

Rhylynn shrugged nonchalantly. "I like Pokémon."

Izzy's grin grew wider as Rhylynn started the vehicle, its engine sputtering before roaring to life. Rhylynn was an eccentric person, and her carefree attitude was one of the things that made her so endearing. If only Izzy could be more like her friend. Unfortunately, other people's opinions mattered too much to her, especially her family's. She sighed and leaned back against the cold seat, watching the buildings go by as Rhylynn navigated the truck down the street.

"We could have taken your car," Rhylynn said, glancing over at Izzy.

"No, this is fine. I needed a break from driving."

"Traffic must have been bananas on the highway."

"Don't you mean *crazy?*" Izzy asked, her eyes closed as she listened to the truck chugging along the snow-packed road.

"*Crazy* has a negative vibe to it. Besides, I like saying *bananas.*"

Izzy smiled. "Never change, Rhy Rhy."

"Why would I?" Before Izzy could respond, she added, "We're here."

Izzy slowly opened her eyes. Her breath caught in her throat, and her hands started to tremble. She quickly shoved them into her coat pockets before Rhylynn noticed. They had arrived at the Thai restaurant where Izzy had her incident last October. Izzy had experienced a hallucination that left her screaming and running through the restaurant until a collision with a server had stopped her. She'd later learned that Emily's magic was most likely the cause.

Sensing Izzy's discomfort, Rhylynn tilted her head toward her. "We can try somewhere else if you want, Iz," she offered.

"No . . . I'm fine."

"Are you sure? I wouldn't have come here, but everywhere else is booked. It was either this or Turtle's Place."

"I'm sure," Izzy said, sounding more confident than she felt. "I'd rather not risk getting food poisoning from Turtle's. Besides, it's been a couple of months now. Maybe people have forgotten about my . . . accident."

Sighing, she slid out of the truck after Rhylynn. The building wasn't the issue—it was the evil witch potentially within. She scanned the parking lot, her shoulders relaxing at the sight of no ravens. *Everything is going to be fine*, she reassured herself. But deep down, Izzy knew things didn't always go as planned.

CHAPTER FOUR

SECRETS SERVED WITH A SIDE OF MAGIC

The briny tang of fish sauce clung to the fabric of the chair Izzy sat in. Sighing, she placed the menu on the table, her gaze lingering on the list of dishes. Rhylynn still had her menu pressed close to her face. Her wire glasses had slid down to the end of her nose.

"There's too many options," she finally said.

"I'm getting the Tum Yum soup," Izzy replied.

Rhylynn didn't respond immediately. She set her menu in front of her, closed her eyes, and let her finger hover over the menu.

"What are you doing?"

"Letting fate decide," Rhylynn murmured.

"You can't be serious. What if you get something awful . . . like shrimp rolls? You hate shrimp!"

"Then fate might make my finger slide to the next item," Rhylynn said, smirking.

Izzy shook her head. "You're going to regret this."

"Or I'll end up with a new favourite dish."

As Rhylynn debated over the menu, Izzy's gaze drifted away, drawn to a subtle flicker in the corner of her eye. At first, it was a play of shadows, the dim lighting creating an illusion against the potted ferns that lined the wall. As the light flickered, the ferns seemed to sway, casting shifting shapes that played tricks on the eyes. But then, it happened again—a darker shape, a silhouette that was out of place amid the greenery. It extended out from the shadow of the plants and took on a human-like form. Goosebumps ran down her arms as the shadow paused and wiggled its fingers at her. *Am I imagining this?*

Rhylynn's sharp voice brought her back to the conversation. "Did you hear what I just said?"

Izzy nodded, shifting under the weight of her friend's stare. "Uh, yeah. Sure. Sounds good."

Rhylynn leaned in closer, her long curls brushing against the table. "The movie starts at ten o'clock, so we should be out just before midnight. We'll be cutting it close if you want to see the fireworks down at Zwick's Park."

Izzy stared at the wall again, finding only emptiness where the shadow had been. She pressed her lips together, her mind a whirlpool of confusion and fear as she grappled with the reality of what she'd seen. *It was real, it had to have been. Just like at the market with Lyssa. What does it want?*

Turning back to Rhylynn, Izzy froze, caught off guard by her friend's intense stare. *She knows something is going on.* The silence between them was thick. Unspoken questions hung in the air. Izzy shifted uncomfortably in her seat. *I should tell her*, she thought. Rhylynn would want to help. And right now, Izzy needed all the help she could get.

Rhylynn's eyes flickered away, then narrowed as she peered past Izzy's shoulder. "What is *she* doing here?" she said, her voice a venomous whisper that sliced through the clamour of the restaurant, catching Izzy by surprise. She swivelled around, her gaze landing on a woman with sleek brown hair gliding toward them. A tray of drinks was poised in her hands. As the server drew closer, the badge pinned to her shirt came into focus, revealing the name *Sydney*.

Rhylynn glared at Sydney, pressing her lips into a thin line. Izzy's brow drew together. What could the server have possibly done to provoke her friend? Even on a bad day, Rhylynn was cheerful. This hostility was totally out of character. Izzy's stomach churned as if a heavy stone had lodged itself there. An ominous premonition washed over her— something bad was going to happen.

The shadowed figure materialized along the far wall again as if on cue, dancing wildly about. Its hands waved high above its body as though desperate to get her attention. Izzy glanced at the other patrons. They were engaged in meals and animated conversations, none acknowledging the peculiar spectacle but her.

The shadow continued to dart from one corner to another, its movements erratic, punctuated by odd pointing and gestures. Izzy found herself unable to look away. What was its purpose? A warning, or merely the antics of some bizarre, supernatural entity? Her knowledge of the magical community was limited, based only on what Dax had shared with her, and he had said nothing of this.

Lost in thoughts of her soulmate, Izzy shivered as an unexpected tingling cascaded down her wrist from her bracelet. She touched it, the metal warming beneath her fingers. *Demons!* She glanced around the room, trying to see beyond any potential glamours. Nothing seemed amiss. But something was there. Her bracelet was still warm to the touch, warning her of the approaching danger.

"Hello, Rhylynn," Sydney's voice rose to an unnaturally high pitch as she stopped at their table.

Rhylynn's eyes narrowed. "I thought you quit."

"I, uh . . . I've been ill."

Rhylynn's chair scraped back as she stood up. She turned to Izzy, a muscle ticking in her jaw. "I wouldn't have brought you here if I'd known she was still around."

Sydney's cheeks turned crimson, her fingers quivering as she gripped the tray. Izzy couldn't help but sympathize with the flustered server. *She can't be a demon*, Izzy thought, a frown creasing on her forehead. *Do demons even get embarrassed?*

"It's okay, Rhy Rhy." Izzy motioned toward Rhylynn's seat. "Just sit down."

Rhylynn snatched her coat from the chair and pulled it on over her plaid overalls. "She's friends with Emily!"

"So. I was friends with Melanie, and you still like me."

"Trust me, Izzy. We need to leave."

Sydney's head snapped up. "Don't leave. Please. I'll get you another server," she said, placing a glass of water before Izzy.

Smiling, Izzy picked up her drink. "Thanks!" As she brought it up to her lips, Rhylynn lunged, her hand knocking the glass out of Izzy's grip. It hit the carpet with a thud, water spilling everywhere.

"Rhylynn!" Izzy's eyes widened, her mouth slightly agape as she stared at her friend. Izzy had known Rhylynn for years and never once had her friend lost her temper. Witnessing this new side of Rhylynn left her unsettled. Sydney quickly intervened as Izzy leaned forward to grab the glass, gently placing her hand on Izzy's arm to stop her.

"Don't worry, I can take care of it," she said, setting her tray on the table. She crouched down, grabbed a handful of napkins from her apron, and used them to dab at the spilled water.

Izzy sat up straighter in her seat and caught Rhylynn's gaze. She gave a slight nod in Sydney's direction, her forehead furrowing. She couldn't understand why Rhylynn was acting so rude toward their server. Ignoring Izzy, Rhylynn cast another dark look at Sydney. She slowly brought her hand behind her back, muttering something to herself. Izzy's stomach twisted into a knot. *Something is off with Rhylynn. Maybe we should leave?*

Sydney's soft voice interrupted her thoughts. "Sorry, I didn't catch that?" Izzy said, smiling politely at her.

"I'm so sorry," Sydney murmured, the wet napkins tumbling from her hand revealing a pulsating orb nestled in her palm. The surface of the deep purple sphere was laced with veins of gold that shimmered in the mist swirling around her fingers. Sydney snapped her arm forward, hurling the orb directly at Izzy.

Time slowed. Izzy was rooted to the spot, eyes widening as the glowing sphere spiralled toward her. *This is it*, she thought, her body breaking out in a cold sweat. *I'm going to die.* Instinctively, Izzy raised her arm, her bracelet growing hot against her skin, emitting its own vibrant glow.

The orb never even grazed her skin. Rhylynn's reflexes were sharper. Her protective incantation enveloped Izzy in a warm shield just in time to counter Sydney's attack. Their magic collided with a thunderous clap, igniting the room in a blinding light. A shockwave rippled outward, lifting the table as if it were paper and tossing Izzy aside like a rag doll caught in a gust of wind.

Struggling to stand up, Izzy's ears rang with the deafening screams echoing through the room. Chaos erupted as customers frantically scrambled toward the door, overturning chairs and trampling on broken dishes in their attempts to flee.

The restaurant lay in ruins as if a bomb had ripped through it. Scorch marks blackened the walls, and the carpet now hid under a shimmering layer of broken chandelier crystals. Among the scattered debris, bits of splintered wood were strewn about, tables reduced to nothing more than fuel for the small fires popping up around the room. Despite the flickering flames, all the patrons miraculously remained unharmed.

Rhylynn stood amid the wreckage, her eyes ablaze with a fierce and otherworldly glow. Her curly hair danced around her face, stirred by an unseen breeze that manifested from the raw power coming from her. Tendrils of pink mist seeped from her skin and blanketed the room in a soft, rosy hue.

"*Freezlaxation*," Rhylynn whispered as her eyelids fluttered shut.

When the mist cleared, the air glimmered with a pearlescent sheen. The customers rushing toward the door stopped in their tracks, frozen in time. Meanwhile, the flames devouring the restaurant were suspended in motion, casting an eerie stillness over everything around them.

Rhylynn opened her eyes. The otherworldly glow that had filled them now faded, replaced by the warm, soft brown of her irises. She surveyed the room, her expression darkening as her gaze fell on Sydney. The server was picking herself up from the floor. Her hair had come undone, and blood gathered from a small cut under her eye. She wasn't even fully standing when Rhylynn flew at her, pinning her up against the wall.

"Seriously, Sydney!"

Izzy came up to stand next to Rhylynn. "Wh-what just happened?"

"She threw a memory spell at you!"

"A memory spell? Why would you do that?" Izzy asked, glaring at Sydney.

Sydney's shoulders drooped, but she did not respond.

"Because I spilled your drink," Rhylynn explained. "She put something in it. Just like she did last October. Isn't that right?"

"No, I—" A sob tore through Sydney's body. "Last year…I wasn't trying to hurt her."

"Sure you weren't," Rhylynn scoffed, her voice dripping with disbelief. You were following Emily's orders."

A red flush crawled up Sydney's neck. "Emily didn't order me to do anything," she said defensively. "I owed her a favour . . . and she's my friend. I swear, I had no idea her joke would be so malicious."

Rhylynn's fingers tightened on Sydney's shoulders. "It wasn't a joke, Sydney. It caused her to hallucinate and embarrass herself in front of the entire restaurant. She could have been hurt!"

Sydney lowered her head. "I know." After a moment, she glanced up toward Izzy, her eyes filled with tears. "I'm sorry," she said, rubbing at her nose. "Emily said it would only make you gassy . . . but I-I shouldn't have done it. I really am sorry."

An ache formed in Izzy's throat as she studied the other woman. Sydney's apology carried the weight of sincerity. Izzy, after all, wasn't innocent herself, having orchestrated a rather unkind prank on Emily. How could she fault Sydney for standing by Emily's side? Rhylynn had done the same for her with Melanie and Kyler.

"Let her go, Rhy Rhy."

"I should report her to the council," Rhylynn replied. "Attacking a human not once, but twice!" She pulled back from Sydney, her hands falling to her hips. "They would bind your magic for at least a year. It would serve you right!"

Sydney wrapped her arms tightly around herself and nodded. "I'm sorry," she repeated, her voice barely audible.

Rhylynn sighed and finally turned to Izzy. "Why don't you seem surprised?" she asked, gesturing at the wreckage around them.

"Oh, I am," Izzy replied. "I knew you were a witch. I just never expected you to blow up a place with your magic."

Rhylynn's hands dropped from her hips. "You knew I was a witch?"

"For several months now, actually. Emily too."

"H-how?"

"It's a long story."

After a moment of staring at Izzy, Rhylynn walked over to a nearby table and flipped it back into place. She murmured something under her breath, and moments later, three of the splintered chairs repaired themselves midair before settling down beside the table. "Sit," Rhylynn told Izzy, nodding toward one of the chairs. "You too," she added, gesturing to Sydney.

Once settled at the table, Izzy blurted out, "You're not even breaking a sweat! The last witch I saw who used magic nearly drained himself after three spells. What are you, the wonder woman of witches?"

Sydney spoke up wearily, "She's a Rivers. Her bloodline comes from the first witch."

Izzy gave Rhylynn an appraising look before laughing, startling the other women.

Rhylynn leaned over and brushed her hand against Izzy's forehead. "She's in shock," she said to Sydney.

"I'm not in shock," Izzy pushed Rhylynn's arm away.

"Then what's so funny?" Sydney asked.

Izzy shrugged and replied, "Well . . . the situation, I suppose." She gestured toward the debris scattered around them and continued, "I don't mean this incident. It's just that I've been so scared lately. So helpless. And all this time, my best friend is some all-powerful witch." Izzy wiped the tears from her eyes, still grinning foolishly. "I should have told you sooner."

Rhylynn shook her head slowly and said, "Yeah, you should have. But Izzy, seriously, what the heck is going on?"

Izzy's smile slipped away. The weight of her secrets was taking its toll, and her shoulders sagged. She should be relieved now that she had finally confided in Rhylynn. But it was all becoming too much for Izzy to handle. The attacks, the magic, her confrontation with her mother—it was starting to overwhelm her. *Maybe I'm in shock.*

At that moment, all Izzy yearned for was the simple comfort of her bed. She wanted to fall into a dreamless sleep and emerge only after a week had passed, when the world had righted itself once more.

But instead of giving in to her exhaustion, Izzy lifted her chin up and told Rhylynn everything, not caring that Sydney was listening too. She recounted her astral projection experience and how she was dragged into the demon realms. She spoke about her rescue by an angel, meeting her soulmate and her adventure into an alternative universe. When Izzy got to the part about the psychic vampire attached to Kate, Rhylynn's eyes lit up in understanding.

As Izzy talked, a lightness came over her. She wasn't alone with this knowledge anymore, and more importantly, she finally had someone she could confide in who wouldn't think she was crazy.

"Wowzers!" Rhylynn said, pushing her glasses back up onto the bridge of her nose. "I knew something was happening with you, but this . . . this is just wild."

"Tell me about it," Izzy mumbled.

Bouncing in her seat, Rhylynn asked, "So what's the spirit world like?"

"Well, Orbistia is beautiful. All the souls are brought in by—"

As Izzy began describing the spirit world, Sydney reached across the table and grabbed her arm. Her fingers dug into Izzy's bare skin, not enough to hurt but enough to startle her into silence. "Don't," Sydney hissed, her tan face turning pale. "We aren't meant to know all the details about the spirit world."

Rhylynn's tone turned cold as she spoke. "Get your hand off her arm."

Biting her lip, Sydney quickly let go. "I'm sorry. It's just that knowing too much takes away from our growth and development in this life. The afterlife is supposed to be a mystery."

"What are you saying? That my soul isn't going to evolve?"

"You should let me take your memories," Sydney said dully, still avoiding Izzy's gaze.

"Absolutely not," Rhylynn slammed her hand down on the table. Sydney jolted backward as if Rhylynn had physically hit her. "Relax, Sydney. I'm not going to hurt you." Rhylynn narrowed her eyes. "But no one is erasing Izzy's memories. Tell Emily to bugger off or I'll go to the council."

"Emily didn't ask me to erase Izzy's memories."

"Yeah, right," Rhylynn rolled her eyes. "I honestly don't know why you're friends with her."

Sydney winced but continued, "I'm not lying. This isn't about Emily." She turned to Izzy, her expression serious. "It's your spirit guide. She came to me in a dream. Priscilla, right?"

Heat rushed through Izzy's body at the mention of her spirit guide's name. "Priscilla came to you in a dream?"

Sydney nodded. "Yes. Priscilla said that you've experienced too much of the spirit world and that it's impacting your ability to lead a normal life. She said I needed to erase your memories of the past two months."

Izzy quickly stood up, her chair tumbling backward. "That elf at the Christmas market . . . that was her doing?"

"Yes."

"And the demonic attack the following day, did she have something to do with that too?"

Sydney's eyes widened. "No, Izzy. Your guide would never do that!"

"How do you know you were talking to Izzy's guide, Sydney?" Rhylynn asked. "Maybe it was a demon."

Sydney's back stiffened. "I can tell the difference between demonic and positive energy, Rhylynn."

"How can you be so sure?" Izzy said, wiping her clammy palms on the sides of her jeans.

"I'm not just a witch," Sydney mumbled, her neck turning red again. "I'm a . . . a psychic medium."

Izzy stared at the waitress blankly. Rhylynn jumped in, saying, "It's a rare combination in the supernatural community." She glanced at Sydney and added, "You shouldn't be embarrassed about it."

"Emily said it makes my witch powers weaker," Sydney said, sounding as if she might cry. "I'm a poor spellcaster," she added.

"Well, feck, Emily!" Rhylynn exclaimed.

"Rhylynn!" Izzy covered her mouth with her hand, trying not to laugh.

"Oh, whatever," Rhylynn said and turned back to Sydney. "Seriously, though, don't listen to Emily. She's an arsehole."

"She's lonely. I've known her since we were kids. She's . . ." Sydney's eyes met Izzy's. "She's jealous of you, Izzy."

"Jealous of me? Why?"

"You come from a good family. You have connections and money. Emily's never had any of that."

"That's not an excuse to be a jerk," Rhylynn said.

As the two witches continued to argue about Emily, Izzy's attention was caught by a movement near the door. A woman with a beautiful, embroidered shawl wrapped around her hair inched forward in slow motion. Around Izzy, more and more customers started twitching in the rumble.

"Crap. The spell is starting to wear off," Rhylynn muttered.

Sydney cleared her throat and tugged on the collar of her white blouse. "Izzy," she said in a low tone, "your spirit guide wouldn't have gone through all this trouble if it wasn't important. You should really let me help."

"I'm fine, Sydney," Izzy replied, her voice sharp. "I might be a bit distracted, but that has nothing to do with my memories. I'm on a freaking demon hit list." She paused, glancing around the room. "Priscilla's here now, isn't she? Watching you do her dirty work."

"I-I don't know,"

"She's here." Izzy narrowed her eyes. She stared up toward the ceiling as if her spirit guide were hovering over them. "Stop interfering, Priscilla! And don't act like you're doing this for me. You're trying to cover up your big screw-up!" Izzy smiled. She could envision Priscilla becoming flustered, trying to defend herself to the other guides. *Good*, Izzy thought. *She deserves it.*

"We should reverse the spell now," Sydney said, a note of panic in her voice. Izzy's attention flickered to the door once more. The customers' faces contorted in discomfort as they jerked forward painfully.

"Okay," Rhylynn nodded. "This is going to take a while."

The two witches worked together, moving around with quick and precise movements. They conjured cooling mist from their hands to extinguish small fires and uttered spells to repair the damage to the restaurant. Once the last flame was put out, Rhylynn turned to Sydney, her curls hanging limply around her shoulders.

"Now we need to modify their memories," Rhylynn gestured at a young couple hiding behind an overturned tropical plant. They were awkwardly twitching in each other's arms. Their eyelids slowly lifted open as they glanced up at the two witches.

As Rhylynn circled the room, Sydney trailed closely behind, mimicking her actions by gently touching everyone they crossed paths with and whispering "*Modapto.*" A symphony of rainbow colours danced around each person, weaving new memories into the fabric of their minds.

This is incredible, Izzy thought, taking in the scene. She felt a sharp pang in her chest, and for a moment, she longed to be among them, wielding magic. She pushed the urge down. Maybe in another life. A smile flickered across her face.

Once they were done, Rhylynn's eyelids closed, and her hands lifted into the air. In a commanding voice, she said, "*Normatempus!*" The room spun around Izzy like a carousel gone wild. Then, in an instant, everything snapped back into place with a sharp pop, and the restaurant erupted with chatter and the clanging of utensils.

Sydney leaned heavily against their table, her eyes drooping with exhaustion. "I'm going to leave work early." She slipped away through the maze of tables, heading toward the kitchen.

Rhylynn was equally drained, her chest heaving as she leaned back against the wall.

"Are you okay?" Izzy asked.

"I'm fine, Iz. Just tired," Rhylynn replied, mustering a faint smile. "Magic always has a price."

"Should I take you home?"

Rhylynn pushed herself to her feet, her movements unsteady. "Take me to my grandma's place. She'll fix us both up."

Izzy hesitated, her arm halfway through the sleeve of her jacket. "Fix us both up?"

"I don't know what to do about your demon problem, but your spirit guide—that's one area where I can help."

With Rhylynn leaning against Izzy, the two girls returned to Rhylynn's battered truck. Izzy helped her friend into the passenger side and then slid into the driver's seat. The journey was silent except for the crunch of tires on the fresh snow as Izzy navigated back to her great-aunt's apartment complex, the world outside a blur of white.

They made an impromptu stop at McDonald's, and the aroma of fries soon filled the truck's cab. As Rhylynn took a bite of her burger, there was a faint return of colour to her cheeks. It wasn't much, but the greasy meal gave her some energy. By the time they walked down the familiar hallway to Mrs. River's door, Rhylynn was smiling and laughing at Izzy's jokes again.

Looking at her friend, Izzy felt safe. Everything was going to be all right. Rhylynn would find a way to safeguard Izzy's memories. Hopefully, once that was done, Izzy could try to reach out to Dax for some answers about the demonic attack. He would know what to do. Perhaps Sydney might even be willing to provide some assistance. After all, she was a medium. She had ties to the spirit world.

Rhylynn stepped around Izzy and knocked on her grandmother's door. It slowly creaked open, and a faint aroma of herbs wafted out to welcome them. Izzy's pulse quickened. She stood on the threshold of an entirely new world. Dax had opened the door to the supernatural, and now Rhylynn was guiding her through it.

CHAPTER FIVE

A Sip of Enchantment

"Hello?" The door inched open, revealing an older woman whose dyed-red hair formed a wild halo around her face. She wore a long, rose-coloured bathrobe cinched tightly at her waist. The tips of her flowered slippers were visible beneath the hem. Her green eyes flashed in recognition as they fell on Rhylynn. "Did you forget something, dear?"

"No, Gran," Rhylynn replied, "something came up, and we need your help."

Lila shifted in the doorframe, obscuring Izzy's view of the apartment. An awkward moment of silence ensued. Finally, Lila relented, "Well, all right, but the place is a mess, Rhylynn. Just give me a moment to clean up." She tilted her head subtly toward Izzy.

"It's okay, Gran." Rhylynn stepped forward, but Lila was quick to block her path.

"I need to put some things away first, Rhylynn."

"Izzy knows about us. It's okay."

Lila's gaze fell on Izzy, and her eyebrows shot up. "She knows?" She leaned out into the hall, scanning around to see if they were alone. In a hushed voice, she turned to Izzy and asked, "You know?"

Izzy nodded, her words lost to the sudden dryness of her mouth. Why was Lila acting so paranoid? Was it really that big of a deal that Izzy knew? Surely, she couldn't have been the first human to discover the existence of witches.

Mrs. Rivers stepped back from the threshold, gesturing for them to enter. As she locked the door behind them, Izzy followed Rhylynn further into the apartment. It resembled her great-aunt's apartment's layout, but the styling was entirely its own. Audrey's place was filled with cat figurines and had family photos covering every wall, while Lila's offered a calming sea of soft creams and pale browns.

A white loveseat sat against one wall beside a bookshelf. A matching recliner held a neatly folded crocheted blanket in a nearby corner. The walls were mostly bare, except for a family portrait. Izzy recognized Rhylynn in the middle, grinning broadly next to a small, impish-looking child. *That must be her little sister*, Izzy thought. She hadn't met the rest of Rhylynn's family yet, other than Mrs. Rivers.

An old Lucille Ball film was playing on the television—laughter roared out of the flatscreen as the audience reacted to something the actress did. Lila shuffled past Izzy and flicked the set off, her face flushed red as she clasped and unclasped her hands. "Izzy, why don't you take a seat. I'll go put on a pot of tea." She gave a pointed cough and moved toward the kitchen. "Rhylynn, care to join me?" Her tone left no room for argument.

With a reassuring smile to Izzy, Rhylynn trailed after her grandmother.

The room remained silent except for the steady hiss of the radiator in the corner. Curiosity took hold as Izzy slowly wandered around. *This is a witch's apartment?* Her heart sank a little. Where were the whimsical signs of magic that she'd imagined? No bubbling cauldron, no sly feline with tales to tell. Mrs. Rivers had insisted on cleaning, but for what? The home held none of the magic she had expected to find.

Sighing, Izzy collapsed into the recliner. She settled back into it, only to jump forward as a loud ringing erupted from her jacket pocket. She fumbled around in her coat and managed to pull out her phone. *MOM* flashed on the display screen.

Izzy swiped at the red button with trembling hands, disconnecting the call. *I'll message her later—maybe tomorrow*, she thought, shoving the phone back into her pocket. She wasn't going to let her mother ruin this moment. Whatever Michelle had to say could wait until the morning. *Let her feel what it's like to be ignored for once.*

Pushing aside thoughts of her mother, Izzy picked up a folded newspaper resting on the TV tray beside her. With nothing better to do, she began flipping through the pages.

On December 26th, 2023, the Belleville Occult Operations Unit successfully detained the warlock who had been using the Whirligigium *spell to terrorize non-magical individuals. In a chilling scene, law enforcement discovered three humans suspended and spinning in midair, the duration of their enchantment unknown.*

The magical signature was traced back to forty-one-year-old Joey MacLellan from the Tweed area. Mr. MacLellan has since been turned over to the Ontario High Council for . . .

Joey McLellan . . . Izzy had heard about this case. He had been arrested for assault. The radio station hadn't mentioned anything about humans floating in the air—that's something she would have remembered. She shivered, goosebumps crawling along her arm. A magical cover-up. What else was the supernatural community hiding?

Izzy kept flipping through the newspaper until she came across the advertisement section. She read aloud: "'Betty's Bewitching Broomsticks! These enchanted brooms are simply magical when cleaning those hard-to-reach areas. Just a word of caution—they can be quite temperamental and don't take kindly to being criticized if they miss a spot. According to Beatrice Crankinpop, the author of *250 Cures for Common Magical Maladies*, one of these broomsticks once retaliated by swatting her on the rump.'"

Izzy became completely engrossed by the next pages. The supernatural world unfolded before her as far more organized than she had initially believed. Gone was the notion of small, scattered pockets of witches and other magical beings living among humans. Instead, the newspaper painted a picture of an intricate and complex society.

Magical police forces, educational institutions, stores, even a broomstick taxi service, Izzy thought, her eyes widening. "They've been living right under our noses this whole time!"

Her reverie was pierced by a soft whispering that danced at the edge of her hearing. She lifted her head, her eyes sweeping over the room. Nothing was amiss. Nothing stirred. The kitchen door was closed, Rhylynn and her grandmother still conversing behind it, their voices muffled. A knot tightened in Izzy's stomach. She knew all too well the tone of a scolding. Guilt washed over her, and she sent out a silent plea, hoping her friend wouldn't get into too much trouble for helping her.

The soft whispers started again, prompting Izzy to rise and follow the noise. It drew her to a bookshelf by the loveseat. Framed photos of Rhylynn's family sat on the first two shelves, including one of the late

Mr. Rivers, whose brown eyes bore a striking resemblance to Rhylynn's. On the third shelf, an array of books was lined up neatly, several titles snagging Izzy's attention.

Curious, Izzy pulled one off. The cover art displayed a beautiful sunset set over a sandy beach. A witch wearing a classic pointed hat was held in the embrace of a shirtless man with dark green, furry skin. His horns curled around his skull, brushing against his lover's dark hair. *Forbidden Love by Randi-Lin Sheppard* was scrawled across the cover in elegant script.

Izzy smirked and put the book back. It was clear that Ms. Rivers was into the romance genre. It all made sense now—the friendly rivalry with Audrey over Mr. Smith's affections. She was like a character in her own romance novel.

Smiling, Izzy glanced at the next shelf. Centred among the books was an urn, its black tourmaline surface polished to a muted gleam, a pentagon etched sharply into its side. Nestled beside it were tiny porcelain animal figurines, carefully arranged as if they were part of a larger scene. Izzy couldn't help but think about her great-aunt Audrey's porcelain collection of cats. Maybe Mrs. Rivers wasn't so different from her after all.

One figurine, a small brown owl, stood out from all the rest. It had a chipped ear and was facing the back of the bookshelf as though engaged in silent dialogue with the surrounding ornaments. Intrigued, Izzy leaned closer, her gaze tracing the intricate details of the feathers on its body.

The owl was so lifelike that, without the light reflecting off its ceramic surface, it could have easily been mistaken for a living creature. As if reading her mind, the little owl's head turned. The porcelain clinked as its neck rubbed up against its body.

"Holy crap," Izzy squealed, stumbling back from the bookshelf. Startled by her reaction, the owl teetered and tapped into another figurine, sending it toppling with a clatter.

The room filled with an uproar, resonating with indignant squeaks and grumbles. "Way to go, Franklin! You broke form right in front of the human," a little mouse said, hopping toward the owl.

"Yeah, you nitwit, and you knocked Charlie over," an elephant chimed in, pointing at a porcelain sloth teetering on the edge of the shelf.

"It's not my fault," Franklin replied, rotating his glass head to glare at Izzy. "She was staring at me!"

"So what?" the mouse said, "That's no excuse for breaking form."

"It was making me self-conscious," Franklin muttered, his eyes downcast. "You know how I feel about my chipped ear, Terry."

"Oh, for crying out loud!" Terry's whiskers bristled. "Now she knows about magic, Franklin! Lila is going to have to modify the poor girl's memory."

"Actually, I already knew," Izzy said, inching back toward the shelf.

A little dog wobbled up to her. "Rhylynn told you about magic? Why would she do that?"

Izzy stared in fascination at the cute Pomeranian. Its tiny fox-like face peered up at her. Usually, she didn't like dogs—she was bit by one as a child. But this ceramic puppy was harmless. Smiling, she reached out and scratched between its ears. The dog was cold, its fur smooth.

It bit down on her finger, sinking its teeth into her skin. Yelping in pain, she jerked away. "Why did you do that?" she asked, pressing her finger to her mouth and tasting the metallic tang of blood.

The dog yipped at her in response and wobbled back to his companions, his bottom clinking against the wooden shelf.

Mrs. Rivers' boisterous voice echoed through the air. "They don't like to be touched much, my porcelain pets. Delicate things they are. Here, dear, let me heal that right up!"

Izzy spun around. "I-I'm sorry, Mrs. Rivers. I shouldn't have been snooping."

Lila smiled, revealing her dentures. Chuckling, she said, "It's all right. It's only natural for you to be curious." She took Izzy's finger and brought it closer to her face, examining the small abrasion. "In the future," she added, meeting Izzy's eyes, "be careful not to touch magical items . . . you can never tell which ones might bite."

"Yes, ma'am," Izzy mumbled, sucking in her breath as Lila pressed down on her wound. "*Nanteos!*" A warm, prickly sensation spread over Izzy's hand as Mrs. Rivers cast the spell. Within seconds, the cut was healed entirely, replaced with a fresh layer of skin. "There, good as new," Lila said, giving Izzy a reassuring pat on the shoulder.

Izzy's new skin was soft and a little sensitive as she stroked it with her other hand. She couldn't help but feel envious of Mrs. Rivers, wishing she had reincarnated into a witch's body instead of a human. *All my problems could be solved if I could wield magic,* she thought. The ability to heal oneself and conjure powers would be an obvious choice for anyone. The list of benefits was endless.

Lila's gentle touch interrupted Izzy's thoughts. She led her over to the loveseat. "Thank you," Izzy murmured, sitting beside Rhylynn, whose sullen expression spoke volumes. Izzy's throat tightened, her mouth dry. Rhylynn had undoubtedly gotten herself into trouble by getting involved with Izzy's problems.

As Mrs. Rivers disappeared into the kitchen, Izzy cast her friend an apologetic look. Moments later, Lila returned with a tray of tea and biscuits and set it down on the coffee table. "What do you take in your tea, dear?"

"Oh, um . . . sugar and milk." Izzy reached for the teapot, but it moved of its own accord, slipping out of her grasp and levitating in the air. It tilted, and a stream of fragrant brown liquid poured out, filling the awaiting cup. The room was immediately filled with the heady scent of fresh herbs infused with a subtle floral undertone. Izzy stilled, her lips parting in wonder. The dishes stirred to life, a pitcher splashing milk into her cup and teaspoons clattering as they heaped in sugar.

"Enough dearies, that's enough!" Mrs. Rivers chided the tea set, shooing the spoons away. "Honestly," Lila said, shaking her head in dismay, "sometimes it's easier to do it yourself."

Fixing her tea, Lila settled into the recliner across from Izzy and Rhylynn and took a sip before speaking. "So, Izzy," she said, "it seems your memories need protection." Lila studied Izzy over her steaming cup before continuing. "Are you sure you want to involve yourself in our world?" She gestured toward the bookshelf where the porcelain creatures were lined up near the edge, quietly listening to the unfolding conversation.

"I'm already involved," Izzy said. "Now that I've met Dax . . . my soulmate . . . there's no way I'll let him go. I'll do anything to keep my memories of him." She raised her gaze to meet Lila's. "Please, Mrs. Rivers. Will you help me?"

Lila set her cup down and leaned back in her chair. "Well, I suppose I don't have much choice, do I?" she said. "Your aunt would never forgive me if I said no. Not that she would know, mind you. But I would."

She sighed heavily and stood up, shooting a sharp look at the porcelain animals, who were calling out their objections. "Never you mind now," she said. "This doesn't concern you!" Lila turned and began walking down the narrow hallway, past the small kitchenette. "Come along, girls," she called out over her shoulder.

Exhaling quietly, Izzy set her cup down and stood up. Tucking her trembling hands into her hoodie, she followed Rhylynn down the hall. She was going to keep her memories of the spirit world—of Dax.

She hadn't grasped the full extent of her fear of losing them until she'd met Mrs. Rivers' gaze. What luck that her great-aunt's neighbour was a witch. In another life, she might have had her mind wiped by now.

"The Bind Your Mind Potion," Lila called back to her as they arrived at the end of the hall. The older woman was standing at the opening of another room, her large frame blocking the entranceway. "One spoonful and your memories will remain permanently attached to your brain. It should protect your mind against any memory-erasing spell or potion." With that, she disappeared into the room, the light flickering on as she entered.

Izzy followed behind her. Her skin tingled as she looked around. The space had been magically enlarged, almost double the size of Mrs. Rivers' living room. One side was a wall of glass that overlooked the Bay of Quinte. The view was stunning. Outside, the snow fell softly from the darkened sky, collecting in heaps on the frozen waterfront.

Lila strode past the window toward the back wall, the polished wooden floor creaking under her steps. She flung open a large cabinet and began to rummage through it. "Let's see, a pinch of turmeric," she murmured, grabbing a jar off the shelf, "five dried blueberries, and some orange peelings." She turned to Rhylynn, "Would you mind getting me an egg from the fridge, dear?"

Rhylynn scurried out of the room as Mrs. Rivers approached an empty cauldron in the nearby corner. Within minutes, an unnaturally green fire roared to life underneath it. As she worked, Mrs. Rivers hummed softly to herself, and Izzy bit back her grin. Lila Rivers was full of surprises. She had eclectic taste, ranging from steamy romance novels to Taylor Swift's music.

"I need a drop of sneezewort plant," Mrs. Rivers said without looking up. "Izzy, please take an empty beaker and collect some of the mucus that sneezes out." She gestured toward some low-hanging plants near the doorway.

Reaching around Lila, Izzy snatched a glass beaker from the counter and crossed the room. Rhylynn passed by her carrying the egg. When she saw where Izzy was heading, she wrinkled her nose and turned her head away, a soft chuckle escaping her lips.

Locating the sneezewort plant was easy—it was covered in oozing blisters and hairy warts. As Izzy approached it, the plant sneezed, sending a light mist of mucus through the air. It landed on Izzy's outstretched hand. Recoiling, she rubbed her fingers against her thighs, and the slime soaked into the rough material of her jeans.

Izzy gagged into the sleeve of her sweater before slowly inching toward the plant once again. She collected the next glob of mucus that came flying toward her and hurried back to Mrs. Rivers. Lila took the beaker from Izzy and dumped its contents into the cauldron. It gurgled, the soup turning a bright shade of yellow.

"Next, add the egg and then the powdered dragon claw," Lila said, instructing Rhylynn to crack the egg over the pot. As the new ingredients were added, the potion became fiery red. Lila nodded in approval, her curly hair falling around her round face. "All that's left is the blood of a spongy moth caterpillar. Luckily, there was an infestation in the area this year, so I have more than enough on hand!" She turned to her granddaughter and smiled. "You know what to do, Rhylynn. And please remember to wear gloves. Their fur can cause a rash, dear."

As Rhylynn hurried off to drain a caterpillar, Mrs. Rivers continued stirring the potion. The scent of sulphur and bile rose from it, filling the room. Covering her mouth, Izzy backed up and accidentally bumped against the window.

She turned and pressed her forehead against the cold glass, enjoying the refreshing sensation against her skin. She hoped Lila would finish up soon—her stomach couldn't hold out much longer. Izzy was used to the smell of decay from working in the funeral home, but this was unlike anything she had ever smelled before.

"While we wait for Rhylynn, I might as well perform a spell to open your eyes to all of the supernatural world." Mrs. Rivers approached Izzy and placed a hand atop her head. "*Glamdato!*" she said, pressing down firmly before Izzy could respond. A heavy pressure expanded behind her eyeballs, filling her skull. It faded away a moment later, leaving behind a minor headache.

"That felt terrible," Izzy said, her hand moving to massage her temple.

"Yes, well, magic isn't always pleasant. You should be able to see through all types of glamours now, though."

"Thank you."

Mrs. Rivers moved back to the pot and resumed stirring it with a wooden spoon. A moment later, Rhylynn returned with the last ingredient and tossed the vial of blood into the cauldron. The scent of rust mixed with the other unpleasant odours, and the bubbling soup turned pink. Lila collected some thick liquid into a mug and handed it to Izzy. "Enjoy!"

Enjoy? She expects me to drink this? She glanced over at Rhylynn, who nodded and smiled. Trusting that Rhylynn wouldn't poison her, Izzy brought the cup to her lips. The potion pooled on her tongue. It tasted chalky and bitter. Tilting her head back, she forced herself to swallow. It slid down like thick sludge, settling heavily in her stomach. *Did it even work?* Izzy didn't feel any different. She supposed she should be grateful it hadn't turned her skin blue or, worse, caused her to grow a third eye. Her shoulders sagged. She had just consumed magic. Shouldn't she have felt something?

A sudden popping sensation jolted through her head. Her wavy blonde hair flew as if caught in a gust of wind. It slowly settled back down over her shoulders, now a tangled mess of knots. Mrs. Rivers clapped her hands together, and the cauldron and all the empty vials disappeared. "Just remember, Izzy, the potion will only work on your physical form. If you astral project again, your spirit guide might still be able to erase your memories."

Izzy exchanged a quick glance with Rhylynn. She needed Dax's help, and she missed him. Her eyes flickered closed for a moment, his image coming clearly into her mind—tall, blond, curly haired, and with a smile so wide that it set her pulse racing. It wasn't a question of whether she would astral project again but rather when. *I'll have to be careful,* she thought.

"Now, I may appear fit as a fiddle," Mrs. Rivers continued, "but my old bones are in need of a good night's sleep." She hustled Izzy and Rhylynn out of the room, the door closing behind them with a soft click.

Leading them back down the hall, Lila picked up the conversation. "Rhylynn, I'd like you to be here by three o'clock tomorrow afternoon. I know it's New Year's Eve, and you girls will likely be up all night, but we need to start your advanced training. We'll begin by covering the *Widdershins* jinx, and if you're up for it, we may even try the *Serpentstoneola* spell."

A smile broke out on Rhylynn's face as she nodded in agreement. Izzy's shoulders relaxed. Her friend's sullen mood had dissipated. Despite her initial worries, Izzy hadn't caused too much trouble.

As they said their goodbyes to Lila and left the apartment, Izzy pulled her friend in for a hug. "Thank you," she said, squeezing the smaller woman tighter.

Rhylynn pulled away. "Aw crap, Izzy. We missed the movie!"

Glancing at her wristwatch, Izzy's shoulders drooped slightly. "It's already ten o'clock. I'm sorry, Rhy Rhy. We could always catch the later show . . . but we'd miss the fireworks."

"Nah," Rhylynn said, slinging her arm through Izzy's as they walked toward the elevator. "I have a better idea."

"Oh?"

"Wanna go to a party?"

"Where? I'm not really into the whole club scene."

A sly smile played on Rhylynn's lips as she bumped her shoulder against Izzy's. "I wasn't referring to a human party," she said as they stepped onto the elevator.

The doors glided shut, enclosing Izzy and Rhylynn in the small metal box. The soft hum of the elevator's descent filled the silence, and Izzy's body trembled. *I'm going to a supernatural party!* She couldn't wait to see what the night had in store for her.

CHAPTER SIX

The Tethered Balloon

"So, now that you know all about my kind, do you want to spend the night at my house tonight? Save me from having to sleep in your crappy bed." Rhylynn cast a sidelong glance at Izzy, her lips curling into an impish grin as she maneuvered the truck along the paved road. The snowfall had ceased, leaving a pristine white blanket that shimmered beneath the starlight.

Izzy's gaze lingered on the shadowy silhouettes of trees flanking the highway. They were miles from Belleville now, with only the occasional light of a distant house piercing the night. Her breath cast a mist over the glass, momentarily blurring the view. "My bed isn't crappy," she said, her finger sketching a heart on the fogged window.

"It's a dorm bed. It's crap."

"It's not crap. My mom bought a featherbed to put on it."

Rhylynn's laughter echoed in the confined space of the cab. "If Emily finds out . . ."

Groaning, Izzy turned away from the window to stare at her friend. "I know. It's ridiculous, though, hating me because my mom has money. We aren't even rich."

"To someone that came from nothing, your family would be considered well off." Rhylynn offered Izzy a half-smile. "I'm not trying to stick up for her. It's just that some people have difficulty seeing past the pain of going without."

"I don't think it's only the money though. Wally comes from money, and I'm sure she has a crush on him."

Rhylynn shrugged, her gaze fixated ahead. "Well, you're a likeable person, and she's not. I guess she hates you because you have everything going for you."

Izzy's response was a burst of laughter, which abruptly ended as the truck slowed down and started jolting along the side of the road. A sign soon appeared, indicating they had reached the H.R. Frink Conservation Area.

As the vehicle came to a stop, Izzy let out a bitter sigh. "Yeah, I have everything going for me, all right. My dad's dead, I've pretty much ruined any chance of a relationship with my mom, my boyfriend is a ghost, and the queen of demons has a hit out on me."

"Emily doesn't know all of that."

"I know . . . Even if she did, I doubt she would care. She'd find something positive and hate me for it."

"Like that you *have* a boyfriend?" Rhylynn said, her hand reaching over to turn off the ignition. As the deep rumble of the truck's engine died, the warmth inside the cab began to fade away.

"Yeah." Izzy caught Rhylynn smirking and asked, "What's so funny?"

Rhylynn stepped out of the truck, and the door slammed shut with a loud bang that reverberated through the silent forest. Following suit, Izzy emerged from the passenger side and joined Rhylynn outside. "Well?" she said, folding her arms across her chest. "Out with it!"

"Your boyfriend's a ghost. You do know how weird that sounds, right?" Rhylynn asked as she led them into the woods. She paused, murmuring something, and then two bright, glowing balls of light floated up and out of her hands. With a flick of her wrist, she sent the glowing spheres ahead of them, illuminating a path through the forest.

"Yes, I suppose it's a bit weird. But he's not just a ghost, Rhylynn. Dax is my soulmate."

"So, how does that work exactly?" Rhylynn asked as they trudged through the underbrush, her thick rubber boots snapping twigs. "Your relationship will always be long-distance, and you'll never date, you know, a living person?"

The two women walked silently for a moment, their footsteps echoing on the path. The cold bit into Izzy's fingers, and she shoved them into her pockets for warmth. Rhylynn's words echoed in her mind, and she couldn't help but wonder if she was making a mistake. Was she really going to spend the rest of her life alone, pining for Dax? The truth was, she didn't know if she would ever see him again. Despite her efforts to astral project, she had yet to make progress. And even if she did, would Dax want her to wait for him? It was hard to say.

A tear streaked down Izzy's cheek. The world around her became a watercolour blur, and she swallowed hard. She didn't want anyone else but Dax. It was irrational, considering she barely knew him. But her soul recognized him. Their connection was something she would never forget. She couldn't move on. She refused to.

So, where did that leave her? Destined for a life without marriage, children, or grandchildren—with only her career as a social worker. As fulfilling as it would be, it wouldn't last forever. Eventually, she would retire, and then what? Loneliness. A gnawing unease coiled in her stomach, tightening its grip as it ascended to her throat. All those years of waiting to reunite with her soulmate seemed like an eternity. What was the point of enduring such an isolated life?

Brushing away the tear, Izzy glanced at Rhylynn. Her friend was silent, an expectant look on her face, waiting for a response Izzy couldn't give. Anything she said would only lead to more questions, and she wasn't prepared to answer them, so she deflected. "Where exactly are we going?" she asked, sidestepping a large rock jutting from the ground.

Rhylynn raised an eyebrow but didn't push the issue. Instead, she pointed to a dim light flickering through the trees ahead. "Some of my friends are throwing a bonfire . . . for supes only, of course," she said with a grin.

"Supernaturals," Izzy murmured, a thrill running through her body at the word. She wondered what kind of creatures she would meet tonight. "Will they care that I'm with you?" she asked as her boots crackled against a frozen puddle.

"Probably not," Rhylynn replied. "Most of them are tired of hiding from humans, especially the warlocks. There's a push to reveal ourselves, but the World Council of Supernatural Beings is against it. Gran's actually a member, although you'd never guess it."

A rustling from behind cut their conversation short. Izzy's muscles locked tight, mirroring Rhylynn's rigid posture as another rustle whispered through the darkness. *Probably nothing*, she tried to convince herself. But Rhylynn's pale face suggested otherwise.

"Should we—"

Rhylynn held up her hand to silence Izzy. The atmosphere grew tense as her fingertips crackled with electric energy, and she stepped forward, positioning herself in front of Izzy. The forest was eerily silent as if a predator were lurking in the shadows. Rhylynn's voice shattered the stillness as she called out, "Show yourself!"

A lean figure stepped out from the woods. His dark hair cascaded around his face in waves, and his brown eyes glowed with an unnatural light. The faint smell of autumn leaves lingered around him despite the trees now being bare of any foliage but the blanketing snow.

Izzy exhaled loudly, and before Rhylynn could stop her, she bounded past her friend into the man's arms. "Lovepreet," she said, stepping back from him, "you scared the bejesus out of me! I thought you were a wolf . . . or a—"

"A supe? Because that's what he is," Rhylynn said as she moved toward them. "A werewolf, right?"

"Yes," he said softly. As he gazed at Rhylynn, a goofy grin spread across his handsome features. Izzy shuffled her feet, pulling back from them. Lovepreet stepped in closer to Rhylynn. "How did you know?"

"Y-you smell like the autumn wind," Rhylynn said, brushing a hand through her hair. "It's my favourite time of the year," she added, averting her eyes.

Feeling as if she should save her friend from embarrassment, Izzy jumped into the conversation. "I go to college with Lovepreet," she said to Rhylynn. "He's also the lead singer in the Gravediggers . . . You know, that band Kyler is in."

Lovepreet's smile faded at the mention of her ex-boyfriend. "Izzy, I am truly sorry to learn of your heartbreak."

"Trust me, I'm not heartbroken," Izzy replied as she thought about Kyler. In truth, she was happy to be rid of him. She no longer had to endure his narrow-minded opinions and groping hands. She frowned, reflecting on the cost of that freedom: her friendship with Melanie.

"I am glad you are doing well, Izzy," Lovepreet said, his gaze drifting over to Rhylynn again. "I didn't realize you were of the supernatural kind."

A chuckle bubbled up from Izzy's throat. "I'm as human as it gets. Just Rhylynn's plus-one for the night."

"Are you heading to the bonfire?" Rhylynn gestured toward the flickering lights through the trees.

"I was not aware there was a party happening tonight . . . I come out here to run during full moons.

"Lovepreet's an international student," Izzy explained to Rhylynn. "He came to Canada at the start of the school year."

A crimson flush coloured Rhylynn's cheeks. "Oh. Sorry, I assumed you would know about the party since you're a supe too."

Silence descended, awkward and heavy. Izzy nudged Rhylynn, gesturing for her to invite Lovepreet along. Rhylynn remained quiet, glancing every now and then at Lovepreet and quickly looking away before he could notice.

A flicker of amusement crossed Izzy mind as she took in her friend's behaviour. Rhylynn was never at a loss for words. Her attraction to Lovepreet was evident, and judging by how he returned her glances, the feeling was mutual.

Stamping her feet to warm them, Izzy gazed toward the distant light that promised the comfort of a fire. Impatient, she turned to Lovepreet. "Well, why don't you come with us? Rhylynn can introduce you around. Right, Rhy Rhy?"

Rhylynn blinked, snapping out of her love-stricken trance. "Yes!" she said, her voice ringing with enthusiasm. "Come with us! It'll be fun!" Her courage returned in a rush, and she boldly slipped her hand into his, tugging him forward down the winding path that led through the forest. Lovepreet's eyes widened, but he didn't object, allowing Rhylynn to lead him deeper into the woods.

Izzy trailed a few steps behind, grinning at their entwined hands. Maybe something good would come from their connection. They were both such great people, and they deserved to find happiness.

Most people would be terrified to discover that their friend was a werewolf, but for Izzy, there was only excitement bubbling up inside her. How many others around her were hiding their true identities? She had a feeling that the night ahead would be full of even more surprises.

She trailed behind her friends as they continued up the path. A faint vibration buzzed in her pocket, signalling the arrival of a text message. *Probably Arlo.* A smile tugged at her lips as she thought about her charismatic housemate. She swiped open her screen, expecting to see a comical photo of a gangly redheaded man wearing a sparkly top hat and oversized New Year's Eve sunglasses. Instead, she saw two words from her mother: *Call me.*

Heat bubbled up in her chest, rising to her shoulders and flushing her face. *Call her? Why? So she can tell me that I'm being selfish? That I'm ruining all her plans? She can't even let me have this one night?* Clenching her jaw, Izzy switched her phone to silent and shoved it back into her jacket. *Out of sight, out of mind,* she thought as she hastened to catch up with her friends.

The path led them to an open clearing, where a bonfire crackled and popped in the centre. The flames shot up high, illuminating the area with an orange and red glow and casting a frenzy of shadows around the snow-covered ground. Sparks pirouetted into the darkened sky above, winking out like fleeting stars. Approaching the fire, Izzy inhaled the tangy scent of charred wood.

A group of people sat around the bonfire, perched on logs and stumps, some strumming on musical instruments. In contrast, others simply listened, drinks clutched in their hands. Soft melodies filled the air, mingling with the murmur of conversation and laughter.

As Izzy surveyed her surroundings, her gaze landed on a small group of creatures huddled together, away from the rest. Their skin varied, with some smooth as polished stone, while others had a soft down in different shades. There were men with twisted tusks protruding from their jaws and women with eyes that were oversized and expressive. Each creature had its own distinct appearance that set it apart from the others.

The air was filled with laughter as a few group members used their magic to transform their fingers into sparklers, playfully carving intricate designs and patterns in the darkness. Several nearby witches glared at them from overtop bottles marked *Maplelicious Honeycooler*. Their hands glowed with green flames as they warmed their drinks.

Izzy's chest tightened as she walked past the strange group of creatures, and a sheen of cold sweat coated her forehead. *Demons?* Her fingers instinctively wrapped around the bracelet on her wrist. It was cool to the touch. Maybe these were just creatures with demonic blood in them. But they resembled the creature that had attempted to poison her at the Christmas market. *Why would Rhylynn bring me to a party with these . . . things here?* She glanced at her friend, but Rhylynn was oblivious to the monstrous group, her attention entirely focused on Lovepreet.

Rhylynn led them through the crowd and over to a different group of people huddled together. "Hey, guys," she said, dropping Lovepreet's hand as she sat beside a man with long, orange hair pulled into a ponytail. His skin was abnormally pale.

"Hey, Rhy Rhy," he said, leaning over to give her a one-armed hug. He held a thermos full of a thick, red liquid in his free hand.

Izzy suppressed a shudder at the vampire before her. She glanced over at Lovepreet, but he didn't seem worried. On the contrary, he was staring at the vampire's arm, still draped over Rhylynn's shoulder. *Jealous,* Izzy thought, a smile tugging at her mouth. *He's definitely into her.*

Rhylynn rested her head on the man's shoulder and said, "Ronnie is my uncle."

"Great uncle," Ronnie corrected, flashing his fangs at Izzy. He gestured to the other side of him. "Take a seat, love," he said. "I don't bite."

As Izzy dropped down to perch on the log, Ronnie gestured toward a man who, like Lovepreet, had an unnatural glow in his eyes. The man was approaching from the other side of the fire. "Jace, baby, how about rustling up a few more coolers for my friends."

Jace bent down, reaching into a burlap bag, and retrieved three Maplelicious Honeycoolers. "Sure thing, love," he said, flashing Ronnie a doting smile. After handing one to Izzy, he took a seat beside her.

Izzy grasped the cool bottle, its surface slick against her palm. "Here," Rhylynn offered, leaning over to touch Izzy's drink. A burst of green flames appeared around the glass, dancing gently around Izzy's fingers without burning her. Soon after, the bottle started to warm up in her hand. "It tastes better when it's warm," Rhylynn explained.

Popping the top off her cooler, Izzy brought it to her lips. The sweet scent of maple entwined with honey wafted toward her, and as she took a tentative sip, relaxation instantly washed over her. It was accompanied by a warm, soothing sensation that flowed down to her toes. She turned to Jace, her shyness dissipating, and asked bluntly, "So, you and Ronnie, huh? Are you two dating?"

He nodded. "Yup, nearly a year now."

"Aren't vampires and werewolves supposed to hate each other?"

"Nah," Jace said, taking a sip of his drink. "That's a myth. My kind gets along fine with vamps." He leaned in closer, lowering his voice to a whisper. "It's the witches and warlocks that have a hate on for each other." His gaze drifted over to the group of demon-like creatures who were now using their magic to fling snowballs at each other.

"Warlocks? I thought they were demons," Izzy said. It made sense now. Priscilla would never send a demon after her.

Rhylynn leaned across Ronnie, her voice coming out in a quiet hiss. "Don't let them hear you compare them to demons, Izzy. It's a huge insult. They don't carry any demonic blood."

Izzy glanced at the nearest warlock, studying his twisted horns and pig-like snout. "They must get that a lot."

"Mostly from witches," Jace replied, flashing Rhylynn an apologetic glance.

"Why don't you like warlocks, Rhy Rhy?"

"I don't hate them personally," Rhylynn began. "It's some old, stupid feud that has gotten out of hand between our two groups. Many witches see warlocks as being weak because their magic does not seem as strong as ours. But their magic is weaker because they use so much of their energy glamouring themselves to look human. If they didn't have to hide who they really are, I imagine they would be as strong as us or possibly even stronger. I—"

An ear-piercing shriek echoed through the air. Izzy's bracelet grew warm against her skin. Around her, some people leaped to their feet, abandoning their beverages as they assumed defensive positions. Others, like Izzy, remained frozen, unsure of what was happening.

The sky boomed with thunder, and at the edge of the woods, electricity crackled in the air, covering the figure of a woman. The sharp scent of ozone permeated the atmosphere. Goosebumps spread along Izzy's arm as she stood and edged closer to Rhylynn. Electricity shot out from the woman's outstretched fingers, zigzagging toward Izzy.

A hand snaked out from behind the woman, yanking on her arm. "Emily, stop!" The contact was enough to shatter the young witch's concentration. The electricity fizzled out, leaving scorch marks on the ground. Izzy's housemate, Emily, stood glaring at Izzy, her plain face twisted into an ugly snarl.

Emily jerked her arm away. "Let go of me, Sydney!"

Sydney reached for Emily to pull her back again. "We should leave," she said, trying to turn her around.

"I'm not going anywhere," Emily snarled, shoving Sydney hard.

Caught off balance, Sydney lost her footing and stumbled to the ground. Her lower lip trembled, tears welling up in her brown eyes. Izzy's throat thickened. Despite their history, Sydney wasn't a bad person. She evidently cared for Emily, even if the sentiment didn't seem to be reciprocated.

Disregarding her fallen friend, Emily marched forward, her finger jabbing in Rhylynn's direction. "Did you tell her? Did you? You told her that I'm a—"

"A bitch?" Izzy retorted, closing the distance between them. Heat surged through her body as she glared at her roommate and crossed her arms. "Rhylynn didn't need to tell me that. I already knew."

A ripple of laughter rolled through the gathering of warlocks. Their snowball fight was forgotten as they had turned to watch the spectacle unfold. Emily's hand clenched into a tight fist at her side, her mouth quivering as she stared at Izzy. On her wrist, Izzy's bracelet began to pulse, warmth radiating from the thin band. Yet, she didn't need it to warn her of danger this time. She already knew what Emily was capable of. Suddenly, provoking the witch didn't seem like a wise decision.

Emily's attack came so quickly it nearly caught Izzy off guard. A dazzling bolt of electricity hurtled toward Izzy, only to be swiftly intercepted by Lovepreet, who positioned himself as a shield to protect her. He stood firm, unflinching as the hex collided with him. There was a moment, suspended and still, before the spell reversed course. It careened back to Emily and caught her in the face with an audible crack.

For a brief instance, nothing happened. Then, slowly at first, Emily's features stretched and swelled. Her head filled out and rose like a balloon being pumped full of air. Her eyes shifted to the sides of her skull, and her nose and mouth stretched outward comically. Emily let out a series of high-pitched squeals, frantically clutching at her ballooning head. Around her, the laughter rose. Nobody moved to help. Izzy's pulse pounded in her ears as she witnessed the transformation. Emily ascended gradually, her feet leaving the ground inch by inch as if the air was hesitating to take her.

A strange lightheaded sensation came over Izzy as she watched Emily bobbing around in the air. She sank back onto the log, massaging her temples. Lovepreet settled beside her. Izzy turned to him, her mouth agape. "I-I don't understand," she said, touching his chest. "How did that not hurt you?"

"Hexes do not work on werewolf skin," he said, wrapping her in a comforting hug. "Perhaps we should leave?" he asked, his eyes connecting with Rhylynn's.

Emily's shrieks pierced the air as her head continued expanding in size. Sydney jumped in the air underneath her, frantically trying to grab Emily's flailing feet. Finally, with the help of another witch, she got Izzy's housemate secured to the ground.

"I can't even get away from her in my own community," Emily sobbed.

A momentary pang of guilt hit Izzy. Leaning toward Rhylynn, she said, "Maybe you should go help her."

"Yeah, um, no. That was meant for you, remember," Rhylynn said, her gaze narrowing at Emily as a rope was fastened to her ankle and then tethered to Sydney. "Besides," she needs a potion to reverse that, and it will take at least a day to brew. Serves her right."

The crowd parted, a silent reverence falling over them as Sydney left. Emily followed, bobbing awkwardly in the sky above. Izzy continued to watch Emily's form grow smaller and smaller long after the party resumed. Eventually, she reached down to retrieve her Maplelicious Honeycooler. Taking a sip, she found it had grown cold, its sweetness concentrated into a syrupy residue that lingered on her tongue.

Rhylynn was leaning close to Lovepreet, deep in conversation, and Ronnie and Jace had disappeared together off into the woods. As the time drew closer to twelve o'clock, a hush fell over the gathering. Then, as if on cue, the sky came alive with a symphony of colours and lights, each magical firework blooming against the canvas of the night.

Magic was in the air, and her friends were nearby, yet an inexplicable sense of loneliness came over Izzy. As the last sparks disappeared into the night sky, the empty space beside her became a painful reminder of Dax's absence. No one else could ever fill that void.

CHAPTER SEVEN

The Shadow's Embrace

Soft whistling floated through the small room, punctuated by the occasional grunt. Izzy peered across to where Rhylynn lay in her bed, her chest's steady rise and fall marking the rhythm of her deep slumber. A cold breeze blew through the cracked window, disrupting the room's stillness. Izzy shivered, tightened her grip on the comforter, and curled up on the narrow spare bed.

Shadows from the overhead fan flickered across the wainscoting of Rhylynn's bedroom walls. Izzy froze. For a moment, she'd glimpsed the familiar shadow that had been present throughout her week. But when she blinked, the figure had dissipated, swallowed again by the darkness.

Sighing, she closed her eyes. The magical explosion at the restaurant and the incident with Emily weighed heavily on her mind. And then there were the supernatural attacks she had endured in Toronto during the holidays. *Is this my life now?* she thought. Would things have been simpler if she had let Priscilla erase her memories? Drifting toward sleep, her mind lingered on the image of her soulmate.

The minutes slipped by in the quiet room, disturbed only by Rhylynn's gentle snoring and the occasional creak of a bed as the girls shifted. Izzy stirred, feeling the discomfort of the twisted sheets around her legs. She kicked the comforter to the foot of her bed, the cool air a brief relief against her warm skin. Her blond hair spread out like a halo on the pillow, her expression relaxed. Calmness and peace held sway for a short time until, without warning, Izzy's eyes flew open.

A relentless buzzing swelled in her ears, escalating to a crescendo that left her quivering uncontrollably. In a futile attempt to shield herself from the noise, she tried to reach for her ears only to find she couldn't move.

Paralysis gripped her body, pinning her to the bed as if an invisible adhesive bound her.

Adrenaline surged through her veins. A tingling began in her fingertips and swiftly engulfed her. Izzy's entire body buzzed as if charged with electricity, and then a series of unsettling pops rippled through her. She knew what was happening. The pull toward the spiritual realm was strong, and she couldn't resist it if she wanted to see Dax again. *Calm down*, she chided herself. *Breathe in, Breathe out. It's almost over.* Gradually, she surrendered to the separation, and in one final pop, everything went quiet. The heaviness of her limbs and the cold breeze circulating around the room faded away.

Izzy blinked, finding herself in control of herself once more. She rolled onto her side, only to discover that she no longer rested on the bed. Several inches below, her physical body lay still. The only sign of life was the rhythmic motion of her chest as she breathed. A long, shimmering cord stretched from her spirit to her physical body. The shining tether slowly disappeared from sight. However, she could still sense its existence. It gently tugged at the back of her neck as she hovered in midair.

"Finally!" someone said from near the door.

She instantly recognized the voice, and joy rushed through her. *Dax!* In her eagerness to sit up, she inadvertently flipped over, her body floating awkwardly as she grappled to gain her footing.

Boisterous laughter filled the room, and Izzy's cheeks reddened. "You can come help anytime now, Dax," she called out as she scrambled to stand up.

A gentle touch on her elbow guided her body back to an upright position. Her feet hovered an inch above the floor as if standing on a cushion of air. Dax's hand dropped to meet hers, their fingers intertwining.

"Close your eyes," he whispered from behind her. Her stomach fluttered at the sound of his voice. She obeyed and leaned into him, surrendering to the energy coursing between them. Warmth enveloped Izzy, and at that moment, she wanted nothing more than to stay wrapped in his embrace forever.

He felt the connection too. She was sure of it. His voice quivered with emotion when he spoke next. "You need to imagine that you can feel all your senses. Like touch," he said softly, trailing his fingers along her bare arm.

She shivered, pressing herself closer to him. She could definitely feel his touch.

Dax chuckled as he continued, "Visualize your feet on the ground. You control your energy signature. If you want to experience the senses, you will. It's all a matter of perspective."

Her shoulders relaxed, and a gentle smile tugged at the corners of her mouth. She turned, her gaze locking onto her soulmate.

"It would have been helpful to know all that last time."

Dax reached up, his fingers rubbing at the back of his neck as he smiled shyly at her. "Sorry, Iz. I was just so excited to be with you. I didn't think about it."

"It's okay. Honestly, I think I naturally started doing it by the time I met you. You did mention something about not feeling pain as a spirit, but I never thought to ask you why not."

"Yeah. But I should have been more on it," he said, looking at her sheepishly. "I can't believe you're here again though," he continued, tenderly brushing her cheek. "I've been hanging around, hoping that it would happen . . . but I didn't think we would get this lucky twice."

Something clicked in Izzy's mind, like the final puzzle piece falling into place. "It was you, wasn't it?" she asked. "You're the shadow person!" Dax had been by her side this whole time, trying to keep her safe. Izzy beamed up at him, a silly grin spreading across her face.

"Yeah. It was me. I was trying to warn you about what Priscilla was up to, but I had to leave whenever she was around. She would report me to the Orbistian Council if she found out I was following you. She's such a stickler for rules."

"You know," Izzy said, reaching out to pull him closer, "most girls would find your behaviour pretty creepy. Very stalkerish." She leaned against him, her lips brushing gently against his. "I find it oddly comforting though."

She raised her hand to thread her fingers through his curly hair, her grip tightening as their kiss deepened. Electric currents crackled between them, energy surging through their connection and into Izzy, filling her completely. When they eventually parted, a radiant light bathed their skin, replacing the faint luminescent glow that had been there before.

"Izzy," Dax breathed. The way he said her name conveyed a depth of emotion that went beyond mere words. What they had shared in that moment, their bond and the intensity of their experience, transcended any definition of love.

"I know," she murmured, her hand rising to touch his face. Every aspect of him felt achingly familiar—the scar on his chin, the stubble on his cheeks, and the warm caress of his voice. Even though her memories remained incomplete, her soul recognized him, yearned for him, and felt an overwhelming sense of fulfillment in his presence.

Her arms encircled Dax's neck as she leaned in for another kiss. Their lips met in an electrifying moment, but a sudden, jarring cough ripped through the room, startling them apart. *Priscilla*, Izzy thought, gritting her teeth.

CHAPTER EIGHT

Caught between Worlds

Izzy's shoulders slumped as she leaned against Dax. Instead of the portly, little spirit guide she had been expecting, a tall, lithe teenage girl stood at the door. She wore faded bell-bottom jeans and a white tank top featuring a duck flipping someone off. *Duck you*, the bold, slanted letters beneath the image declared.

The corners of the girl's mouth quirked upward, and she said, "Go find a shaggin' wagon or something. This is my place."

Izzy's mouth dropped open. "Excuse me?"

The teenager's fingers skimmed through her short hair, a spark of mirth dancing in her eyes. "Get a room," she replied.

Warmth spread across Izzy's cheeks. "We were just kissing," she sputtered. "Who are you anyway?"

"Darla Rivers."

"What are you doing in Rhylynn's house?"

Darla sauntered over to Izzy's bed and unceremoniously plopped down at its end. "It was my house first," she said, collapsing back onto the pillow beside Izzy's body. Catching Izzy's baffled expression, she added, "In case you haven't figured it out, I'm the resident ghost. Died in '76, choking on a pizza crust. Right here in this room, actually." Her gaze drifted along the blue walls, lost in memory.

A sharp ache throbbed in Izzy's chest as she stared at the ghostly teenager. Darla had spent years in the shadows of Rhylynn's house, all alone. It was heartbreaking. "I'm so sorry," Izzy said softly. She searched Darla's face. "Why are you still here?"

Darla laced her fingers behind her head and cast a dramatic eye roll toward the ceiling. "Oh, they have tried numerous times over the years to make me leave, but this is my crib, and I'm not going anywhere!"

"They?"

Darla's gaze drifted to Izzy's. "Priscilla and her merry band of so-called guides," she said, her nostrils flaring as she scowled. "They're pretty lousy at their job, don't you think? Considering I died so young."

"Priscilla is your guide too?" Izzy's fingers clenched around Dax's hand. Her guts twisted at the mention of her guide's name.

"Yeah. She's like a total mother hen. Kind of gets on your nerves."

"She wants to erase my memories of the spirit world," Izzy said, her lips pressing into a line. She raised her gaze to meet Dax's, his expression mirroring hers.

"We should get going," he said. "Before Priscilla gets here. She would have been alerted that you left your body again."

Darla glanced upward, as if she could sense something. "She's almost here," she said, her nose wrinkling slightly. "It's like that great-aunt who tries to hug you every time you walk by—after so many years, you get really good at recognizing her gross perfume. Makes it easier to avoid her." She glanced back at Izzy. "You have less than a minute."

Releasing Dax's hand, Izzy rushed toward the nightstand beside Rhylynn's bed. She dropped to her knees and began scanning the wall frantically. "We need to use the Electricity Network!" She stood up and started pacing along the edge of the room, searching for an available outlet. Piles of dirty clothes and stacks of books obstructed her view.

"You don't have time for that," Darla said, one corner of her mouth quirked upward as Izzy circled the room. "Hide in the closet."

The closet Darla was referring to was shielded by a bead curtain instead of a door. Squinting, Izzy could discern the dark outline of Rhylynn's dresser wedged in the back. Dax nudged Izzy forward. As she moved through the beaded curtain, a wave of unsettling tingles flowed through her spectral form.

She melted into the closet's corner with Dax, a tapestry of dresses, skirts, and cozy sweaters obscuring her form. Peering through the beads, Izzy caught only fragmented glimpses of the bedroom.

A swirl of emerald fog crept through the room, unveiling a stocky woman with wild, curly brown locks. Pausing, she tucked her orange and blue striped tie into her crisp navy blazer with deft fingers. She stood upright, a slight arch in her back, as her gaze swept over the room.

Izzy's breath caught—an instinctive response, though unnecessary in her spirit form. Rooted in place, she cast a silent plea into the void, hoping Priscilla would overlook their hiding spot. Regret washed over her. She had been given another moment with Dax, and she'd blown it. Why hadn't they seized the opportunity to leave? As tears dripped off her chin, she dared not wipe at them lest the movement give away their presence.

Priscilla's cry shattered the silence as she stamped her foot on the carpet. "That Roger," she said, "abandoning his post. . . again . . . unbelievable!" Her voice lowered to a grumble, fingers worrying the raven brooch pinned on her blazer. "I ought to report him," she continued, eyes darting around with fervent energy. Her gaze settled on Darla, who was nonchalantly stretched out on the bed, a smirk on her lips.

"Darla!" Priscilla's hands went to her uniform, smoothing down her jacket as she tried to regain her composure. "Why, I am surprised to see you here, my dear. You usually try to avoid my visits! Have you changed your mind then? Shall I bring you back with me?" Her eyes pleaded with Darla to say yes.

"Um, no. I was just checking out all of the action in here."

A gleeful expression danced across Priscilla's features. "You witnessed Izzy's astral projection? Do you know where she went?"

Izzy's form went taut, a shiver of tension climbing her spine. Was Darla going to give away their hiding spot? It was hard to tell with the teenager. She was amused by everything. Turning them in could be a form of entertainment for her. On the other hand, maybe not. Darla had made it clear that she didn't like their spirit guide.

Darla propped herself up, her legs slicing carelessly through Izzy's physical body as she perched on the bed's edge. "What will you give me if I tell you?"

Priscilla's brows shot up. "Give you? What could I possibly give you?"

Rising to her feet, Darla closed the distance between herself and the guide, folding her arms defiantly across her chest. Her gaze bore down on Priscilla. "How about you bugger off and leave me in peace, permanently? No more visits?"

"You know I can't do that. It's my job to guide you home safely!"

"This is my home."

"Darla, I'm just about at my wits end with you!" Priscilla ran her hand through her hair, the curls becoming a tangled mess under her fingers. "Why is everyone making things so much more difficult than they have to be?" she said, her voice rising to a shrill pitch.

Stepping back, Darla lifted her hands in a placating gesture. "Geez, Louise! Chill out. They took off into the Electrical Network as I walked into the room."

A moment of silence hung in the air before Priscilla spoke in a somewhat strangled voice, "They?" A shadow of understanding passed over her face. "Of course, he would be with her!" She turned to Darla, her mouth twitching in displeasure. "That's the problem with soulmates. Drawn to each other like moths to a flame, they are. Always meddling in each other's incarnated lives, never allowing each other the opportunity for self-growth!"

"Wow, aren't you the romantic type," Darla said.

Priscilla pivoted and frowned at Darla before flicking a gold coin into the air. "*Pasporta Dorasalite*," she said. A jagged green line appeared before her, pulsating gently. Without a word of goodbye, she strode forward and vanished into the portal. As it shut, a hush fell over the room like the gentle release of a long-held breath. Rhylynn let out a soft moan from her bed and rolled over onto her side. Her arm hung off the mattress, but she remained asleep.

The air softened, the tension fading as Darla glanced at the closet. "You love birds can come out now."

Izzy emerged from the closet, followed closely by Dax. She gazed at the teenager and warmth coursed through her body, and she was tempted to hug the girl. She hadn't revealed them to Priscilla. Sensing that Darla wasn't the hugging type, she instead thanked her.

Darla gave a nonchalant shrug. "It was fun to jerk Prissy's pants around. She really has it out for the two of you, eh?"

"You have no idea," Izzy muttered, a shadow falling across her features.

"Now Roger, on the other hand," Darla continued, "he's pretty chill."

Izzy's eyes widened as she processed Darla's words. "You have *both* Roger and Priscilla as your spirit guides, too?" she asked. Confusion creased her brow as she glanced at Dax. "Does everyone share the same spirit guides? Didn't Priscilla say there was a Department of Spirit Guides or something like that?"

"Department of Spiritual Guidance and Support," Dax clarified, a wry smile curving his lips. "Millions of different souls act as spirit guides. You two seem to have rotten luck getting Priscilla." He smiled and added, "Don't worry. Once you return to Orbistia, she will be reassigned to someone else. You won't have to see her again if you don't want to."

"Well, since I don't plan on leaving anytime soon, I guess I am stuck with her," Darla said, settling down next to Rhylynn. She gazed down at her affectionately and continued, "I've made a happy little afterlife for myself here, playing the pet poltergeist for my brother's family when I'm not with my mother."

"Your brother?" Izzy asked.

"Rhylynn's dad, Dwayne. I told you, this used to be my house. It's been in the family for years."

"Oh . . . Why would you want to stay here?"

A shadow passed over Darla's face, and her voice was low when she spoke next. "I'm not leaving without my mom."

"Your mom? You mean Mrs. Rivers—Lila? You've been waiting all this time for her?"

Darla nodded, her back stiffening. "She needs me. Since I died, she's been . . . My presence brings her comfort. I know it does."

Izzy's thoughts drifted back to her own mother. Michelle needed her—so much that it felt suffocating. *Weekly dinners, continuing the family business . . . and I've always complied. Because it's my mom.*

Darla could have reincarnated by now and embraced a whole new existence. Similarly, Izzy had put her own life on hold for her mother. *I could have started university sooner and seen more of this world, but I haven't because of Mom.* Izzy realized they were both trapped by a sense of loyalty and love.

"I've heard it all before. I don't care." Darla's voice brought Izzy back from her thoughts. The younger girl stood with her arms crossed, glaring at Dax as he tried to reason with her.

Dax softened his tone and continued, "I just meant your mom wouldn't want—"

"I'm done talking about this."

Recognizing the finality in Darla's tone, Izzy tactfully changed the subject. "Well, I would appreciate it if you could refrain from your poltergeist duties until morning. Don't wake my body up. I'd like more time with Dax before I'm pulled back to it." She stepped closer to her soulmate, threading her fingers through his.

Darla shrugged. "Whatever. Just don't be making out anywhere in the house." She stood up, walking toward the bedroom door. "Your ride's there," she said, pointing to the side table beside Rhylynn's bed. "Later days!"

Izzy watched her disappear through the wall. The thought of Darla existing here, a silent spectator in the Rivers' lives, was depressing. "What will happen to her?" she asked Dax once the other ghost was out of earshot.

"Ghosts can only remain earthbound for so long. If Priscilla can't convince Darla to leave, she'll eventually send an angel to collect her." He ran a hand through his hair. "She's missing out on so much . . . I don't understand why she won't go. She has to realize her mother wouldn't want this for her."

"Sometimes, it's hard to see beyond what you've been taught to believe. It's difficult to put yourself first when loyalty to your parents has always been your main priority."

"Why does it sound like you are speaking from experience?"

Izzy dropped her gaze from Dax's. She was, of course, referring to her own relationship with her mother, but she didn't want to talk about that. Not now. Instead, she changed the topic.

"Did you ever find the bloodstone for Marlo?"

The light dimmed from Dax's eyes. He let go of her hand and raked his fingers through his blond curls. "No," he admitted. "Maddy's information said that the talisman was last seen with Sarah Good in Salem, Massachusetts. I went there, but it was gone. I couldn't find any leads."

"She was hanged after the birth of her child, right? Maybe it was buried with her?"

"It wasn't."

"How do you know?"

Dax glanced away, the tips of his ears turning red.

"You didn't!"

"It was the only way to check," he said, his face now flushed. "I didn't have to go down far. She was buried in a shallow grave. I let myself sink into the ground."

"And . . . ?"

"There was nothing there but dirt."

"That's morbid. You know that, right?"

"I doubt she would care. Her soul's likely reincarnated by now. Besides, there was nothing left. Her body had completely decomposed."

"Maybe you had the wrong spot. Weren't all the accused witches buried in unmarked graves?"

"Maddy had the exact coordinates."

"Oh. Well, I guess Marlo's out of luck then? If you can't find it . . ."

"I *have* to find it, Izzy."

"Can't he just give you a different artifact to hunt down? You have no clues as to where the talisman could be. It's like looking for a needle in a haystack."

Shaking his head, Dax replied, "I went back to Marlo after I searched the grave. He told me to check New Orleans. The city is teeming with dark objects and magic."

"Why does he want the talisman so badly? It seems a little suspicious, don't you think, how persistent he is about you finding it?" Izzy folded her arms across her chest, fixing Dax with a pointed look.

"If Marlo were a dark god, he wouldn't be allowed in Sparklafcx, Iz," Dax replied firmly. "He's a bit odd, but he's not a bad man."

"You didn't want me making a deal with him, remember? You called him a 'shifty character.'"

"You're referring to when you rushed into a magical binding deal with a stranger in a moment of impulse? Yeah, I remember getting upset about that."

"It wasn't an impulsive move. Priscilla was about to catch us in Marlo's store. She was trying to erase my memories! I had no other option."

"You're right. Using the shop's back entrance to escape wasn't a good option at all."

"Yes, well . . ." Izzy blushed and looked away, an embarrassed grin creeping across her face.

"Marlo's weird, I'll grant you that. But he isn't evil. While I don't like you being indebted to him, I don't believe he's plotting to take over the spirit world using dark artifacts."

"Okay . . . So he's not after world domination. But why is he so fixated on this bloodstone? Why is it so important?"

"Marlo said the talisman was created by an English plantation owner in the mid-1650s. A dark and twisted man—not surprising, given his involvement in slavery. He murdered a number of people over a decade, using voodoo to infuse their blood into a bloodstone. The man was killed in an uprising by his slaves before he could harness its power. Sarah Good was a descendant of this man, which explains how she came to possess it. I doubt she was strong enough to sense its power. If she had, she would have known what it could do."

"Which is . . ."

"The stone is incredibly powerful. With the right ritual, it could be used to achieve immortality. And immortality in the wrong hands could be very dangerous."

"No one should have that kind of power," Izzy murmured, rubbing the goosebumps that had formed along her arm.

"We need to remove that talisman from the playing field. Things like that aren't meant to exist."

Izzy's face dropped, and she glanced away, trying to conceal her reaction. She wasn't quick enough though. Dax gently cupped her face, guiding it back so her eyes met his again.

"What is it?" he asked.

"It's just . . . well, I was hoping we could spend time together just hanging out in Orbistia—not chasing down a dark artifact."

Dax's expression softened as he pulled her into his arms. "You're right. I can find it later. You won't be in the spirit world for long. We should make the most of our time together."

Izzy's gut tightened. She was being selfish, and she knew it. Sighing, she stepped back from him. "No, this is more important than us. We need to find it. Two heads are better than one, right? Maybe we'll get lucky."

Leaning over, Dax pressed a soft kiss to her lips. "And then we can relax on the beaches of Orbistia," he said.

"To New Orleans then?" Izzy replied, smiling tightly.

"To New Orleans!" Dax led her over to the wall that Darla had pointed out. As his fingers brushed against the outlet, a warm current flowed through her, pulling her through the tiny prong holes into a world of dark, twisting tunnels.

CHAPTER NINE

Spirits on Bourbon Steet

Izzy and Dax emerged from the dark tunnel amid a crackling blue light. Standing up, she found herself in a crowded bar. A prickling sensation—the kiss of static—danced over her skin. She fought to smooth her hair, which rebelled in every direction. A chuckle escaped her lips as she looked at Dax. His hair appeared as if it had been in a playful scuffle with a balloon. Reaching out, she brushed it down, attempting to tame his curls.

The room they now found themselves in was abuzz with lively chatter as people mingled under high ceiling beams. At the rear, a bar showcased exquisite stained glass, which was bathed in the glow of soft overhead lights. Behind the counter, bartenders moved with purpose, tending to a steady stream of patrons flowing into the establishment.

Izzy glanced at a widescreen TV attached to a nearby wall. She watched as the fleur-de-lis glided down its mast, unleashing a shower of white sparks that lit the night with a spectacular glow. The iconic flower reached the bottom of its pole, and an eruption of fireworks unfurled across the sky, painting it with brilliant hues. Ribbons of red, blue, and gold crackled above the crowd while the number *2024* flashed in rainbow colours on mounted screens around Jackson Square. Simultaneously, the band across from the newscaster began playing "Auld Lang Syne."

"We missed it!" Izzy said.

"Miss what?" Dax asked.

"The dropping of the fleur-de-lis. I thought . . . I was hoping that we could ring the new year in together." Izzy swallowed hard and then bit her lip to keep from crying. "If we hadn't had to hide from Priscilla, we might have made it here in time. We missed half of the Skyscuttle game because of her, and now this! She ruins everything!"

"It's New Year's Day for the next twenty-three hours," Dax said softly. He reached over and brushed her hair back so that they were looking at each other. "Technically, we are ringing the first day of the new year in together."

Izzy offered her soulmate a weak smile. He was trying, she'd give him that. But that wasn't the same thing. The slow buildup of excitement leading to midnight, the magical electricity crackling in the air, and the childish joy of watching fireworks light up the night sky—those things were captured in one moment. There was nothing magic about New Year's Day.

He's right though. A small voice rose up in her mind, pushing back against the negative thoughts threatening to pull her down. The first moments of 2024 would always be memorable because they were spending them together. And that was better than just one brief moment.

Leaning against Dax, Izzy settled back into him, watching the fireworks on the television set. The scene changed to show a newscaster speaking to a somewhat famous actor. Beside them, an elderly musician with a trumpet pressed to his lips swayed on the spot, his bowler hat teetering on his head. A younger man with a drum slung around his neck beat out a rhythm next to him while beaming at the crowd.

The warm trumpet notes floated out from the television, barely reaching Izzy's ears through the noise of the bar. She closed her eyes, tuning out the rambunctious laughter coming from a nearby booth.

"I felt so alone at the party," she murmured, shifting against Dax.

"I was there. You just couldn't see me."

"As a shadow."

"Yeah. And it takes a lot of energy for spirits to manipulate shadows, you know. But you're worth it." He kissed Izzy on the top of her head.

"I wish we could be together all the time."

"I know. But Izzy . . ."

An awkward silence hung in the air. Izzy glanced at Dax, who was biting his lip, his face marked by uncertainty.

"What is it?"

Dax reached out and brushed a finger against her cheek. "I want you to be happy," he said.

"I am happy."

"Yeah. But I mean in this life too. You can love me and still love someone else . . . You reincarnated for a reason. To experience life—self-growth. You can't do that if you are always thinking of me . . ."

Izzy stared up at Dax, her pulse hammering in her ears. "You want me to date other people?"

"No—yes . . . I don't know," Dax said, his voice faltering. "I just don't want you throwing your incarnated life away for me."

"I'm not."

"You don't want to get married someday . . . have kids? These are experiences you would be missing out on."

"I don't care."

"Izzy—"

"Dax, don't. I know what I want, and it's you. Even if it's years before I see you again, it will always be you. Now that I know about you, about our connection . . ." Her hand rose, fingers gently tracing the stubble along his cheek. "When I'm with you, no one else matters. And when I'm not, all I can think about is the moment we can be together again."

"But you're going to get lonely. You could live a long life. I *want* you to live a long life. Are you sure you don't want Priscilla to—"

"No," Izzy cut in abruptly, her hand falling from his face. "You gave up your reincarnation meeting for me, remember."

"Yes, but—"

"Did you ever reschedule it?"

"No. I—"

"And you've been following me around, keeping tabs on me over the holidays?"

"Well, yes, but I was trying to protect you."

"Dax, *you're* putting *your life* on hold for me!"

"It's different."

"It isn't. You could have reincarnated by now. Think about all the experiences *you're* missing!"

Dax's gaze fell to the floor, and he lapsed into silence. Izzy watched him, feeling a tightness in her chest. They were postponing their own lives just for the rare moments they could share—maybe two or three times in the next seventy years? *Why does this have to be so complicated?* she wondered, fighting back the tears that threatened to spill down her cheeks.

Laughter filled the air as a group of men took their places on nearby stools. The bartender slid mint juleps across the counter to them, the crisp scent of mint mingling with the sweet, oaky notes of bourbon and permeating the cozy space. Simultaneously, the spicy aroma of freshly served gumbo wafted from the adjacent booths, pulling Izzy out of her reverie and into the room's lively ambiance.

A woman—draped in dangling beads and sporting a tall hat emblazoned with *Happy New Year 2024* sauntered by, her body gliding through them. Izzy recoiled, an uncomfortable tingling sensation crawling across her skin.

"I'll never get used to that," she said, wrapping her arms around herself.

Dax shifted his gaze back to her. "You might have to if you want to make it outside," he said, nodding toward the throng of partiers.

"I guess we should get going." Izzy took a step forward, then paused. "Hold on a second," she muttered, squeezing her eyes shut. Moments later, her pyjamas transformed into black jeans and a thin, zip-up sweater. Opening her eyes, she flashed a crooked smile at Dax. "I know they can't see me, but it feels odd walking around in my night clothes."

"Even if they could see you, I doubt anyone would care," Dax said. He gestured toward some of the more extravagant costumes in the room. "Everyone is out to have a good time tonight."

"You're probably right," Izzy said, swerving around a man wearing a glittering bodysuit. As they stepped out onto the red-bricked sidewalk, a new wave of patrons stumbled into the bar. One man passed through Izzy, her form compressing and bouncing back into place. He halted, glancing at where she stood. For a moment, Izzy felt visible under his stare.

Izzy watched the man disappear into the bar. It was possible he had a sixth sense. After all, New Orleans thrived with those who claimed to commune with spirits. Perhaps, among the many self-proclaimed psychics and mediums in the city, there were a few who were authentic. *Like Sydney*, she thought.

Dax's gentle tug pulled Izzy from her reverie. He steered her from the doorway. "Everything okay?" he asked.

"Yes. I thought that man saw me. Maybe he's a medium?"

"Maybe. Or sensitive to spirits."

"It was just weird . . ." Izzy peered behind her. The man was gone. She took a step forward. "It's not important. Let's go."

Bourbon Street unfurled ahead, alive with a stream of tourists and locals heading to Jackson Square. Izzy and Dax skirted the edge, hugging the line of buildings. The street was a parade of bars and clubs, with the soulful strains of blues and jazz floating out each time a door swung open. The aromas of cocktails and Cajun spices hung heavily in the air, tempting Izzy's senses.

New Orleans had always captivated her father, and now she knew why. The city vibrated with life, its air charged with infectious excitement. Jamie Adams had spent nearly a year here during his gap year before college. He often entertained his children with tales from that time—like his stint as a street performer. One time, Jamie had stationed himself on a corner in Jackson Square, strumming his guitar with gusto and belting out a Bryan Adams song, only to be joined by a stray dog that howled out of tune. He told Izzy that his performance ended abruptly when the dog chose his open guitar case as its makeshift bathroom.

Izzy smiled at the memory. She let the city's vibrant energy encircle her, dissolving her tension. A sense of calm settled within her as she passed beneath the balconies hanging over the street. Beads and trinkets swayed from the wrought iron.

"So, why didn't you call your mom back?" Dax asked.

Izzy nearly stumbled, catching herself at the last second. Tension crept back into her shoulders, her posture stiffening. "Let's not talk about my mother, okay?"

"I've never seen you ignore a call from her before."

"The old me wouldn't have dared," Izzy mumbled.

"I was there when you told her about university."

"So, you saw how well she took that then."

"I think she was just in shock."

"Yeah, shocked that I finally grew a backbone."

"You're angry."

Izzy halted abruptly, her hands balling into fists at her sides. "I'm not just angry. I'm furious. It's always about what she wants and what the family expects. When is it my turn? Why doesn't what I want matter?"

"What you want matters," Dax reassured her, gently wiping a tear from her cheek. "I'm sure she's just trying to do what she thinks is best for you. Sometimes, people struggle with change. She's had time to think over your news now. Give her a chance. Call her when you get home."

"I've given her plenty of chances, Dax. Over the years, I've tried to connect and spend time together, but she's never shown any interest. She's not doing what's best for me. She's looking out for herself." Izzy wiped her face, her hand coming away wet. "Honestly, I hope I never wake up. I don't want to call her back."

"Izzy—"

"No. I'm done talking about her. Just drop it, please!" Brushing past him, Izzy hurried down the street. She reached up, pulling at her hair, twisting it roughly between her fingers. When no pain followed, she exhaled a weary sigh and let her hair fall back into place. *Spirits can't feel pain*, she reminded herself.

Glancing around, she focused on the people in the street, letting the outlandish costumes and bizarre behaviours distract her from thoughts of her mother. In the gutter, a woman retched, her friend holding her hair back as the sharp stench of vomit filled the air. Nearby, a man lay passed out on the sidewalk, his pockets picked clean. After a long moment, Izzy's heartbeat slowed, and her body gradually relaxed.

"Where should we look first?" she finally asked Dax. He had been giving her space, following quietly behind her. She offered him a small smile, signalling that she was okay.

"Our best bet is to find a medium. Then we can at least talk to someone," he replied.

"Okay . . . so where can we find—"

"Here on Bourbon Street."

"Oh, great! Well, this part should be easy."

It wasn't easy. They roamed the street for twenty minutes amid the festive throngs of partygoers, searching vainly for a medium. No one even glanced their way, and many simply passed through them as if they were air—a sensation Izzy was reluctantly getting used to.

"This is pointless," she grumbled, watching Dax lean into a storefront window. A chill ran down her spine as he pressed his face through the glass. The unsettling feeling of being watched crept over her, and slowly, she turned to look over her shoulder.

Near the crowd's edge, a man caught Izzy's attention. His attire—jeans and a t-shirt, with beads looped around his neck—was unremarkable, no different from anyone else. It was the man from the bar—the one that had walked through her at the door. A tingle crept up the nape of her neck, dancing across her scalp.

The man's dark eyes bore into hers. Izzy turned her head, feigning interest in graffiti scrawled across the sidewalk. She was sure he had seen her. *He must be a medium*, she thought. While finding a medium should have come as a relief—they were searching for one, after all—it wasn't. Something was unsettling about him, and it stirred a nauseous, edgy feeling within her.

She moved closer to her soulmate, threading her fingers through his. His eyes brightened as he turned to face her, and he nodded toward the window.

"We're in luck! I saw movement in the back."

"And you're sure it's a medium in there?"

"Yes. The store's called *Beyond the Veil*."

"All right, let's go in," Izzy said eagerly. She needed to escape the penetrating stare of the man on the street. She could still feel him watching her. He wanted something, but she wasn't about to stick around to find out what. She slid through the glass pane, following Dax into the darkened room.

CHAPTER TEN

A Dark Prophecy

"This isn't creepy at all," Izzy murmured, eyeing a shelf lined with shrunken heads against the far wall. Their mouths were crudely sewn shut, and coarse black hair obscured many of their faces.

"It's New Orleans," Dax replied with a shrug. "The tourists expect it."

"Shrunken heads are associated with the Jivaroan people of Ecuador and Peru, not New Orleans. It would make more sense to have Mardi Gras masks."

"Yeah. But Mardi Gras masks aren't spooky. Voodoo heads are, and most tourists aren't walking encyclopedias like you," Dax said, grinning. "Besides, they're not real. They're made of wax."

Passing through a door, they entered a small room. A wooden table, pushed against the wall, was draped with a midnight-blue, velvet cloth adorned with silver stars, creating a mystical vibe. At the centre of the table sat a crystal ball.

"It doesn't look like anyone is here, Dax."

"Someone is. I saw the door shut through the window. Come on," he replied, leading her to another door. "The medium must live behind the store."

"Hopefully, they aren't just a charlatan," Izzy muttered as she passed through the wooden entrance.

Her mind lingered on the strange man outside who had been watching them. A potential medium was right there, and she had walked away from him. He might have had all the answers they needed. A twinge of guilt gnawed at her, but she dismissed it.

Izzy stepped into another cramped room. She surveyed the small kitchenette tucked against the far wall, where a hot plate replaced a traditional stove. Across the room, a line of clean clothes hung, emitting a musty scent as if they had been washed in haste.

Dax stood beside a single bed with a sagging mattress. A gaunt man with deep-set eyes was propped up against a pillow, his nose buried in a mystery novel. Izzy watched as Dax waved his hands in front of the man's eyes, occasionally brushing his fingers across the man's face.

"A fake medium then?" Izzy asked, sighing.

"I don't think so," Dax replied. "Sometimes their gifts aren't strong enough to see or hear us, but they can still feel our presence."

As if to prove his point, the man wrinkled his nose and leaned back into his pillow, away from Dax's hand. Smiling, Dax leaned in and gently tapped him on his shoulder.

"All right, already!" the man exclaimed, tossing his book aside. "Stop touchin' me!" His blanket fell away as he swung his legs over the edge of the bed and stood up. Muttering under his breath, he shuffled over to a nearby shelf and pulled down a battered black box.

They returned to the sitting room and watched as he carefully shifted the crystal ball aside and placed the box on the table. He flicked on the lamp, and the room lit up. Sheer cloth hung from the ceilings, and a frayed braided rug sprawled across the floor.

"Disturbing me in my own time," the man grumbled, arranging an ancient-looking Ouija board crafted from darkened wood. The letters had faded from extensive use. He positioned a smooth planchette next to it and glanced around the room as though searching for them.

"What do you want?" he asked. "I'm not here to contact your loved ones. Don't have time for that."

"Cheerful guy, isn't he?" Izzy muttered.

Dax leaned over the table, his lips pressed tightly as he concentrated on guiding the planchette across the Ouija board, slowly spelling out *bloodstone.*

The medium snorted. "You're bugging me about a bloodstone? You can find them at any crystal shop!"

Dax carefully spelled *special* and *negative energy.*

Izzy watched as the medium's complexion turned ashen. "A bloodstone infused with negative energy . . ." He rubbed at his jaw and leaned back in his seat. "I was at a gem expo a few weeks ago," he mumbled, his eyes losing focus as he recounted the memory. "There was this witch there—Alice Dame from the UK. Nasty woman. She's even on the World Council of Supernatural Beings watch list. She bought a heart-shaped bloodstone pendant—quite the dark object, though I doubt the seller knew that. The negative energy off it? Strong. I felt it all the way across the room."

Where in the UK?

"Burley," the medium responded. "But don't ask me where. I don't mess with the dark arts, so I'd have no reason to—" He paused suddenly, tilting his head toward the ceiling as if hearing something distant. "Spiders," he declared, his gaze fixing on Izzy.

She knew he couldn't see her, yet a shiver ran through her. What did spiders have to do with the bloodstone?

"Spiders," the medium resumed, his voice lowering ominously, "are coming for you, girl. Spiders and darkness."

Explain, Dax hastily spelled out, his eyes flickering to Izzy with concern.

"I only know what the voices tell me," the medium replied, his hand thudding onto the table. "If you're looking for a reading, better find a psychic."

"We should leave," Izzy muttered. "He gave us what we asked for." His words echoed in her mind, drudging up memories of Christmas Day. *Spiders and darkness. The Realm of Nightmares . . .* At that moment, all she wanted was to escape the medium and his chilling prophecy.

Dax nodded. *Thank you.* He finished spelling out the word and stepped back from the planchette.

"Yes, well, what choice did I have?" the medium asked as he carefully packed away the board. "You would've kept on until I helped. It's a bit rude, don't you think? Invading my private space like that. Most folks in this line of work wouldn't stand for it." He crossed his arms and glared at the empty room around him.

Izzy glanced at Dax, feeling her cheeks warm. The medium was right. It was rude. But what choice did they have? With downcast eyes, she left the room.

"I feel awful," she confessed as Dax caught up.

"I know . . . If only we had more time."

Izzy sighed. "But we don't." She was already too aware that, sooner than she'd like, she would be pulled back into her physical body.

They stepped out into the bustling street. Intoxicated partygoers wandered by, their drinks sloshing as they sang and stumbled along the sidewalk. Dax quickly pulled Izzy against the wall to avoid a young couple who passed by, wrapped in each other and oblivious to the world around them.

"Izzy?"

"Hmm?"

"What do you think he meant—'spiders and darkness'?"

A cold chill washed over Izzy as she recalled the nightmare from the previous week. In the excitement of astral projecting again, she had forgotten all about it. "I meant to tell you earlier . . ."

"Tell me what?"

Izzy quickly described her dream and the demonic creature she had awakened to find perched on her chest.

"It tried to *kill* you?"

"Yes. I didn't think demons could physically hurt people?"

"Most can't. A hag must have attacked you," Dax said, his arms tightening around her.

"My bracelet broke it down into its base form. It's gone."

"But the threat isn't," Dax murmured. "Queen Mara is the ruler of the Realm of Nightmares . . . The Kingdom of Nachtmahr. The demon we saved Kate from was one of hers."

"So she wants revenge," Izzy said.

"Seems like it. She hates souls, even dark ones, and you defeated one of her pets. Izzy, this is bad. Really bad. We need to go see Marlo now. He will know what to do."

"We can't, Dax. We need to find the bloodstone!"

"It can wait. This is more important," Dax countered, rummaging through his jacket. "Where's my Meli coin?" he muttered, emptying his pocket.

"No, I'm not going to see Marlo. The bloodstone matters more than just one person. If Alice gets it—"

"I don't care."

"Well, I do. What if she uses it? What if she hurts someone? I can't live with that. Besides, I have you with me. If anything comes at me, you can protect me. Or the bracelet—"

"And what if Queen Mara shows up, Izzy. I can't fight off a dark god. Neither can you. We don't even know if the bracelet is that powerful. I'm not willing to risk it."

"I am. And it's my choice." Izzy crossed her arms and glared at her soulmate. "I'm not going to Marlo for help. Not yet. Let's finish this first. We're so close! We know where the bloodstone is."

"We know it's in Burley. But finding it could take hours or even days. A dark witch won't just have her address listed anywhere."

"We have to try."

Dax sighed, his hands falling from his pockets. "Izzy . . ."

She smiled inwardly, knowing she had won. Dax would never make her choices for her. She might still be getting to know him, but this she knew for sure. He was worried for her, with very good reason. If Mara did show up in person . . . Izzy shook her head. She couldn't think about that. They had to find the bloodstone and stop Alice from whatever she had planned.

A group of young people passed by them, laughing and looking carefree. For a moment, Izzy envied them. They had no harrowing quests in their future, no dark gods hunting them down. Just a couple of friends, ringing in the new year together.

She watched as they stopped in front of a store a few feet away. The sign on the storefront advertised *Zulie's Hard Pressed Ritual Prepared Graveyard Dirt—Ideal for revenge and hexing spells!* Beside it, a sign advertising *Lucky Rabbit's Feet* was prominently displayed, with a sale price of $6.95. Other items—gris-gris bags, peculiar dolls, waxen skulls, and beads—filled the cluttered shelves.

The women in the group discussed visiting the shop in the morning while their male companions lingered by the window, capturing selfies and playfully shoving each other. One man reached into the pocket of his jeans, but his hand returned empty. "My phone's gone! Someone stole my phone!"

One of the women—a short, plump girl with dark skin and deep dimples—turned to him and rolled her eyes. "Well, what do you expect, Kade? You left your phone in your back pocket."

"My dad is going to be so pissed," Kade groaned as the group drifted away from the store.

Izzy moved closer, transfixed by the storefront display. "Is any of this actually real?" she asked, nodding toward a small wax doll ensnared in twine. A needle protruded from its neck.

Dax stepped forward, scrutinizing the display through the dusty pane. "Voodoo is real—a distinct form of magic. But this"—he waved dismissively at the crowded shelves—"is for show. A lure for tourists." His finger directed her gaze to a bottle labelled as graveyard dirt. "It wouldn't surprise me if they swept that off their floor."

Dax pressed his face closer to the glass, eyeing the lower shelves. "Now this," he murmured, his eyebrows drawing together, "is an authentic magical item! I bet the shop owner doesn't even know it."

His finger lingered near a silver ring set with an unusual blue gem that caught the dim light. Crude etchings adorned the sides, giving it an arcane presence. Affixed to it, a label proclaimed, *Ancient Shaman Ring, available for $200.*

"I can feel the magic rolling of this," Dax said, his hand passing through the window and wrapping around the ring. "This was made by one of the gods. I have no idea what it does, but Marlo would know. We should bring it back to him . . . *when* we bring him the bloodstone," Dax said, catching her expression. "It could be dangerous." He guided the ring through the glass pane and offered it to Izzy.

"How did you do that?" she asked, taking it from his outstretched hand. She brought it closer to her face, captivated by the myriad shades of blue swirling within the gem.

"A spirit can interact with the physical world. It just requires focus and drains some of our energy. But this ring is imbued with magic. That makes it easier for spirits to touch. Magical objects can also be transported between our realm and the spirit world, much like the bracelet I gave you," he explained, glancing at her wrist.

"What are these weird markings on it?"

Dax moved in to look, their heads close together over the artifact. "These symbols are not of this universe. That's all the more reason to take it to Marlo. He's not from around here either."

"It's not from our uni . . ." Izzy's words faded as the bracelet on her wrist ignited with a brilliant glow, illuminating the shadowed street. It thrummed against her skin, growing warm—a beacon of impending peril.

A hushed incantation unfurled behind them. "*Paracapturar.*"

There was just a moment, a heartbeat, to meet Dax's gaze—one of shared disbelief—before Izzy's form crumpled inward, her torso collapsing toward her thighs as an unseen force yanked her backward. As she shrank and was drawn into the narrow confines of a bottle, the piercing eyes of the mysterious man from the bar met hers.

She tumbled back, his face receding rapidly until she hit the bottom with a soft thud. A cork popped into place, sealing her and Dax off from the world.

CHAPTER ELEVEN

A Feast for Spiders

The bottom of the bottle was impenetrable, crafted from thick glass. Izzy tried in vain to pass her ethereal form through it. They were trapped. Despite the soft glow from her body, it was dark inside the man's jacket. A hand brushed against Izzy's, fingers closing around her own. Her heartbeat sped up, and she almost tore her hand away. But then, her soulmate's familiar voice filled the cramped space.

"It's just me, Iz."

"It's dark. I can hardly see you."

"Hold on a second."

There was a rustling sound, and then a soft white light bloomed between them, pushing back the dark. Dax's face emerged from the shadows, his eyes glowing orbs. Clutched in his hand was a white stone.

"Moonstone," Dax said, handing her the small rock. "It's enchanted to glow in the dark. Most souls carry one around."

Izzy turned the stone in her palm, its smooth surface soothing against her skin. As she did, the tightness in her shoulders eased. "What are we in?"

"An obsidian bottle—a prison for souls—although this one seems crudely made. The ones back in Orbistia are of finer craftsmanship."

"Why would someone capture us, Dax?"

"I'm not sure . . . maybe it has something to do with that ring? Do you still have it?"

"Crap, the ring!" Izzy had forgotten all about it. Handing the moonstone back to Dax, she felt along the floor.

As Dax said, the bottle was shoddily made. The base was uneven, with raised, rough patches that crumbled under Izzy's fingers. Despite her efforts to break through, the obsidian remained stubbornly intact.

Sighing, she resumed her search for the ring. Her hand eventually brushed against a small object. Grabbing it, she slipped the band onto her finger. The cool metal was snug against her skin.

"Found it."

"Good."

They sat in silence, curled up together, tumbling apart every now and then as their glass prison slid around in the man's pocket. Izzy scrambled back to Dax each time, arms reaching out, desperately searching for him.

Terrible images invaded her mind. Demons, large and grotesque, rose up beneath her closed eyelids. Elongated fangs pierced into her soul, siphoning her essence until nothing was left. This was Queen Mara's work, no doubt. She wanted Izzy dead, and now she was bringing them back to whatever nightmarish realm she ruled.

Dax's arm trembled around her. Izzy's chin fell to her chest, guilt gnawing at her. They were in this mess because of her.

"I'm sorry," she whispered.

"For what?"

"This is my fault."

"Why would you say that?"

"It has to be Mara," she murmured, her voice quivering. "You were right. We should have gone to Marlo when we had the chance." A sob caught in her throat. "I'm so sorry for dragging you into this mess."

"You're my soulmate, Izzy. We're in this together. Besides, this probably has nothing to do with Mara."

Izzy didn't respond. She still felt responsible. That nagging sense that something was off about their captor, she had shrugged it off. *I could have prevented this*, she thought, sniffling. She had believed that he was a medium, like Sydney, but clearly he was something else, something darker.

Sydney! Of course, Izzy could ask the waitress for help. Once her body woke up, she would be sucked out of the bottle and returned to her physical form. And then, Sydney could get a message to Dax's sister in the spirit realm. Izzy sagged against Dax, and she took a deep, steadying breath.

"What's wrong?" Dax asked.

"Everything is going to be okay. Once I wake up, I'll contact Maddy, and she can send help to you. We just have to get through the next couple of hours."

"It won't work, Iz."

"Of course, it'll work! I'll wake up at some point. I won't stay trapped in here."

"But you won't wake up. This prison is designed to trap souls. If your body starts to wake, you won't be able to return to it. You'll remain in a coma, and eventually, you'll die."

Dizziness washed over Izzy. She would never see her family—Lyssa, Eddie, Kate, Aunt Audrey . . . and her mother—again. She had never returned her mom's last call, leaving things unresolved, and maybe Dax was right. Perhaps her mother had been reaching out to reconcile. Now, Michelle would never get that chance. She would lose Izzy, just as she had lost Jamie.

Her mother's world had crumbled when Izzy's father passed away. That's when her attempts to control every facet of Izzy and her siblings' lives truly began. A vivid image of her mother's tear-stained face flashed in Izzy's mind, causing her chest to constrict. She fidgeted, overwhelmed by the realization that she was about to cause more pain in her mom's life.

Desperate to escape these thoughts, Izzy's mind wandered to Rhylynn. Izzy pictured her friend waking, rubbing the sleep from her eyes, and padding over to Izzy's bed to rouse her. But she wouldn't find Izzy responsive. She might laugh at first, assuming Izzy was just a deep sleeper. But as her efforts—shaking Izzy, casting numerous spells—grew more desperate, nothing would change. *She's going to blame herself*, Izzy thought, a lump rising in her throat. *I did this . . . I did this to my friends and family.*

Her pulse pounded loud in the dark silence of their prison. They were going to be trapped here forever. Unless—What if they took her out to torture her? She didn't want to think about it, but if it gave her the opportunity to escape . . .

"Do you feel that?" Dax whispered, releasing Izzy to stand up. "We stopped moving."

The bottle jolted, and Dax flew against the far wall. Moments later, a blinding light pierced through the murky glass. Their tiny cell rocked violently as their captor pulled it out of his pocket. Izzy's stomach churned, and she fought back nausea as their surroundings spun. The man hoisted the bottle overhead, placing it on a shelf above.

Staggering to the glass wall, Izzy pressed her face against it. *It's like looking through sunglasses.* A pervasive darkness tinged everything.

The room was cramped, filled with an array of items. An open cabinet on the far wall cradled more obsidian bottles. Within some, a sickly green mist churned. In others, minuscule figures banged against the glass, their cries muffled and indistinct.

Dax stepped up beside Izzy. Under the dim lighting, his mouth was set in a thin line.

"What?"

"See the bottles over there—the ones with the green mist."

"Yeah."

"That only happens to souls if they've been drained of all their energy. You lose the ability to take on your human form and become a cloud of thought."

"Like what I did to that psychic vampire that attacked Kate?"

"You reduced it to its purest form. It'll recover in a decade. But this—this takes centuries, even with your spirit family's energy to help you."

Izzy slumped against the wall, staring at Dax with blurry eyes. "What are we going to do?" she asked, the words barely a breath.

He sat down beside her and drew her into his arms. Neither spoke. They just held each other in silence. Time stilled. Across the room, other trapped souls slumped in defeat within their glass prisons. They waited . . . and waited . . . and waited. For Izzy, it was excruciating. There was nothing to wait for but their turn to be siphoned of life.

Dax finally broke the silence. "There's something I need to tell you," he said, pulling away to meet her gaze.

"What is it?"

"I kept something from you . . . about the bloodstone."

"What do you mean? Why would you hide something from me?"

"I . . ." Dax averted his eyes, his fingers nervously twisting the hem of his shirt.

"Dax, what is it?"

"Marlo mentioned a prophecy concerning the bloodstone," Dax confessed. "I didn't want to worry you. It's vague, could mean anything."

"Just tell me."

Dax met her gaze slowly. "If the bloodstone is used, a river will meet its end."

"That doesn't make any sense. A river will meet its end?" Izzy cocked her eyebrow, her forehead wrinkling as she thought over Dax's words. *Why did he think I'd be worried? Unless . . . Rhylynn!* A chill swept through her as she thought of her friend. *Rhylynn Rivers . . . a river will meet its end.*

"You think it refers to Rhylynn?" she asked, her voice breaking.

"I'm not sure. Maybe . . . She's descended from a line of powerful witches. If Alice Dame gets her hands on the bloodstone, she'll likely target her rivals first. I could be wrong, but . . ."

"But you don't think you are."

"No," Dax replied, his expression sombre.

"We need to get out of here." Izzy jumped up and strode to the glass wall, running her hands over its surface, searching for any sign of weakness.

"We can't do anything, Izzy. I already told you, there's no way out."

"We'll get out." Heat flared through Izzy's body, and she clenched her jaw shut. They had to stop Alice Dame from using the bloodstone. *I won't let anything happen to Rhylynn*, she thought, slamming her fist against the bottle.

When that failed, Izzy threw herself against the wall in a desperate attempt to topple it. Minutes dragged on as her attempts grew increasingly frantic until she finally slumped to the ground beside Dax, tears streaming from her eyes.

"I'm not giving up," she said, wiping at her face.

"I know. I'll help. Maybe together—"

The bedroom door swung open with a loud bang as the man returned, now clad in a stained sweatsuit, his brown hair mussed from sleep. He rubbed his eyes and yawned as he took in the surroundings, his gaze eventually settling on the shelf their bottle was on. Instinctively, Izzy pressed closer to Dax.

Their kidnapper approached them. For one heart-stopping moment, Izzy believed he would select their bottle. But instead, he extended his hand and took down the one next to theirs. Inside, the tiny figure hurled itself against the glass—a desperate, final effort to break free. The man removed the cork and lifted the bottle to his mouth, tilting it back to seal his lips around the opening.

Horrified, Izzy could only watch as the small figure curled into the fetal position. A soft white light floated from its form, drifting toward the man's open mouth. The figure's screams diminished to feeble pleas for help, its body fading to a sickly pale green. In a matter of seconds, it dissipated into smoke, vanishing, leaving behind nothing but a lingering mist.

As the man turned to face them, Izzy recoiled from the wall, her breath coming in uneven, shuddering gasps. Their captor placed the bottle back on the shelf, his eyes pitch black, the whites gone. Dax let out a strangled noise and staggered toward Izzy.

His voice dropped to a whisper. "He's a dark soul."

"What?"

"A soul that has gone completely dark—evil. I-I think he has possessed a witch's body. He used a spell to trap us."

"Demonic possession?" Izzy's voice quivered, her body folding, arms wrapping tightly around her knees.

Dax nodded solemnly, his gaze flickering to the shadowed corners of their cell. "Sort of. When a demon possesses a body, it morphs it. It becomes contorted and abnormally strong. A demon doesn't know how to act human, so it will do destructive and odd things, like self-harm, swearing, vomiting . . . the things you see in movies." He paused, inhaling deeply to steady his wobbly voice. "A dark soul needs permission to take over a body," he continued. "He must be stealing energy to perform dark magic."

Her eyes burned as she looked up into Dax's. "How does Orbistia allow this to happen?"

"It's a big universe, Izzy. The Guard and the angels can't be everywhere at once. Sometimes, things slip through the cracks. When dark magic is used, it also complicates things. It's hard to detect, and the spirit guides aren't always around watching."

Izzy frowned and turned back toward their captor. He was squatting in the middle of the room beside a throw rug. In one deft motion, he tossed it aside, revealing a trap door set into the floor. The door clattered against the ground when he yanked it open.

A twisted smile stretched across his taunt skin as the dark soul reached into the hidden compartment and pulled out a dishevelled-looking man. Chains bound the captured man's hands and feet, and a filthy red handkerchief was knotted tightly around his mouth. With a swift jerk, the dark soul tore away the cloth, and a raw cry of pain escaped the man's lips.

Tears carved through the grime on his cheeks, forging muddy rivulets. "Please," he said, staring at their captor, "let me go. My wife—"

"I don't care," the dark soul said dismissively.

"My kids . . . P-please—"

"I *don't* care." The dark soul flexed his fingers, and black sparks shot out. The shimmering magic swirled around the chains on the other man, shaking them until, with a sudden and violent clatter, they broke free and tumbled to the floor.

The dark soul stared down at his captive, a sneer creeping onto his face. "Give it your best shot," he said cruelly, nodding toward the door.

Gingerly, the man massaged his wrists.

He looks like he's been confined in the dark for days, Izzy thought, staring at his pale face. She pictured him all alone, probably haunted by thoughts of his children. A strangled sob broke free, and she pressed her hand against her chest. He was going to die, and his family would remain oblivious to his fate.

The man stumbled toward the exit. His body—weakened by neglect—betrayed him, and he fell. With a desperate army crawl, he fought his way across the floor, only making it halfway before the dark soul approached. The possessed witch pressed his heel into the man's back.

The man cried out, his head tilting upward, giving Izzy a clear view. Harsh lines of healed slashes marred his visage, and one eye was grotesquely swollen—the telltale signs of repeated abuse. This was not the first time the dark soul had toyed with him.

"I'm tired of this game," the dark soul said, feigning a yawn. "You humans break too easily."

"Let me go!"

"One last riddle then? Guess it right, and I let you go. Guess it wrong . . ." Laughing, he lifted his foot from the man.

"A person skilled in the art of lies, whose mother wouldn't recognize them, that good is their disguise. Next, think of a griddle, what goes in the middle, and how the ending of *end* is also the beginning of *descend*. Finally, give me the sound most often heard when trying to remember a long-forgotten word. Now put them together, and what do you hear? What sort of creature evokes such fear?"

As the final word of the riddle hung in the air, a chill ran down Izzy's spine. Her heart lurched as the man burst into tears. She didn't blame him. She had no idea what the dark soul meant. *Think of a griddle, and what goes in the middle?* Was he talking about a pancake or the letter *D*? She had never been good at solving riddles. The whole situation reminded her of a cat playing with a mouse, and she couldn't shake off the feeling that things were about to take a turn for the worse.

A gleeful look crossed the dark soul's face, and a long, drawn-out laugh poured from his mouth. "No answer? Here, let me give you a hint." He pointed a finger at the man, black energy crackling around it. "*Borborygm!*"

A stream of magic flowed into the man. He cried out, his hands grasping at his belly as a deep, guttural rumble resonated through the room. Drops of sweat streamed down his contorted face.

Horrified, Izzy watched his belly expand and balloon out as though he were months into pregnancy. His t-shirt rode up, revealing pale skin etched with hideous, purple veins. Something sinister moved beneath, desperate for release.

Spiders, Izzy thought, the answer to the riddle coming to her.

Her hand flew to her mouth as several spiders crawled out of the man's nose. He swatted at them, trying to brush them off his face. A moment later, his bulging stomach erupted, a fountain of blood spraying upward. From the carnage, thick black spiders emerged, swarming over his body. His intestines tumbled out in a grotesque display on the floor. His screams dwindled to silence within moments as the spiders consumed him. Soon, all that was left was a pile of bones. Having finished their meal, they skittered across the floor, disappearing under the door into the early morning hours.

CHAPTER TWELVE

THE GORGON'S GAZE

As the last spider scuttled away, the dark soul collected the bones in a Tupperware container. He approached a nearby folding table and dumped the human remains on it. An array of items—black candles, human teeth, and the carcass of a decaying rat—was already scattered across the surface.

Unfamiliar with the dark arts, Izzy watched, transfixed, as the man began his grim work. His hands hovered over the bones, murmuring incantations that made his palm glow a fiery red reminiscent of an oven's heating elements. Within moments, the bones imploded, dissolving into a mound of fine ash.

Izzy retreated from the grisly sight and crumpled to the floor, her back against the bottle's wall. A bitter taste filled her mouth. The sight of cremated bodies was nothing new to her. She had assisted her sister with the process multiple times before. But this—this was the desecration of a human body. This man had not simply ended a life. He had erased an existence, reduced a person to unrecognizable ash, and stolen away the right to a final farewell.

"Why?" Izzy asked, her voice cracking.

"Bone dust of a murdered man. It's a powerful ingredient," Dax replied.

"He's a monster!"

"He was probably a serial killer in his past life. The way he tortured that man . . ."

Izzy shuddered. "I'm going to be sick."

"Block out the feeling. You're a spirit. You don't have to feel it."

"No," Izzy said. "Blocking out emotions is why that man is a murderer. I won't be like him!"

Dax's hand gently rested on Izzy's shoulder, filling her with reassurance. "You could never be like him," he said, his voice low. Their eyes met, and they were once again entangled in the deep and powerful connection they shared.

Izzy moved to place her hand over his and gasped. An intense, throbbing sensation passed between their touching skin. Energy coursed through her petite frame, filling her with a lightness that left her happier. With every breath, the tightness in her body loosened, the heat of her anger dissolving away.

"You did that on purpose," she said, pulling her hand back.

"You needed the energy boost, Iz," he replied. "It's okay to feel those emotions. Just don't drown in them. We've got to stay sharp. If we want to . . ." Dax narrowed his eyes and stepped back from her. Something had captured his attention. Izzy's head snapped toward the direction he was looking. A bluish-white mist was materializing in the room.

At first, it was just a shapeless cloud, but gradually, it took on the form of a burly man. The muscles rippled beneath his skin as he stepped forward, his features solidifying. He wore a starched white dress shirt neatly tucked into his pants. The newcomer cleared his throat loudly. Their captor whirled around, his mouth dropping open.

"Beau," a new voice said with such coldness that the temperature in the room dropped by a few degrees.

Sweat beaded on the dark soul's forehead as he swallowed hard. "Connor—I wasn't expecting you so soon!"

Connor narrowed his eyes at the ashes on the table. He walked over and pinched the dust. Lifting it to his nose, he inhaled deeply. A growl rumbled from his throat, his lips peeling back, exposing his teeth. "You've been killing the humans again."

"J-just the one, sir. He got out of hand—almost escaped. I had no choice."

"You signed a contract agreeing to send us two captives a month, did you not?"

"Y-yes."

"Where are my captives, Beau?"

Beau stepped backward, bumping up against the shelving unit where Izzy and Dax's bottle perched. The fragile prison wobbled and clinked against its neighbour but remained upright. Izzy could no longer see Beau, yet his desperate tone floated up to her. "I-I had them, but then . . . things got out of control. I had to kill them. Just give me a little more time, I can—"

Connor strode forward, his blue eyes ablaze with an eerie, fiery light. He slammed Beau up against the shelving unit. The dark soul's red hair came into view.

Dax moved away from the glass, tugging Izzy along with him. "That man—he's a demigod! This isn't good, Iz."

"None of this is good, Dax."

"I mean on a bigger scale. Beyond our situation. Demigods work for the gods. In this case, a dark god. Something big—"

The shelving unit rattled as Connor shook Beau. Their bottle tipped over, falling onto its side. It rolled into the one beside it, knocking it off the shelf. The bottle fell, shattering on the hardwood floor. Glass shards sprayed across the room as the green mist that had been contained within spilled out, coiling upward and vanishing into the ceiling.

"Hey! Look what you did!"

Connor shook him again, his grip tightening until Beau's gasps for air filled the room. Izzy, seizing the moment, pushed herself onto her knees. She scrambled toward the now reachable neck of their bottle, her feet kicking out against the cork. It wouldn't budge.

"It won't pop out," she said, sliding out to sit next to Dax.

"The only way we get out is if the jar breaks open."

"Maybe they will shake the shelf again."

"Maybe . . ."

Hope blossomed in her chest as she pressed her face against the glass. Despite her soulmate's lack of optimism, she held onto the belief that they would escape. All they needed to do was bide their time and be patient—though patience was not her strongest suit. But it was their only choice.

She scanned the room for the two men and found they had moved toward the centre. Beau was struggling to his feet, his hands rubbing at his throat. Bright red marks stood out on his neck from where Connor's fingers had been.

"You signed a deal with Medusa," Connor said as he adjusted his suit. "I warned her not to trust this job to someone like you. Serial killers have no impulse control." Beau winced at the insult but stayed quiet, shrinking away from Connor.

Dax glanced at Izzy. "Medusa is second in command for the Kingdom of Hellstone now that Satan is gone. Zeus captured him during the War for Orbistia."

Izzy raised her eyebrow. "Medusa as in snakes for hair Medusa? Seriously?"

"After all the things you've experienced lately, this is surprising to you?"

Before Izzy could respond, Beau gave a high-pitched squeal, drawing their attention back to the two men. He had backed away from Connor, his mouth hanging open like a gaping fish. "Please, no!" he begged.

Connor advanced toward Beau, a switchblade glinting in his hand. Izzy's breath caught in her throat. She didn't necessarily care what happened to the dark soul—he was evil, after all. But he was possessing someone, and that person might be innocent.

She needn't have worried. Connor brushed past the quivering dark soul, knocking him aside. Izzy's eyes widened as he took the blade and cut across his open palm. Blood immediately welled up, spilling over his fingers. He brought his hand to the wall and smeared an oval onto it.

Stepping backward, he muttered an incantation. The inside of the oval shimmered and transformed into a mirror. A beautiful woman with alabaster skin appeared in the reflection. Serpents extended from her head, draping down her body. Their black coils glistened in the light. Her mouth twisted into a snarl as she took in the scene.

"Connor, you are interrupting my torture party. This had better be important."

"Medusa, my great commander," Connor said, bowing before the mirror. "We have had a setback in our plans for Fight Island. It seems that several of the dark souls that Mammon has loaned to us have reneged on their contracts," he explained, nodding over at Beau.

The snakes hissed as Medusa bared her fangs. "They dare break a contract with me?"

"It appears so." Connor reached over and grabbed Beau by the neck, dragging him closer to the mirror. The dark soul recoiled from the image of Medusa. His chest heaved, and he broke out sobbing.

"This one, Beau 9895401, killed the promised captives rather than turning them over."

Beau's sobs grew louder as he tried to pull away from Connor. The demigod yanked him back roughly, forcing him down to his knees.

"I couldn't help myself! They were so easy to capture using this witch's body! I was going to get more for you!" Beau twisted out of Connor's grasp and stood up, sticking his finger in the man's face. "He came early," he spat out.

"Enough!" Medusa said, her lip curling upward. "How dare you speak to your superiors in such a manner! We have granted you the opportunity to serve the Kingdom of Hellstone and have given you access to a physical body, a magical one at that. This is how you demonstrate your appreciation?"

The snakes draped around Medusa's neck rose, snapping at the mirror. Her eyes took on a blood-red sheen, and a moment later, Beau fell to the ground howling, clutching at his face. Medusa smiled and leaned back in her chair, watching Beau writhe around on the floor. Her snakes settled around her neck, and she stroked them absentmindedly. After a long moment, she allowed her eyes to return to their normal shade of brown.

"You have two days, and I want four captives now." Turning to Connor, Medusa continued, "Keep him alive as a reminder to others not to cross me. If he strays from orders again, kill him and have his soul sent to Queen Mara for her little torture games. I am sure her beasties would love a new chew toy. I'll be speaking to King Mammon about the choice of dark souls he has sent me."

The mirror rippled, and Medusa's image distorted and then faded away. In her cell, Izzy stood with her fist against her mouth. Medusa was terrifying, and she wasn't even the ruler of Hellstone. Izzy shuddered. She never wanted to meet Queen Mara. Pressing closer to the glass, she could make out Beau still thrashing about on the floor.

"I'll be back in two days," Connor told him. As the words left his mouth, his body began flaking away. Moments later, he was gone.

Beau slowly rose to his feet. Izzy inhaled sharply. The dark soul's face was grotesquely deformed on one side as if it had been melted and then frozen in place. His left eye had been dislodged from its socket and now dangled, swinging against his disfigured cheek.

Beau reached up, tentatively touching his skin, and let out a piercing scream. The noise sent Izzy back into Dax's arms. She buried her face in his jacket, trying to block out Beau's cries, which seemed to go on and on. She desperately wanted to wake up from this nightmare, but that wasn't an option.

CHAPTER THIRTEEN

THE SEVERED BOND

From their cell, Izzy and Dax watched Beau frantically run between his bathroom and potion table, attempting to heal the damage he had sustained. None of his efforts were successful. One potion sent smoke pouring out of his ears. Eventually, he depleted his magical energy, exhausting himself with various spells.

At last, he emerged from his bedroom, clutching a small, compact jar. He opened it and slathered smooth cream over his face, coating it until it was masked in white. Immediately, he screamed, his hands clawing at his skin as he bolted into his bathroom.

Dax couldn't suppress a grin. "What an idiot," he said. "Firedrake ointment is for sore muscles, not open wounds."

"What's it do?"

"It sends intense heat to wherever you spread it."

A sharp, high-pitched chittering filled the room. Izzy peered through the glass. Around her, souls clapped and banged against glass walls as they laughed. A smile touched Izzy's lips. Despite their captivity, the trapped souls felt a fleeting, twisted sense of triumph at Beau's mishap.

Dax stepped up next to Izzy, and his body lightly brushed against hers. She leaned into him, resting her head on the curve of his shoulder. "So Mammon and Mara . . . they both have their own kingdom? I remember the acting troupe in Sparklafex presenting something about Mammon and the War for Orbistia."

"Yeah. Mammon rules the Kingdom of Midas. The realm of greed and pride."

"How many demonic kingdoms are there?

"Too many . . ."

"What are they like?"

"Worse than what you experienced in the Realm of Nightmares. You were on the outskirts of Mara's kingdom. The actual city is much more terrifying, from what I've been told. Any soul that's ever escaped ended up in the healing realm . . . indefinitely."

Izzy's body tensed up at the mere mention of the Realm of Nightmares. The haunting memories of her time there would often wake her up at night, leaving her drenched in sweat.

She shivered and snuggled closer to Dax. As he pulled her into a protective embrace, a sudden and loud series of knocks on the door shattered the stillness.

Beau emerged from the bathroom, his face a mix of burns and the remnants of Medusa's curse. The knocking continued, each thud shaking the frame. Straightening up, Beau reached for the knob. He paused, touching his disfigured cheek. With a muttered incantation, a glamour unfolded over his head, concealing the melted skin and sagging eye.

Beau opened the door a crack, shielding whoever was at the door from seeing inside. "Yes?"

"It's three in the morning!" a male voice boomed out. "What the hell is going on in there? You woke my kid up with your yelling!"

Sweat beaded on Beau's forehead as his glamour flickered. Pink magic glowed briefly at his fingertips before dying. Clenching his fist, he trembled, struggling to keep the illusion intact.

"His energy is wearing out," Dax whispered to Izzy, his voice holding a note of alarm.

"That's a good thing."

"Is it?" Dax gestured toward the prisons across from them. "He'll be looking to one of us to recharge."

Before Izzy could reply, an eruption of curses from the front door interrupted them. A hand thrust through the narrow opening, pushing Beau off balance. He staggered, nearly falling, and as he steadied himself, his failing glamour revealed his disfigurement.

A man appeared in the doorway. He had a thick beard covering his chin and wore faded flannel pyjama pants tucked into work boots. The ends of his undone bootlaces clicked against the wood flooring as he stepped into the room.

"I'm done with this conversation, man. Knock off the noise. If I have to come back down here—" He stopped mid-sentence, his eyes locking onto Beau's melted face. "What the hell—"

"*Immbolisi!*" A slender magic jet burst from Beau's hand, coiling around the larger man like a serpent. His body seized up, and he toppled to the ground with a thunderous crash. The tremor dislodged a glass prison perched on the edge of a shelf, sending it crashing down to shatter on the floor.

A small figure emerged from the debris, gradually regaining her average size and form. Before Beau could react, she vaulted across the room, weaving around him to plunge into the nearest electrical socket. In the next instant, she had disappeared.

"See what you've done!" The dark soul started kicking the other man in the face. Izzy winced at the sickening crunch of a nose breaking. Blood sprayed across the hardwood floor. Beau didn't relent, his feet striking the man's head and abdomen repeatedly. He hurled curses until his voice rasped with hoarseness. All the while, the victim lay immobilized, his gaze fixed and glassy. Blood cascaded from his face, which was now disfigured beyond recognition.

Pausing to regain his breath, Beau stooped to haul his neighbour toward the trapdoor. With a grunt, he rolled the stiff figure into the dark hole, the body falling awkwardly into the cramped space. Beau pushed the rug into place and then fell back against the wall, panting heavily.

Izzy slammed her fist on the glass. "He can't get away with this!"

"He won't." Dax leaned in and took hold of Izzy's hand, squeezing it. "We're going to get out. That soul escaped! She'll bring back help!"

Hope shone in her soulmate's eyes for the first time since they had been captured. He pulled her into his arms and kissed the top of her head. His body shook against hers as he laughed, his voice growing louder. Soon enough, she was laughing too, and they both sank to the bottom of the jar, their limbs tangled in a heap.

Dax leaned back to gaze at Izzy, smiling broadly. "I know it's awful that we're celebrating—what happened to that man was horrific—but Izzy, you're going to be with your family again, and I'm going to see Maddy. Everything will be okay."

They wouldn't be trapped for much longer. Someone would come to their rescue. Warmth rose in Izzy's chest, and peace settled over her.

She couldn't help but hope that they would have a chance at one more adventure before her body inevitably drew her spirit back into her corporeal form.

And then the world turned upside down on them again. Quite literally. Izzy found herself falling from Dax's arms and slamming into the neck of the bottle. Dax fell against her, wedging her further into the small opening. She gagged as a foul odour—a mixture of stale coffee and morning breath—blew against them. Pressing back against Dax, she scrambled to get away.

The reality of their situation dawned on her. *We're not going to escape.* Dax had been right all along. Beau had chosen their jar to recharge his energy.

A cold emptiness took hold in Izzy's body, and an eerie sensation spread throughout her limbs. Her thoughts scattered in all directions, her energy gradually draining away. Leaning against Dax, her eyelids fluttered closed. Behind the veil of her lashes, she caught a glimpse of her life force, streaming out like a ribbon of light, winding its way toward the open mouth of the bottle.

A loud crack echoed through the room, followed by a blinding white flash. Her gut twisted, and a sense of weightiness washed over her. A moment later, the world shattered around her as their prison hit the ground.

Nausea overwhelmed Izzy as her body stretched and expanded at an alarming rate. Her eyes snapped open to a room that seemed to hurtle toward her as she grew. She staggered backward and collided with Dax. He was just as disoriented. Before she could grasp what was happening, a metal bowl flew through her, crashing with a loud bang against the far wall.

Dax quickly grabbed her elbow and pulled her out of the way as another object flew past her ear. They pressed up against the cabinet, sinking into it. A bizarre cocktail of horror and glee bubbled up inside of Izzy as she watched her captive come under attack.

Beau was backed against the bathroom door, blood trailing from a fresh wound on his head. In his grip, he brandished a knife, flailing it around. A petite woman with straight black hair approached, each step marked by the heavy thump of combat boots against the wooden floor. She stopped a few feet away, her face etched with indifference.

"I don't have time for this," she said flatly.

Her arm recoiled, and then, with a deft motion, she sent the whip lashing out toward Beau. Its crack split the air, the leather coiling with precision around his neck. She tugged sharply, sending the dark soul staggering.

Beau collapsed to his knees, desperately clawing at the whip. His complexion turned a ghastly shade of purple, each gasp a struggle for air. White flames sprang to life along the whip, searing into his flesh. The acrid scent of burning skin permeated the air. Izzy fought the urge to gag.

She's going to kill him! Izzy gazed at Beau, biting her lip. The dark soul needed to be stopped. Clearly, the woman had the upper hand and could just as easily capture him as kill him. But was murder the right response? Did he deserve it? Probably. Yet it wasn't Beau alone who would die. He was possessing an innocent person—someone who didn't deserve this fate. There had to be another way to remove the dark soul from the witch's body.

Nodding, Izzy squared her shoulders, bracing herself for what she had to do. Marching over to where Beau was slowly dying, she stopped in front of the other woman and raised her hands in a placating gesture. "You can't kill him! He's possessing someone!"

The woman ignored Izzy. She yanked the whip harder. Flames leaped up, searing into Beau's neck with great ferocity. Unable to scream, the dark soul could only emit weird, gurgling noises. In desperation, he clawed at his neck, tearing his own flesh in a frantic attempt to escape.

"Stop!" Izzy stepped forward, closing the gap between herself and the woman. "You can't just kill him!" She reached out, her fingers slipping through the woman's shoulder like mist.

The woman's eyes flashed. Without warning, she raised her free hand and flicked her wrist. A solid gust of wind encircled Izzy and Dax, lifting them up. They were hurled across to the other side of the room. The weight of the air against her formed an impenetrable barrier between Izzy and the other woman. She remained trapped despite her efforts to push back against the invisible force. Once again, she was a helpless spectator to the events unfolding before her.

Heat prickled up Izzy's throat as she glared at the other woman. Hot tears welled in her eyes as she watched blood slither down the whip, staining Beau's white shirt with crimson. A gruesome crack echoed as his neck gave way, and in the next breath, his head detached, hitting the floor with a wet thud. It rolled, coming to rest a few feet from Izzy.

With the barrier gone, she lurched forward, collapsing to her knees by the severed head. Her world spun again for a moment, her gaze locking with the glossy eye dangling from its socket. She should have been relieved that her captor was dead. Instead, a dark rage grew within her and threatened to spill out into the room.

CHAPTER FOURTEEN

GHOSTS OF THE FRENCH QUARTER

Scrambling backward, Izzy bumped into Dax's legs. He bent down and helped her to her feet, wrapping his arm protectively around her waist.

"You okay?"

A hard line formed at her mouth as she glowered at the dark-haired woman. A silver badge on her leather jacket glinted in the light. Etched into the metal was a demon skull wrapped in chains.

"I'm fine," Izzy said, straightening to her full height.

"She's a demon hunter, Izzy." Dax's voice carried a note of warning. "She was just doing her job."

Ignoring him, Izzy marched toward the other woman, who was now kneeling by the headless body, an obsidian bottle in her hand. It was adorned with ancient runes and intricate designs, resembling the bottle in which they had been imprisoned but far more beautifully crafted.

"What is your pr—"

The woman lifted her finger to her lips, issuing a soft shush. Izzy inhaled sharply, steeling herself to speak, and then froze. Her mouth fell agape as a dense plume of black smoke began to spiral upward from the jagged opening in the corpse's neck.

Extending the bottle close to the mist, the demon hunter murmured, "*Paracapturar!*" The fog changed direction, swirling toward the bottle's opening. When the last wisp had been drawn inside, she sealed the decanter with a cork and tucked it in her jacket pocket.

A second mist rose from the body, emanating the same white glow as Izzy's, though marred by streaks of grey. Izzy's eyes widened as the mist took on Beau's form. Only it wasn't Beau. This was the spirit of the body's true owner, his face now whole. Tears were streaming down his cheeks, fading back into his body as they fell off his chin.

His gaze swept the room, coming to rest on his mangled corpse. A raw howl tore from his throat as he crumpled to his knees. Ignoring the man, the demon hunter rose to her feet. She moved toward the nearby desk and started rifling through its contents.

Dax approached Izzy, exchanging a warning glance with her before bending down to comfort the distraught soul. Izzy's fingers twitched at her side, slowly curling into fists. She understood Dax's caution, but she really didn't care if this strange woman held some higher title in Orbistia. Sure, she had captured the dark soul possessing the body, but she was also a murderer.

A flurry of thoughts screamed through her mind. *She hasn't even acknowledged the man. How could she be so callous? She caused this!*

Walking up to the desk, she stepped beside the demon hunter and slammed her fist down, expecting a loud thud. However, her interruption didn't have the desired effect. Instead of striking the wood, her hand sank through the wood, plunging deep into it. She had forgotten about Dax's earlier lesson on controlling her energy signature.

"You have a funny way of saying thank you," the demon hunter said in a cool tone.

A heat stained Izzy's neck as she struggled to extract her arms from the desk. "Excuse me?"

"I saved your butt. You'd be vapour right now if it weren't for me."

Tensing her abdominal muscles, Izzy mustered all her strength and hoisted her body upward, her arms materializing with a sickening pop. A shiver rippled across her skin, leaving a trail of goosebumps in its wake. She rubbed her arms to ward off the uncomfortable sensation. Peeking through the veil of her hair, she caught sight of the demon hunter watching with an amused smirk painting her features.

"Thank you," Izzy said, her teeth clenched as she forced the words out.

"You're welcome," the woman said. "Now get out of my way." She reached through Izzy's body, gripping the desk drawer and pulling it open.

"What the heck is wrong with you?" Izzy recoiled, a chill passing through her as the woman's arm ghosted through her body. She instinctively dropped her arms to her stomach, holding it protectively.

"I told you to move."

"You're a cold person. You know that, right?"

"So I've been told."

"You didn't have to kill him." Izzy gestured toward the soul who was still sobbing near his body.

With a heavy sigh, the demon hunter shoved the door closed. "Look . . . what's your name?"

"Izzy."

"I'm Elena. Izzy, that carnie's life was over. That dark soul murdered a lot of people, and he did a crappy job at hiding his tracks. It was only a matter of time before he was caught. I probably did the guy a favour. At least now he won't waste his life in a jail cell."

"You don't know that for sure! Who are you to—"

A brilliant green light filled the room. Shielding her eyes, Izzy looked over to Dax. This had to be the man's spirit guide coming to collect the carnie. *What if it's Priscilla?* She inched backward, her muscles tensing.

A man stepped forward, his features becoming clear. He had thinning hair, round, owl-like eyes, and a bristly mustache that needed a trim.

Definitely not Priscilla. Izzy exhaled loudly. She couldn't believe how close they had come to getting caught again. Dax shared her sentiment, his shoulders relaxing as he moved to stand next to her.

They nodded at the spirit guide as they backed away, granting him an unobstructed view of the decapitated body. He flinched as he surveyed the gruesome scene. His gaze drifted over to the body's soul—the carnie—who remained hunched over his own lifeless form.

"Edmund!"

The soul straightened, his mouth agape as he regarded the spirit guide. "I-I don't know you."

The guide's smile broadened at Edmund, and he extended his hand. "Peter 6645875. Your appointed spirit guide. How nice to finally meet you soul to soul!"

"Spirit guide?"

"I've been watching over you your whole life, Ed."

"Why didn't you warn me?"

"Warn you of what?"

Edmund stood up, his tall figure towering over Peter. He pointed, his hand trembling, to the decapitated head. "The demon!" he said, his voice shrill.

Peter's eyebrows arched together. "What demon?"

"The one controlling my body! He told me he was an angel—that I would serve a higher purpose." Edmund's voice broke, a new wave of sobs erupting from him.

"Dark soul," Elena clarified, stepping toward Peter. "Not a demon."

Peter's eyes brightened as Elena acknowledged him. "Ah, Orbistia's greatest demon hunter," he said. "That explains why you're here. I suppose you caught it?"

"Yes. An alert came out that he was here. One of his captives made it back to Orbistia. I've been after this one for a while now. He's been leaving bodies all over the French Quarter. The media have dubbed him the Voodoo Viper. It's Beau 9895401."

"I've heard of him. A famous serial killer in a past life, wasn't he?"

Elena nodded, her eyes darkening. "He gave his spirit guide the slip several months ago. A demon must be—"

A terrible wailing filled the room. Edmund had collapsed near his severed head, trying to pick it up. His face crumbled as his hands kept slipping through the skull like mist.

"Oh, dear," Peter said, his expression pinched. "It's a shame they haven't figured out how to extract a dark soul without killing the carnie body." He sighed and continued, "I need to take him to the Astral Sorting Station." He turned to bid Elena farewell, but she had already retreated into the bedroom.

"Not exactly a warm woman, is she?" Izzy said, glaring at Elena's retreating form.

"Oh, well, demigods have a lot on their plate, my dear. Demon hunting, minding the Realm of Shadows . . . they're a busy bunch. Not much time for pleasantries."

"She's a demigod? Well, that explains everything!"

"Excuse me?"

"The dark soul was working with a demigod. Elena reminds me of him. Cold, heartless, acts like she's bett—"

"You should contact the Orbistian Council when you take Edmund back," Dax said, putting his arm around the spirit guide and steering him away from Izzy. "The dark soul was also working with Medusa."

"Medusa!"

"Yes," Dax continued, gesturing toward the shelving unit. "There are other souls trapped here. Some of them will need to be taken to the healing realm."

"My goodness," Peter said, glancing at the shelf and then at Edmund, who had curled up into a ball beside his head. "Of course, I will contact Councilman Mark immediately."

Dax nodded and dropped his arm from Peter's shoulder. The spirit guide shuffled toward Edmund and crouched down next to him. "Come now, son. Let me take you home," he said softly. Hooking his arm around Edmund, Peter supported the other man in rising to his feet. A moment later, they were gone, the portal closing up behind them.

"We should go," Dax said. He moved toward an electrical outlet, but a gentle touch from Izzy stopped him.

Her eyes narrowed into slits as she tilted her head at the bedroom door. "I want to talk to her."

"Izzy, don't. It's not worth it. We need to go now. The bloodstone, remember?"

"It would be rude not to say goodbye," Izzy said, striding past Dax and into the bedroom. She paused at the threshold, her eyebrows pinched together as she surveyed the disarray. The room was a mess, with half-empty soda cans scattered on the floor, creating sticky puddles on the hardwood. Dirty laundry was strewn about the small space, and a lone sock dangled from the brim of the overflowing garbage can.

Elena was yanking the mattress off the unmade bed, her hands moving along the bedframe. "How is she doing that?" Izzy asked Dax. "Wouldn't that use up all her energy?"

"She's not just a spirit, Iz. She's a demigod. They can do things we can't."

"She's still a spirit, though?"

"Yeah. One with special powers. In Orbistia, there's this competition every—"

Elena grunted and shoved the mattress back on the bed. "There's nothing here," she mumbled, raking her hands through her hair. Her gaze came to rest on Izzy and Dax. "Why are you still here?" She folded her arms across her chest and looked away, just above their heads.

Warmth flushed up Izzy's neck. The demigod's indifference to them set her blood boiling. *This woman is supposed to be a protector of Orbistia? How is it that narcissists are always the ones in power?*

Dax reached up, pressing his hand gently on the small of Izzy's back. Ignoring him, she took a step closer to Elena. The stress of the last week had finally taken its toll on her. Izzy glared at the other woman. She wanted nothing more than to knock Elena down a peg and eliminate her air of superiority.

"You could have just told me there was no other way to save Edmond," she said.

"There wasn't time for explanations." Elena brushed past her and opened the closet. She began rummaging through shelves, tossing items to the floor.

"It would have taken two seconds!"

"It's not my job to explain things to you, carnie."

Izzy bristled, and she bit down hard on her lip. Her eyes flickered over to Dax. His shoulders were tense, and he was fidgeting with the hem of his jacket. Izzy closed her eyes, drawing in a deep breath. Fighting with the demigod wasn't going to achieve anything. Dax was quiet, but his body language spoke volumes. He wanted to go. *I should be looking for the bloodstone, not wasting time in arguments.*

Sighing, she stepped back from Elena. "Let's go before the council gets here."

Elena stiffened and then slowly turned her head toward Izzy. "Why would the council be coming here?"

"Because of the trapped souls."

"Trapped souls?" She dropped the shoebox she held and settled her hands on her hips. "Explain!"

Izzy arched an eyebrow. "Now you're interested in what I have to say?"

"What trapped souls?"

"I don't know how you missed them in your extensive search of the apartment. What are you looking for anyway?"

"Proof the dark soul was working with a demon. I suspect he was." Elena brushed past Izzy and strode toward the doorway, her gaze locked on Dax's transparent form. She marched through him without hesitation, his body stretching before recoiling into its original shape. Dax's jaw tensed, yet he kept silent.

"Where are they?" Elena called out from the living room.

"On shelves. Where bottles are normally stored," Izzy said, smirking. Elena didn't respond. A moment later, she let out a string of profanity. Izzy's lips quirked into a grin as she trailed after Dax into the main room. Elena was pacing around, a manic look in her eyes. She came to a sudden halt.

"There must be one hundred bottles here. At least fifty in the cupboard alone," she said, gesturing toward a nearby cabinet, its wooden door flung open. "This many souls, the amount of dark magic he was using . . . I knew it! He's involved with demons!"

"Dark gods, actually," Dax corrected, gently grasping Izzy's arm. "We really need to get going," he murmured into her ear.

She nodded. "Where should we—"

"Dark gods? Are you for real? Why didn't you mention this earlier?" Elena said.

"When should I have brought it up? When you were killing Edmond? Or should I have slipped it in while you were insulting me?" Izzy twisted the ring around on her finger, heat spreading through her body as she glared at Elena.

"Now is not the time for dramatics, carnie."

"Stop calling me that. I have a name."

Dax stepped in between the two women. "The dark soul works for Medusa," he said, nudging Izzy toward the wall. He pointed to the rug that Elena was standing on. "There's a man, by the way, under your feet."

Elena glanced down, her jaw dropping open. As she flung aside the rug, Izzy and Dax edged toward the nearest electrical outlet. It was half concealed behind a pair of muddy workboots leaning up near the door. Izzy bent toward it, the blend of wet soil and aged leather filling her senses. *Smells like Dad. I wish the Electrical Network could take us to him. Maybe once we leave here, we can—*

For the second time, green light filled the room.

"You there, don't leave," a voice commanded. His tone left no room for argument. Against her better judgment, Izzy slowly straightened up, twisting around to stare at the newcomer. A man strode toward her, his purple robes swishing against the ground. A gold belt hung around his thick stomach.

"Councilman Mark," Dax whispered against her ear.

The man halted several feet away, a slight frown on his face. "Peter advised me of the situation. Are you the captured souls he referred to?"

"Yes, sir." Dax shifted in front of Izzy, partly hiding her from view. "There are others, though," he said, nodding toward the open cabinet.

The councilman glanced over at the jars, his nostrils flaring as he studied the tiny figures inside. They were pounding at their glass prisons, screaming unintelligibly. *Likely upset that they haven't been released yet*, Izzy thought, her guilt gnawing at her. She should have let them out as soon as she had escaped.

"Peter said Medusa was involved in this. Explain."

Once again, Dax spoke for them. "The dark soul was capturing humans for Medusa—for something called Fight Island."

"Fight Island?" The councilman stilled. "Elena," he said without taking his eyes off Dax.

The demigod looked up from her position on the floor. She had dragged the captive from the hidden compartment and had laid him out beside the dark hole. The man's face was bruised and bleeding.

"Yes, sir."

"Your findings?"

"Nothing yet."

"Continue looking. I want information on this Fight Island. Interview the dark soul as well," he continued. Report everything to me—only me."

"Yes, sir," Elena said, standing and walking back into the bedroom. The sound of objects tumbling to the floor echoed from the closet as she resumed her search.

"I expect a full report from both of you," the councilman said, his gaze shifting past Dax to lock onto Izzy. "You're an astral projector? Your memories will need to be e—"

The room flashed green again. The councilman flinched as a stream of people poured out of a new portal. Within moments, the space became crowded with guides, members of the Guard, and other Orbistian officials. The murmuring of voices grew louder as they wandered through the cramped room.

"You," Mark said, nodding toward a nearby guide. "Come here."

A thin, dark-haired woman approached, her steps hesitant. "Yes, sir?" she asked, wringing her hands.

"We have a situation. There are a hundred or so imprisoned Orbistians, many of whom will need to be taken to the healing realm." He tilted his head toward the injured man lying frozen on the floor. "That Carnie will also need his memory wiped."

"Yes, sir. I'll see to i—"

An overly bright voice sang out through the room. "All right, everyone, here is what we need to do. James, you will lead those completely drained directly to the healing realm. Barty, I want you to wipe the memories of any astral projectors and send them back to their bodies. Those that are recently deceased will need to be taken to the Astral Sorting Station."

At the sound of her spirit guide's shrill voice, Izzy grimaced. *Priscilla! How is it that she's always showing up?* Thankfully, Priscilla hadn't noticed them yet. Dax slipped his fingers around Izzy's wrist and pulled her down with him as he dropped toward the floor. His hand disappeared through the workboots as he searched for the electrical socket.

"Stop!" A sharp voice called out. "Isabelle Adams! You stop right there!"

Izzy looked up, her eyes locking with Priscilla's. *If looks could kill,* Izzy thought. Priscilla set off toward Izzy, her plump lips forming a firm line. And then everything disappeared. Izzy was sucked into the Electrical Network, swallowed up by its black tunnels.

CHAPTER FIFTEEN

DENYING DEATH

Izzy tumbled out of the electrical socket and landed in an unceremonious heap on the floor. Rising to her feet, she brushed back her hair, smoothing the pieces still floating upward. She glanced around, taking in the off-white walls and the simple furniture decorating the small room she had fallen into.

In a nearby bed, an older woman slept, her grey hair matted to her head. Faint sunlight streamed in through the lace curtains, slowly lighting up the room.

"Where are we?" Izzy whispered.

"Burley, United Kingdom. I'm pretty sure this is a long-term care home."

"Why did you bring us here?"

"The medium said the bloodstone is somewhere in this village, remember."

Izzy glanced at the digital clock next to the bed. *It's nine in the morning! That would be . . . four back in Ontario.* "We don't have much time to find it," she said.

"I know. We'll have to walk around and look for another medium."

"Easier said than done," Izzy grumbled as they made their way out of the room and into the hallway.

"By the way, it looks like we were both wrong."

"About what?"

"Why we were captured. It had nothing to do with the ring we found or Mara. We were just in the wrong place at the wrong time. Rotten luck."

"I'd say so," Izzy replied, her fingers tracing the grain of the wooden banister along the hallway.

"It is interesting though," Dax continued.

"What?"

"Mammon is working with Medusa on something."

"The whole Fight Island thing?"

"Yeah, the dark gods rarely collaborate. They're too busy fighting among themselves. The last alliance was during their assault on Orbistia."

"And the Siege of Sparklafex."

"Yes. Loki would be interested to know that Mammon is working with another dark god."

"Loki?"

"Do you remember the reenactment we watched in Sparklafex—the one where Loki defeated Mammon during the siege?"

"Oh, right."

"Marlo is good friends with Loki. I'll update him when we get back. I know Elena is investigating things, but Loki would want to look into it too."

"Wouldn't Councilman Mark fill him in? He's a light god, isn't he?"

"He is. But he tends to get left out of things . . . He doesn't really fit in with the other gods even though he is an Orbistian."

"Really, that's . . . Oh right. He's a god of mischief, isn't he? Or is that just a legend?"

"Legends are based on some truth," Dax said, smiling.

They reached the staircase. It was wide and covered in thick carpeting. An electric chair lift—a supportive device to help the long-term care home occupants down the stairs—was attached to the side. Dax paused, pulling Izzy to a stop.

"About what happened back there with Elena—"

"I know, I was an emotional mess. I shouldn't have gotten into it with her. I wasted a lot of our time. I'm sorry, Dax."

"Actually, I wanted to tell you I was proud of you. You were assertive with her—far from being an emotional mess."

"You think so? I'm always getting into arguments. Eddie says I have a bad temper sometimes."

"No. You call people out on their behaviour—make them self-reflect. It's a good thing. Without that, people wouldn't grow."

Izzy's cheeks grew warm. *Emotional, hot-tempered, irrational*—all words she had heard before. Words that left her feeling ashamed. *Assertive* was a new one. It was positive. It made her feel . . . strong. Lightness blossomed within her chest. She glanced shyly up at Dax.

He crooked his mouth into a smile, and her breath caught. *That smile.* Her pulse hammered louder as she flicked her gaze up to meet his. The world around them ceased to exist. Nothing else mattered. Just Dax. *My soulmate.* She wanted nothing more than to merge her soul with his and just exist with him.

He leaned down, his lips inches away from hers. His breath was warm against her skin. Inhaling sharply, she caught a whiff of vanilla. His scent—soothing and familiar. She closed her eyes, stretching up on her tiptoes as she moved to press their mouths together.

But her lips found nothing. He had pulled away. Her eyelids slowly opened. Dax's head was tilted away from hers. His eyes narrowed at a dark form as it moved down the hall, half-hidden in the shadows. It disappeared into one of the bedrooms, slipping through the door as if it weren't there.

"Demon," Dax said.

A heavy weight settled in Izzy's chest. *Demons. In a long-term care home.* An image of her Aunt Audrey flashed before her—Izzy imagined her curled up sleeping, her frail body wracked with coughs as a dark form rose up above her. Slimy tentacles reached down toward her head, sliding across her thin skin.

No! Izzy straightened her back, pulling herself up to her full height. *I won't let that happen, not to anyone.* She moved quickly down the hall.

A hand wrapped around her elbow, forcing her to stop. "Weapons first," Dax said. He let go and whispered, *"Advo Telum."* A boomerang materialized in his hand, the polished grain of its wood bathed in a radiant sheen. Along its curved body ran elegant carvings, each line thrumming with energy.

Nodding, Izzy closed her eyes, visualizing her own spirit weapon. *"Advo Telum,"* she murmured. Her fingers wrapped around the hilt, the earthy scent of aged leather filling her nostrils. She opened her eyes. A Viking sword rested in her hand. Its long, steel blade was etched with Norse runes that glowed, casting a brilliant light on the walls.

She started forward again, pausing before the last door at the end of the hall. Pressing her sword against the dull wood, she watched it sink in. Dax brushed up against her, his boomerang gripped tightly in his hand.

She lifted her eyes to meet his. "Together then?"

"Always."

Her vision blurred as she passed through the wood, her form twisting and stretching like an elastic band before snapping back to its original shape. She found herself on the other side, in a room mirroring the one they'd arrived in. Drawn curtains shrouded the space in semidarkness while slender shafts of sunlight poured around the edges, draping the figure on the bed in a patchwork of light and shadow.

Izzy inched forward, eyes scanning the room. She wrinkled her nose as she inhaled the sharp antiseptic scent clinging to the coverlets tucked around the man asleep on the bed. His breathing was laboured, his lips dry and cracked. One hand rested above the sheets, gripping the coarse fabric.

A skeletal creature emerged from the shadows, wrapped in a long, brown cloak. Two pinpricks of light shone where its face should have been, piercing through the darkness and fixing on Izzy. She sucked in a deep breath, steadying her arm as she raised her sword.

The creature blinked, its bony hands lowering its hood. A cascade of wispy, white hair tumbled out, framing its thin face. Izzy's stomach lurched at the creature's appearance—chalky white skin stretched tightly over its cheekbones, cloudy eyes, and dry, cracked lips. It resembled the man lying between them.

Dax let his boomerang fade away as he slipped past Izzy. *What is he doing?* She reached out, grabbing his sleeve.

"Not a demon, Iz," he said. "A grim reaper."

She tightened her hold on his jacket, pulling him back. Grim reapers were bearers of death. Murderers. It had to be demonic in nature. How could her soulmate not know this?

"Relax, Izzy. Reapers work for Orbistia."

"Are you sure, because it looks—"

"I'll explain later," he murmured.

Reluctantly, she loosened her fingers, letting her hand drop to her side. They stepped up to the bed to stand across from the reaper. It was still staring at them, a blank expression on its gnarled face.

"Have you come to escort his soul home?" It asked, its voice coming out dry and cracked.

"No. We're just passing through." Dax's gaze drifted to the bed. "It's his time, is it?"

The reaper nodded, its hand drifting toward the man's creased forehead.

"Don't touch him!" Izzy said, her voice harsh.

The reaper paused, tilting its head at her. "You object?"

"You're going to murder him. Of course, I object!"

"This man is living with pancreatic cancer."

The reaper crooked a finger toward Izzy, gesturing for her to step closer. The muscles between her shoulder blades tightened, but she shuffled over, taking care to maintain her distance from the strange Orbisian.

The reaper traced the man's mouth with its finger. "His mouth is so dry he cannot swallow anymore. The staff moisten his lips with water . . . when they have time." It gestured toward a small tray next to the bed, which held a small cup of water and a sponge. "His body is shutting down, and he feels every moment of it."

Sweat glistened on the man's brow. He moaned, his lips quivering. A silence fell on the room as they watched him sleep. Izzy reached out, her hand hovering over his, but then remembered she couldn't touch him. She felt a sharp pang in her chest as he moaned again. Tears welled in her eyes, and she glanced away, focusing on the starch-white bedsheets.

"Hasn't he suffered enough, child?"

Her jaw twitched, but she didn't respond.

"Should I leave him to suffer until his heart gives out? He'll feel everything. Thirst. Pain."

"Doesn't that go against free will? Who are you to decide when he dies."

"I decide nothing. The choice is his."

"What do you mean?"

The reaper reached over, its hand resting on the man's head. "His guides visit him in his dreams," it said. "He asked them for help. He wants to move on." The reaper peered up at Izzy, its murky eyes locking onto hers. "Death is just a step toward another life."

A glow pulsed from its fingers, disappearing into the man's skin. "First, I send them comfort," it said.

Izzy leaned forward, her mouth opening slightly as she stared at the man. His expression softened under the reaper's touch, and a serene smile spread across his face.

"Then I end their pain," the reaper continued. It lifted its arm, a large scythe gripped in its hand. Before Izzy had time to react, it brought it down and gently tapped the tool against the man's head. The man's breath hitched, and a low, faltering crackle cut through the quiet room. Then, the sound dwindled away, leaving an eerie silence behind.

Izzy gasped and she staggered into Dax. He held her, wrapping his arms around her. "It's okay, Iz. Look."

She lifted her chin and gazed toward the dead man's body. A shimmering light floated from the pores of his skin, slowly taking the shape of an older man. "Thank you," he said, tears leaking down his nose as he stared at the reaper. "That was dreadful. I've been yearning to leave that wretched body for months now."

The reaper nodded as it tucked its scythe back into its cloak. The man glanced down at his corpse, blinking rapidly as tears continued to spill down his face. He reached up to brush them away and then jerked his arm back. "My face! I still look half-dead! I thought I'd at least come out of this looking healthy again!" Glancing over at the reaper, he added, "Don't say I'm to be stranded in this form!"

"No, sir," Dax said, giving the man a reassuring smile. "Once you cross over, you'll learn to control your energy signature. Then you can change your appearance."

"Oh, thank heavens! What a relief. I can hardly reunite with my Elizabeth looking like—"

The room filled with a green light, marking the entrance of the man's spirit guide, a tall woman with straight black hair and warm-toned skin. She moved toward him, her lips pulled into a gentle smile.

"Ah, Yuko-san." The man stepped forward, offering a slight bow. "Thank you kindly for arranging this, my dear."

Yuko bowed in return. "Are you ready, John?"

"As prepared as I'll ever be."

John took his guide's arm, and a moment later, they were gone, leaving Izzy and Dax alone with the reaper. It grinned at Izzy, revealing brown, rotted teeth. "You see," it rasped, "a death that was eagerly welcomed—a peaceful release from this life."

Izzy forced herself not to recoil from the reaper. It was terrifying. How people didn't run screaming from it was beyond her. *It looks like a demon. What are the gods thinking, sending this creature to end the lives of dying people?*

Clearing her throat, she managed to say, "I suppose if it's what people want . . . but I don't understand. Why take on this form?"

The reaper stilled. An awkward silence ensued before it finally spoke. "To the man, I was beautiful. Angelic."

"But this is your true form?"

"Yes. For now . . . I resemble the souls I am meant to help."

"Why?"

"To remind me of my purpose on Earth."

"Why would the gods force that on you? It's—"

"Izzy," Dax said, touching her back. "Grim reapers are souls from the Realm of Shadows. They agree to take on this role to work off their bad karma. It's a way for them to brighten their souls. Once they are no longer tinged with darkness, they are allowed back into Orbistia."

"The Realm of Shadows?"

"A world without colour," the reaper whispered. "A prison."

"Souls on the verge of going dark—we call them greys—they're imprisoned in the Realm of Shadows," Dax explained. "The gods don't want them near Orbistia."

"That awful," Izzy said. "Aren't there other supports in place to help you? Like counselling . . . or rehabilitation?" She motioned at the reaper. "This just seems traumatizing."

A dark look flashed in the reaper's eyes. "Being a reaper is a humbling experience. It's also the quickest and most effective route to being reborn again."

"How long do you have to do this?"

"As long as it takes." It pulled its hood back up, concealing its face. "I have one more soul to attend to here. If you will excuse me . . ." It brushed past them, disappearing through the bedroom door.

A hollow feeling settled in Izzy's chest. What horrible things had the reaper done to get segregated to such a place? *Was it a murderer?* She shivered.

"I know what you are thinking," Dax said.

"What?"

"Greys aren't necessarily murderers, Izzy. They're souls who have continually made poor life choices—fraud, abuse, theft, bullying—that sort of thing. It can take multiple incarnations for your soul to turn grey." He moved his hand to her elbow, gently turning her toward the door.

"The reaper isn't a bad spirit. It's made mistakes. Some are worse than others. What matters is that it's trying to do better. That's what all Orbistians work toward—doing better. Some souls just have to work at it more than others."

CHAPTER SIXTEEN

THE UNHINGED HEDGE GHOST

The long-term care home's lawn was blanketed with fresh snow. A wooden cart, worn and bent with age, was parked near the front doors. It was hitched to a gaunt horse, whose hide was stretched tight over its bony frame. Like the grim reaper, the horse had murky eyes and brittle white hair.

The support staff, absorbed in their morning routines, paid no attention to the spectral cart as they made their way into the building. A car passed right through it while letting out a young nurse. Untroubled, the ghostly horse flexed and regained its form as the vehicle pulled away.

Circling the horse warily, Izzy kept her distance. "Another lost soul paying for their sins?" she asked.

"Probably," Dax said. "Thousands of souls live in the Realm of Shadows, and there are only so many grim reaper jobs. The horse adds to the image, I suppose."

"The gods sure do like their theatrics, don't they?"

"You have no idea," Dax said, his lips twitching.

As they strolled down the narrow street, the pristine white snow under their feet remained untouched, leaving no trace of their footprints. Thick bushes and towering trees formed a natural canopy on both sides of the road, and occasionally, the pair glimpsed grand homes peeking out from behind the lush greenery. Small, ornamental wooden fences surrounded each property, serving more as decorative boundaries than actual enclosures.

One estate held a white brick building with several horses grazing in the yard. Their muzzles were buried in the snow as they searched for patches of grass. Izzy gestured toward the animals. "Should be interesting when the homeowners wake up."

Dax snorted. "They won't care. This village is known for letting horses and cattle roam around."

"Seriously?"

"Yeah." He slowed down, pausing in front of the house. The smallest horse raised its head, gazing at him. Its ears twitched, and then it bent down, resuming its search for food. Dax's gaze softened. "Animals can see spirits, you know. Some get spooked, but most don't seem bothered by us."

"Too bad they can't speak—point us in the right direction to the bloodstone." Izzy drew in a long breath. "Dax, how are we supposed to find it? It's not like we can ask anyone!" She fought back a wave of despair. Her body was going to wake up soon. She'd be pulled away from Dax, leaving him with the impossible task of finding the talisman alone. *It could be years before I see him again*, she thought, wiping at her face.

"Well, we could ask them," Dax said, pointing over her shoulder.

Whirling around, Izzy peered into the overgrown hedge behind her. Two sets of eyes blinked out from within the leafy foliage. She jerked backward, falling against Dax. "Jeepers!"

Dax stepped around Izzy, arms extended from his body with his palms facing upward as he approached the hedge. "Hello," he called out, his mouth curving into a friendly smile.

The eyes narrowed into slits—a silent warning. Izzy shifted uncomfortably in her spot. *They don't want us here.*

"Hi," Dax tried again. "I don't suppose you could help us. We are looking for someone."

Izzy reached out, her fingers curling around his arm. "We should go," she said, tugging him back a step.

"They might know where the talisman is."

"Dax, let's just—"

"Listen to the girl." An older man stepped out of the hedge, followed closely by a woman wearing a pale blue dress with a cinched waist and sleeves that billowed out. She regarded Izzy with a stormy look from under the brim of her feathered hat.

"Excuse me?" Dax said, taken aback.

The man scowled. "Away with you!" He squared his shoulders, his chest inflating. His suit strained at the seams, the silver buttons threatening to fly off. "You shall find no aid from us."

"Sir, we're trying to find—"

"Don't bother rummaging around for answers here, young man. We haven't got what you're after," the woman said, her gaze flickering between Izzy and Dax.

"You don't even know what we're looking for!"

"We don't want your kind here. Carry on your way."

"Our kind?"

"Spirits or guides, whichever name you claim, we desire no part in your business!"

Izzy pressed against Dax's side, stretching up to whisper in his ear. "They don't realize that they're dead."

"We are quite cognizant of our ethereal nature, thank you," the man said. He lifted a hand to his bowler hat, his thinning hair visible beneath the brim as he straightened it.

Dax blinked and reached up to scratch at his head. "Forgive me for saying this . . . but you two look like you've been dead for at least a hundred years. I-I don't understand. Why haven't your guides taken you away by now? It's unhealthy for a soul to be stuck in the physical realm this long."

The man's face brightened, a grin stretching across his cheeks. "Our Frances, she's got a knack for sending those other chaps packing, hasn't she, Lynda?"

"George!"

The man glanced at Lynda, whose face had turned a bright shade of red. His eyes widened, realizing his mistake.

"Whose Frances?" Izzy asked.

"Never you mind," Lynda replied sharply. She shook her head, loose strands of vibrant orange hair escaping her updo. Tears sprang from her eyes. "N-Never you m-mind!"

She's unhinged. Izzy squeezed Dax's arm, and he reached up, interlocking his fingers with hers. They watched as George moved to console Lynda, lowering his voice to talk to her in a soothing tone.

A harsh creak sounded nearby. Turning away from the hysterical ghost, Izzy scanned the nearby hedges, searching for the source of the noise. "Lynda? George?" a voice called out. "What's happening?"

The hedge rustled as someone drew closer. A moment later, a human emerged from a hidden path, her curly white hair tangled with brambles. She paused, scanning her surroundings, and her gaze coming to rest on the distraught ghost.

"Oh, my word. Lynda, what's the matter, dear?" She moved to touch the other woman, her hand hovering over her shoulder.

"I'm sorry, ma'am, I think we upset your friend," Dax said.

"Oh?"

"They were spying on us through the hedge and—"

"Spying!" George looked up sharply. "Investigating the situation, we were! The recently deceased catch wind of our Frances and they'll start traipsing across the countryside, demanding a word with her. I won't tolerate it!"

"Move along," Lynda said, her voice rising to a piercing screech.

Frances drew in a deep breath and gazed toward the sky. "Now, Lynda and George, while I do appreciate your help—I really do—there is no need to chase these two away," she said, exasperation creeping into her voice. She glanced at Izzy, her eyes lingering on her neck. "Why, this girl isn't even dead. Look, you can see the outline of her astral cord between her shoulder blades."

George busied himself with straightening his vest. Meanwhile, Lynda continued to glare at Izzy, her frail body heaving with silent sobs.

Izzy's fingers crept into her hair, pulling at a stray strand. Lynda's stare bore into her, unsettling in its intensity. Something about the woman just wasn't right. With any luck, they would learn what they need from Frances and be on their way. She didn't want to spend any more time around these individuals than she absolutely had to.

"I'm terribly sorry," Frances said to them. "Would you mind forgiving George and Lynda? They are distant kin and are very protective of me." She smiled warmly at her ancestors before adding, "Frances Smith's my name, just so you know."

"I'm Dax, and this is my soulmate, Izzy."

"Soulmates? How sweet." She winced as she turned toward the hedge, rubbing at her hip. "Would it be too much trouble to continue our chat inside the house? I could do with a sit-down and wouldn't say no to a cup of tea."

With a slow nod, Izzy followed the older woman down a narrow path through the hedge. Ahead, an iron gate stood ajar. Behind her, she could still hear Lynda muttering unintelligible words under her breath as George nudged her forward. The weight of Lynda's stare pressed against Izzy's back. Her shoulders slumped. A cup of tea usually meant for an extended visit. It looked like they weren't leaving anytime soon.

CHAPTER SEVENTEEN

A Home among Headstones

An itchy, tingly sensation washed over Izzy as she stepped over the gate's threshold. Her shoulders shook as unease engulfed her. And then, it dissipated, slipping away like a current of water. She glanced back at Dax, catching the subtle twitch in his jaw. *He felt it too.*

"It's the barrier spell. It keeps the guides at bay," Frances was saying.

"You're a psychic medium . . . and a witch?" Izzy asked.

"Yes."

"I thought that was rare? To have both gifts, I mean."

"It is, dear. We're a rather small community. There's only six others like me in the UK that I know of."

Frances gestured toward a tall, whitewashed chapel in the middle of the lawn. All around it were tombstones, many of which had started to crumble with age. A narrow pathway, cleared of snow, led up to the building. "Let's get inside, shall we? It's too chilly to be out here chattering."

Izzy glanced at a nearby tombstone, its name weathered beyond recognition. "You live here . . . in a graveyard?"

"Yes, I own the chapel," Frances replied, leading them down the pathway. She paused to let everyone in before shutting the heavy wooden door with a soft thud.

A large room opened up before them. Bright light streamed through the stained-glass windows, casting colourful patterns on the polished hardwood. A neatly arranged kitchen with modern appliances and sleek countertops occupied the space of the former altar, and plush living room pieces had taken the place of the pews. Above the entrance, a small loft had been built, accessible via a set of stairs that spiralled down to the side.

While it still retained much of its original architecture, it had been transformed into a cozy, unconventional home.

After hanging up her coat, Frances led them over to the kitchen. A black iron kettle sat on the stove, already filled with water. She flicked the stovetop on and then settled down at a small oak table near the window to wait.

"Mum and Dad moved to Newfoundland just before I came along, yet Burley's always been a bit like home too. Spent all my summers here with my grandparents," Frances said. "When this old chapel came up for grabs, well, I couldn't resist. Packed up my life and set it down right back here."

"You have a beautiful home, but . . . why buy a chapel? Weren't you worried about ghosts?" Izzy asked, glancing at Lynda. She was standing near the fridge, a scowl on her face.

"The only spirits around are George and Lynda," Frances said tenderly. "My great-aunt had the same gifts as I do. She put a spell on the graveyard and made it so they could stay. I maintain it. They're laid to rest here, you know." She lowered her voice and whispered, "Lynda is still attached to her body—what precious little is left of her."

A high-pitched wail sounded, and Izzy jolted forward, sinking into the side of the table. Lynda had crept up closer, coming to stand behind her. A continuous scream tore from Lynda's throat, her fingers tangled in her hair, clawing at her scalp. Her updo came loose, her hair falling in waves to frame her narrow face.

George rushed over, his mouth quivering beneath his thick mustache. He gently took Lynda by the hand and led her out of the room, tears glistening in his eyes.

Frances let out a deep sigh, her eyelids fluttering shut briefly. "You see, Lynda's getting restless, been here longer than she ought to have. It's wearing her spirit thin. It's time for her to let go. And George, god love him, he's sticking by her, even though he's been set to leave a good while now."

The kettle's shrill whine pierced the room. Frances stood up and moved toward the stove. As she made her tea, Izzy sidled closer to the window. Peering out, she could make out George standing near a distant tree, watching Lynda as she dropped down near a tombstone. She had her fist over her mouth, her screams muffled.

Izzy had to wonder if George and Lynda were soulmates. After all, he had stuck around this long for her. The devastation on his face as he watched Lynda break down was heart-wrenching. A sharp pang stabbed through Izzy's chest, and she looked away. *Will this be Dax and I in another fifty years? Tethered to each other by love, both hurting but unwilling to do anything about it?*

She glanced at Dax, her throat tightening. *I should let him go*, she thought, fighting back tears. *I'm like Lynda, keeping him tethered to me . . .*

Yet deep down, she knew she wouldn't. They were like two atoms irresistibly drawn together. Separation was unthinkable. She moved to stand next to him, entwining her fingers in his as Frances took her seat, a steaming cup of tea in her hand.

"Now, my dears, what brings you to Burley?"

"We're trying to find Alice Dame. Do you know of her?" Dax asked.

Frances's hand shook, her tea sloshing out of the cup. She uttered an apology and set about mopping up the mess, ignoring their question.

Izzy exchanged a knowing look with Dax. Frances knew something and obviously didn't want to share it with them.

"Please," Izzy said. "If you know something, tell us. It's important."

Frances tossed the soiled dishcloth in the sink with a thud. "It's important, *really important*, that you let that name slip your mind."

"We can't do that. Please, we don't have much time left. If Alice is in Bur—"

"Get tangled up with Alice Dame, and you'll find yourself out of time permanently."

"We're spirits. Nothing can hurt us," Izzy said. A fleeting image of the sickly green mist swirling around in the obsidian jar flashed through her mind, but she quickly pushed it to the back of her thoughts.

Frances slowly pivoted, facing them once more. The skin around her eyes tightened as she stared at them. "Alice Dame's no one to take lightly. A dark witch, she is. A real threat to the living and the dead alike. That woman is up to no good, I'm telling you. Her coven's been arriving all week, settling in around town. I'd bet she has something big planned. It'd be best for you to steer clear of her."

"We're not defenceless," Izzy said. "Please, Frances. Tell us where Alice is, and we'll be on our way."

"I can't. Not in good conscience."

Izzy felt a heavy weight settle on her shoulders. Frances wasn't going to tell them anything. That much was clear. Time was running down on them. Soon Izzy's physical form would stir, and she would be thrust back into it. Dax would be left to find the bloodstone alone. And it didn't sound like he had a lot of time to get it. Alice was going to use it soon!

Izzy glanced at her soulmate, who was gazing intently at Frances. A coldness crept across Izzy despite the morning light streaming through the window. Dax would have to face Alice alone. And if she was as dangerous as Frances believed her to be . . .

No. That's not going to happen. I won't let it.

Izzy straightened up, steeling herself. "*Advo Telum*," she said firmly. A brilliant white light filled the room as Izzy's spirit weapon materialized in her hand. She raised her sword, angling it slightly above her shoulder as if poised for battle.

Frances pressed backward against the sink. Her jaw slackened, a strangled gasp escaping her lips. Izzy took a step toward the older woman. She paused for effect and loosened her hold on the sword, allowing it to fade back into the ether.

Slumping against the counter, Frances stared at the sword warily. "Your astral cord . . . I assumed you were astral projecting. But you're not, are you? You must be something else to have that much power! Wh-what are you?"

Izzy inwardly cursed, realizing she had overlooked her astral cord. What else could she say to persuade Francis to help her? She locked eyes with the older woman and said, "A demigod."

Frances traced the sign of the cross and inched away toward the window. Izzy's chest tightened as she watched Frances's face pale and her lower lip tremble. She didn't want to frighten her, but brandishing her spirit weapon had seemed like the only way to convince Frances to give them the information on the dark witch. Time wasn't on their side. They needed to know where Alice Dame was now.

Whether out of a desire to help or simply to be rid of them, Frances relented. "Head on to the A35. There's a place, deep in the woods—that's where you'll be finding the dark witch. You'll know when you're close. Death will surround you."

"Thank you . . . I'm sorry if I frightened you."

Frances's jaw tightened, a muscle twitching. Her demeanour shifted as she opened her mouth to reply, and then her eyes grew hazy. When she spoke next, her voice was distant—distracted. "With the heart of a dragon, she is unstoppable. Mind yourself with the dark witch, Izzy Adams. She'll remove you from this world."

Frances's gaze settled on Izzy as the milky whiteness in her eyes cleared. She blinked a few times. "I-I'm not frightened," she said as if the premonition never happened. "But you should be on your way now. I've got a heap of things to do today, and Lynda's none too pleased with you being here."

"Yes, ma'am," Dax said, taking Izzy's hand and leading her away from the older woman. Moving toward the opposite end of the kitchen, they walked through the wall, popping out onto the other side with a sucking noise.

Izzy scanned the yard, relieved that Lynda and George were nowhere in sight. The last thing she wanted was another run-in with the delusional ghosts. *They will be so angry when they discover what I did to Frances.*

Izzy bit her lower lip, shame flooding her as she thought of Frances's quivering jaw. They had gotten what they wanted . . . but at what cost? Izzy knew that the bloodstone couldn't remain with Alice Dame. The damage the dark witch would do with its power . . . She had to be stopped. Yet, resorting to scare tactics and deceit to obtain the bloodstone left Izzy feeling nauseated.

As they crossed the frozen lawn, Izzy's head dropped downward, and she couldn't meet Dax's gaze. They continued in silence, following signs pointing toward the A35. Each step took them closer to the dark witch.

CHAPTER EIGHTEEN

IN THE SHADOW OF SCALED WINGS

Before long, the paved road ended, obstructed by a small, wooden blockade. Beyond it, a narrow dirt path stretched out, flanked by fields of bushes and scattered tree groves. The rising sun brought a bright, crisp light to the landscape as they navigated around free-roaming cattle. Izzy dodged piles of dung on the path, even though she knew it wouldn't touch her ethereal feet.

"Is there a quicker way to get there?" Izzy asked as they hastened along. "Can spirits fly?"

"No, we can float, but that would only slow us down," Dax replied.

"What if she uses the bloodstone, Dax?"

"She won't. We'll make it in time," he reassured her, slowing his pace to pull Izzy to a stop. "About Frances's prediction . . . maybe it's best if you don't come with me."

"Alice can't kill me, Dax. I'm in spirit form. She's just a witch."

"And Beau seemed like just a witch too."

"You can't kill a soul. You told me that. Frances said Alice would 'remove me from this world'—those were her exact words. It's impossible. Frances is wrong."

"I still think—"

Not wanting to talk about Frances or her prediction, Izzy brought the conversation to the earthbound spirits instead. "Is Darla going to end up like Lynda and George?" she asked as she resumed jogging.

Dax hurried alongside her. "I doubt it. They have been dead for over a hundred years. Darla, for less than fifty. I imagine the Department of Lost Souls will be around to get her soon."

"What do you think will happen to Lynda?"

"Once Frances passes on, the barriers will too. Lynda will be sent to the healing realm."

At Frances's name, Izzy lapsed into silence. Her eyes remained fixed on the ground as if she were deeply interested in the bushes inching their way over the path's edges. Next to her, Dax was silent for a moment.

"Izzy, about what you did at Frances—"

"I don't want to talk about it, Dax."

"You did what was necessary."

"Was it though?"

"Yes. She wasn't going to help us."

Warm tears welled up in Izzy's eyes, tracing a path down her face. "It didn't feel right. I shouldn't have done it."

Dax reached out, catching a hold of her elbow. They came to a stop, and he pulled her into a hug. She buried herself into the softness of his jacket, inhaling the familiar scent of vanilla that surrounded him. Drawling back, she sniffled, brushing the tears away with the sleeve of her sweater.

"She was scared, Dax. I-I did that."

"I know . . . Izzy, sometimes doing things for the greater good means doing things we don't like."

"What do you mean?"

Marlo collects dark artifacts to keep them out of the hands of evil beings like Alice Dame. By taking away the bloodstone talisman, we take away some of her power to hurt others."

"It still doesn't feel right."

"It shouldn't feel right. I'm not saying what you did was okay, but don't beat yourself up over it. If we had more time, we could've persuaded Frances or wandered around until we found Alice. But we don't have time. You'll wake up soon."

When Izzy didn't respond, Dax touched her cheek, brushing away a tear with his thumb. Tilting her head upward, she gazed into his eyes, feeling the warmth projecting from them.

"We make mistakes and learn from them," he said, kissing her forehead. "If it makes you feel any better, I contemplated doing the same thing."

"But you wouldn't have. You think before you act, Dax."

He brushed his lips against hers. "Not when it comes to you," he murmured. Deepening the kiss, he pulled Izzy closer. His hands cradled the nape of her neck, fingers weaving through her hair. Warmth flooded through Izzy as her mind exploded into vibrant white sparks. A tingling sensation spread from where his skin met hers, and a soft sigh escaped her lips.

And then darkness swept across her closed eyelids. At first, she imagined it to be nothing more than a cloud's shadow drifting by. But then a gust of wind blew through, powerful enough to bow the surrounding trees, their limbs sweeping low, brushing against the snowy earth.

Breaking the kiss, Izzy looked upward. A strangled sound, half cry, half moan, slipped from her mouth. Her hands found Dax's, her skin growing clammy with a sudden cold sweat.

Shimmering in the sunlight, red scales glinted down at her. The dragon's massive wings spanned as wide as two houses. Side by side, they pushed through the air, sending rhythmic booms resonating over the terrain.

Izzy and Dax stood frozen, their eyes locked on the creature as it passed overhead. With each powerful stroke of its wings, the dragon cleaved the clouds apart, leaving a trail of mist in its wake. It flew into the distance, gradually shrinking until it was no more than a tiny speck on the horizon.

As her heart rate climbed, Izzy touched her chest, feeling the rapid thumping against her palm. She closed her eyes for a moment, willing herself to calm down. *Dragons are real. DRAGONS ARE REAL!* She angled her head up toward Dax, fixing her eyes on him.

"Frances said that Alice would be unstoppable with the heart of a dragon. Dax, what if Alice requires a dragon's heart for whatever she has planned? What if she actually kills the—"

A loud boom rang out, the ground beneath them trembling and scattering stones across the dirt path.

Wide-eyed, Izzy grabbed Dax's arm. "What was that?"

"My guess? A dragon just fell from the sky," Dax said, his face ashen. "We need to run. Now."

Within minutes, a highway came into view, the black asphalt glistening under the wet slush. A breeze blew their way, carrying with it a faint aroma of pine trees mixed with the unpleasant smell of exhaust fumes.

The A35 stretched before them, a straight line in either direction. To the right lay a forest, and to the left, fields of tall bushes. Cars zipped by, oblivious to the two ghosts that stood alongside the road.

Izzy glanced at Dax. "Which way?"

"The woods. Keep an eye out for dying trees and matted-down grass. There's probably a hidden path."

They turned right and continued along the roadside. Silence hung heavy between them, the air thick with tension. Izzy's eyes darted frantically, scanning for the path leading to Alice's property. Moments later, she abruptly stopped.

"What's wrong?"

Izzy didn't speak. Instead, she pointed to the forest's edge ahead of them with a trembling finger. An ancient, gnarled oak tree stood guard between two smaller trees. Hanging from its branch, a man thrashed, his leather boots stretching desperately toward the ground, which was just out of reach.

His gaunt face twisted into a grimace while his grimy fingers clawed at the noose around his neck. With a final grunt, the man's hands fell, brushing against his dark, weathered coat.

"We need to help him!" she said.

"Izzy, wait!"

Dax tried to grab her, but she was too quick and slipped away. Izzy skidded to a stop near the oak tree and reached out to pull at the man's pants. Her hands met with nothing but air. Losing her balance, she tumbled headfirst into the snow.

Coming up to her side, Dax crouched to help Izzy to her feet. He guided her away from the dead man, whose pallor deepened, the natural hue of his face giving way to an ashen tone.

"We need to help him!"

"It's a residual haunting, Iz."

"A what?"

"An imprint of a traumatic event—something that happened here years ago."

"How do you know? It could be real, Dax!" She stepped forward, but Dax quickly wrapped his arms around her, holding her in place.

"Just wait. Any moment now . . ."

The whistling of the wind as it blew around them was the only sound, other than the steady creaking of the rope as the body swung.

"Dax, I—"

The man's legs jerked, a spasm racing through him as his hands flew to his neck. His tricorn hat, which had been lying in the snow near his feet moments before, was now inexplicably perched back atop his head. His complexion returned to its normal, pinkish hue. A guttural moan erupted from him, his eyes wide and stricken, as his fingers clawed desperately at the rope.

"Oh my god," Izzy whispered. Her hand trembled as she pressed it against her mouth.

"It's just an imprint, Iz. The man's soul is long gone. He's probably reincarnated several times since this happened."

Izzy bit her lip, struggling to hold back her tears. "This is . . ."

"I know," Dax murmured, shifting his gaze away from the grisly scene replaying beside him. His body stilled as he caught sight of something in the distance. "Look!"

Just ahead, the branches of a dead tree loomed over a shadowed path, partially obscured by underbrush. The entrance was surrounded by wilted black flowers, emerging from beneath the snow and standing stark against the white, almost as if marking a grave.

"Want to bet that's the way to the evil witch's lair? It fits, with the imprint so close," Dax said. "Dark magic is always stronger around negative energy." He moved toward the path, slipping through the low-hanging branches. "You coming?"

Izzy gave him a wry smile. "Sure! Let's step away from the road and stroll into a dark, dreary forest. What could possibly go wrong?"

Dax's lips curled up into a grin. "Don't worry, fair maiden," he said, offering his hand to her. "I shall protect you from whatever lurks in these woods."

Rolling her eyes, she smirked and pushed past him. As they ventured deeper into the forest, darkness enveloped them, the trees swallowing them up. The path ahead was marked by drooping flowers and the remains of dead animals that guided them through the eerie woods. Each step Izzy took felt heavy, her body reluctant to move forward. Neither of them spoke, the death around them muting their desire to talk.

The path curved sharply, and Izzy stepped around the corner. A cool feeling like cold water, flowed over her, causing a prickling sensation to race up her arms and goosebumps to erupt on her skin. Her stomach lurched, and she stumbled forward, her hands groping the empty air for Dax. But there was nothing there, only the void where he should have been. Izzy was alone.

CHAPTER NINETEEN

THE HOUSE OF HORRORS

"Dax!" Izzy clawed at the air, searching for her soulmate.

Another barrier spell. This one was different than the one Frances had cast. Darker. Meant to harm. The world around her spun, blurring and twisting, distorting everything, and a hot and sticky heat wave blew over her.

She gasped reflexively despite knowing spirits didn't need air. All logic escaped her. Walking blindly, she stumbled through a tree, the pulling and snapping sensation making things worse. And then, it was over.

Dropping to her knees, Izzy wrapped her arms around her body. Waves of hollow retches coursed through her, her midsection squeezing into a tight knot. She leaned forward, her strained breaths filling her ears. Finally, it subsided, leaving her trembling violently.

"Izzy!"

"Dax?"

Izzy's eyes snapped open as a hand gripped her thigh. The tightness in her chest eased as her gaze came to rest on her soulmate. He was curled up next to her.

"Are you okay?"

Dax lifted his head, his face pale and drawn. Nodding slowly, he pulled himself into a sitting position. "I think so. That was meant to kill. If we weren't already ghosts . . ."

"We're close, then?"

"Yes. We're in the dark witch's territory now. We need to move carefully."

"She can't see us, Dax. Frances would've mentioned if Alice was a medium too."

"We can't be sure what we're up against."

Izzy stood up and tried to steady her quivering legs. "You're right," she said, scanning the forest for the path. They had wandered several feet away. "We'll go slow."

As they moved forward, sunlight filtered through the trees, lighting their way. Despite the warmth from the sun, Izzy shivered, a heaviness settling around her. The forest felt off. Unnatural. Nothing stirred—no critters scurrying across the trail or rustling in the trees. *The animals know to stay away.* Izzy swallowed the lump rising in her throat and hurried to catch up with Dax.

The trail ended, revealing a large clearing that was unmistakably man-made. Standing before them was an older Tudor home. It had stark, white, plaster walls, which contrasted sharply with the weathered, black beams crisscrossing its exterior. Dark, diamond-shaped windows were set into the walls, resembling eyes peering out at them. The entire structure was covered with a thatched roof. Plumes of thick black smoke billowed from the chimney, interlaced with a blood-red haze that stained the blue sky.

"Not creepy at all," Izzy muttered, eyeing the smoke as they moved up alongside the house.

Dax dug around in his jacket pocket and, a moment later, pulled out a pair of sunglasses. "Here," he said, popping out one of the lenses. "X-ray shades. Marlo gave them to me. They're illegal but convenient for moments like this."

Izzy took the dark lens and placed it against her eye. The wall dissolved from her vision as she looked through it, revealing the room inside. It was as if she was peering through a picture frame.

A large, open kitchen spread out before them. In the far corner, a cauldron was simmering on the hearth. The fire below crackled, casting long shadows across the walls.

Nearby, set beneath a large, dusty window, was a long, wooden counter. An assortment of items was laid out on it—herbs, cooking utensils, and, more disturbingly, finger bones, a thick and purple severed tongue, and a pile of spiders, their bodies curled inward. In the sink, a bewitched dishcloth scrubbed at a bloodstained cutting board while red-tinged suds formed around it.

A tall, rosy-cheeked woman wearing brown slacks and a grey blouse stood at the counter, holding a small knife. Her eyes were fixed on the objects before her, and her mouth twisted into a grimace. She looked over at another woman, whose hair was set in a mass of curlers. She was seated at a wooden table near the cauldron. They exchanged a few words, and the young woman's shoulders slumped. She picked up the rotting tongue, placed it on the cutting board, and began to slice it into tiny squares.

Dax nudged Izzy, passing her a small tube filled with murky liquid. "Hear-wing Serum. Take a sip."

"You expect me to drink this?"

"Do you want to hear what they're saying?"

"Yes, but—"

"Then down the hatch it goes."

Izzy carefully uncorked the vial and brought it to her nose, inhaling the sweet aroma of honeysuckle. She hesitated, chewing on her lower lip before bringing the glass to her lips. As she let a single drop fall onto her tongue, she was met with an explosion of rich sweetness that made her close her eyes and savour the taste.

She returned the vial to Dax, who finished the remaining liquid in one gulp. "What was in that?" she asked.

"Crushed moth wings and some other stuff."

"What!"

"Shh, listen." Dax gestured toward the house, motioning her to be quiet.

Izzy peered through the wall again, watching the younger witch as she made her way to the hearth and scraped the cut-up tongue into the cauldron. The boiling water began to bubble and foam over the top, hissing violently.

The older witch leaped up, her chair crashing against the wall. She rushed over to the hearth, tripping over the frayed rug that covered the hardwood floor. Her eyes widened as she fell, but the thick cord around her waist sprang to life at the last second. It stretched outward, became rigid, and prevented her from hitting the ground.

"Gran!" The young woman dropped the cutting board, running over to help steady the older witch.

"Mind the cauldron, Charlotte!" She batted her granddaughter's hands away. "You mustn't rush the ingredients in, dearie. Gently does it, and keep stirring!"

The older woman shuffled back over to her chair and dropped heavily onto it. The wood creaked under her thick frame as she leaned back, moaning and reaching down to rub at her hip.

Charlotte paused, the wooden spoon resting in the pot as she gazed at her grandmother. "Gran, isn't there more than enough of the potion for you as well? Why can't Aunt Alice divide it with you?"

Her grandmother jolted upward, her face draining of colour. "Hush, you daft lass. Should my sister catch wind of your words . . ."

"She's out back with that dragon."

"Alice's ears are sharper than you think, Charlotte," her grandmother replied, easing herself back into her chair. "Living forever's no gift," she murmured. "I've no desire to take that potion."

"Have I stirred it enough?" Charlotte asked, sweat soaking her brown hairline.

"That'll do, love. Now, these Snakelers are getting all in a tizzy," she said, patting her hair curlers. "Be a dear and take them out for me, would you?"

"Aye, Gran." Charlotte set the spoon aside and hurried over, a tin clutched in her hand. Bending over her grandmother's head, she began gently unwinding tiny snakes from her hair. They hissed at her, their little forked tongues licking at her fingers as she carefully set them down in the container.

"Easy now, mind the curls," the older witch said as Charlotte tugged at a stubborn snake that wouldn't let go.

After some more coaxing, it finally released its tail, allowing a beautiful white ringlet to bounce into place. Charlotte worked on teasing her grandmother's curls until they were artfully arranged around her face. She handed her the tin lid, and the older woman used it to look at her reflection.

"Thank you, love," she said, gently tweaking one of the curls. "It's come out quite nice, hasn't it?"

"It's fetching, Gran." Charlotte hesitated as if weighing her words. "Wouldn't it be simpler to let me work a charm on your hair?" She nodded toward the snakes, now stiff and lifeless in the tin. "These Snakelers seem rather . . . old-fashioned, wouldn't you say?"

"Rubbish, child! Last time you tried a spell on my hair, it all dropped out!"

"I was only nine!"

"Nine and plenty old enough to do it properly. Anyway, these Snakelers are more than old trinkets. They're family, passed down from my mother—"

The kitchen door flew open with a bang that startled both women. A short man with a pinched expression stormed in, clutching a large chunk of bloody meat. As he marched forward, red dots peppered the floor. He hurled the meat at Charlotte with a grunt, splattering the front of her blouse.

"Chop up that dragon heart and toss it in the cauldron. Be quick about it now. Clare's come back with the human offering." He glanced at the elder lady. "Brenda," he said, with a firm nod, before striding out of the room.

As Charlotte began slicing up the heart, Izzy removed the lens from her eye and turned toward Dax. "They did kill the dragon!" she said, her eyes widening.

A shadow fell across his face. "There will be a lot of death today. She's brewing an immortality spell." He started walking along the side of the house, away from the kitchen. "Come on, we need to check the other rooms."

Izzy hurried after him, tugging at his arm. "They're going to murder someone."

"We can't stop them, Iz."

"We have to try!"

"We would use up all our energy trying, and even then, the best we could do would be to throw some things around. That's hardly going to help." Dax sighed, dullness replacing the usual sparkle in his eyes. "Look, Iz, I'm not happy about it either. I wish we could do more."

"So, contact Elena. She's a demigod. She can help. Send a fire message to her!"

"That only works in Orbistia and Sparklafex. Besides, she's investigating the Fight Island thing—that seemed important too," Dax said, placing his hand on Izzy's shoulder. "We need to find the bloodstone and leave. That's the best way we can help—by taking the dark object away from the witch."

Izzy's mouth opened in protest, but before she could respond, Dax turned and walked through the wall into the house. She stood, silently fuming as she weighed her options. She could go find the human and maybe find a way to release them, give them a fighting chance. It would use up all her energy like Dax said, but it would be worth it. *I have to try.*

A stone lay nearby. Bending down, she reached out, but her fingers slipped through it. She closed her eyes, imagining the smooth surface beneath her fingertips. She reached out again, and again, and again. Nothing. Her eyes welled up with tears, her cheeks burning red. It was useless.

I'd make a lousy poltergeist, she thought. Dax was right. If they took the talisman away from Alice, she might not be able to complete her spell. Maybe she would let the human go. Deep down, she knew that was wishful thinking. *Whoever Alice has is as good as dead.* With her shoulders slumped, she followed Dax into the house.

She stepped into a cramped, shadowy room, barely the size of a walk-in closet. Dax had removed his moonstone and was shining it around, its light casting a dim glow. Looking down, Izzy realized she was standing on a dishevelled bed, its comforter stained and reeking of stale sweat.

She gagged and stepped further into the room, pressing up against her soulmate. "This is disgusting," she whispered, eyeing the overflowing garbage can beside a tilted bookcase. The floor was strewn with rotting fish heads, maggots squirming in the decomposing flesh.

"It's a brownie's room," Dax said. "Most witches have one as their familiar."

"How can you tell?"

"The bed is small, and brownies like fish," Dax explained with a shrug. "It fits."

"If it's Alice's familiar, maybe the bloodstone is in here?"

"I doubt it. She probably has it on her. Still, we should check to be sure."

"You check. I'll explore the rest of the house," Izzy said, glancing at the maggots.

"I don't think splitting up is safe, especially since Frances warned us—"

"We're running out of time, Dax. I'll be fine. It's not like they can see us."

"Still—"

Ignoring him, Izzy stepped through the wall into the next room. It was minimally furnished. Against the far wall stood a single bed with a neatly arranged black coverlet. A modest dresser sat beneath the window. The room might have passed for ordinary if not for the odd items scattered about: a vintage doll with crudely stitched lips sat in a rocking chair, a snakeskin hung over the curtain rods, and, most bizarrely, a human thumb encased in wax was placed by the bed, serving as a grotesque candle.

Izzy moved slowly around the small space, scrutinizing every detail. Besides the candle, two books were neatly piled on the dresser—*Secrets of the Dark Arts: A Guide to Annihilating Your Enemies* and *Killing Can Be Fun: 101 Magical Ways To Do It*—both authored by Alice Dame.

Not morbid at all, Izzy thought, her arms prickling with goosebumps. She continued her search of the room but found nothing. *This is taking too long! We're not going to find it in time!*

A fluttering sensation sprang up in her chest, bringing with it the familiar signs of anxiety. Her mind overflowed with the potential consequences of Alice using the stone. Marlo would be furious, and given that he was a god, that was terrifying. Rhylynn, her closest friend, would be in danger. Above all, a nearly invincible dark witch would be unleashed upon the world.

She bit her lip and gazed out the window. *I need to calm down*, she thought, as a gust of wind lifted the light snow from the ground, swirling it into the air. Outside transformed into a magical wonderland, a stark contrast to the death and decay inside the house.

Her chest rose and fell with each deep breath, steadying her pulse and slowing her racing thoughts. As clarity returned, she turned from the window, her gaze sweeping the room. *If the bloodstone was here, the dark witch wouldn't leave it out in the open. But how do I look for it if I can't move things around!*

The ring on her finger caught the sunlight as she tugged on her tangled hair. Pausing, she drew her hand closer to examine the ancient gem. Dax had said that spirits can interact with magical items. *I should be able to feel the bloodstone then—like this ring we found.* She hadn't had to use any energy to hold it. In fact, she had completely forgotten she was wearing it.

New resolve settled over her as she resumed searching, rummaging through the desk drawers and sweeping her hand beneath the dusty rug on the floor. All she felt was the cool touch of her fingers passing through mundane objects.

It's here, I'll find it, she thought, pushing herself to continue. She checked the pockets of the housecoat hanging next to the rocking chair, then felt under the creepy doll perched on it. Still nothing. Moving to the bed, she sifted through the pillow's stuffing and poked at the mattress. At last, her fingers encountered a cool, smooth object.

Adrenaline surged through her veins as she extracted the item from beneath the mattress. A thin, silver chain hung from her hand, at the end of which dangled a heart-shaped black stone. Red splatters marred its surface, sinking deep and blending into the black. The stone might have been beautiful if not for the negative energy pulsating from it, sending unsettling vibrations into the air.

A cold wave swept over Izzy, leaving an empty ache in her chest. It felt as though all her happiness had been drained away. Shivering, she hastily tucked the necklace into the front pocket of her sweater, concealing the rock from view.

Warmth trickled back into her body, yet a persistent loneliness lingered. She attributed it to the bloodstone's influence but couldn't shake the sensation. Her thoughts wandered to her soulmate. *Where is he? Dax should have joined me by now.* His room was much smaller to search. Absently, she twisted the ends of her long blond hair, pulling sharply as a weight of unease came over her. Something was amiss. She could feel it.

She returned to the far wall and stepped into the brownie's room again. The overpowering stench of rotten fish hit her face, making her gag. Plugging her nose, she quickly scanned around as her eyes began to tear up. Dax wasn't there.

A murmuring sound came from the hallway. The Hear-wing Serum having worn off, Izzy stepped closer to the wall, fumbling around in her pocket for the lens Dax had given her. Izzy pressed it to her eye and peered through the door. The hallway sharpened into view, shrouded in deep shadows and illuminated only by a dim light mounted on the wall.

Dax stood in the centre of the hall, clutching his spirit weapon. Izzy's chest tightened at the sight of his pale face, and she quietly summoned her sword.

She watched a hunched figure move in the shadows, stepping toward Dax. A hand appeared first, the skin paper thin and stretched tight over twisted fingers that clutched a cane. Then an older woman came into view, her eyes narrowed into slits as she glared at Dax. The woman's aura exuded an unsettling energy that sent shivers down Izzy's back. This had to be Alice Dame.

An ugly little man pushed past the woman's skirt to point at Dax. His body was covered in curly grey hair, patchy in spots. "There he is, my mistress. Snuck in he did, right through the wall. Sneaky little spy, he is."

Izzy remained motionless, trying to make sense of the scene before her. The little man reminded her of the tiny creature that usually followed Emily around—a brownie, she now recognized.

"Well done, Wormpus," Alice said, patting the little man on his head. A cruel smile spread across her face as she took in the spirit weapon in Dax's hand.

"That won't be of any use to you, boy," she remarked, pointing her cane at it.

Unfazed, Dax raised his boomerang. With a swift flick of his wrist, he hurled it toward her. It sailed through Alice as though she were nothing but air, then arced gracefully back to his hand without making any impact.

Alice sighed, shaking her head. "I haven't the time for this," she muttered. The air thickened as dark magic began to pool from her gnarled hand, swirling slowly before crackling with sudden intensity around her fingers. It was unlike any magic Izzy had seen before.

"*Alma Immbolisi!*"

Dax took a step backward as a streak of dark magic shot toward him. Time seemed to slow as he turned to run, his movements desperate yet sluggish, as if he were moving through molasses. The magic cascaded around him in a shower of black sparks. He stopped mid-run, his legs frozen in place, suspended in a sprint. Dax's expression remained locked in a moment of panic, his eyes stretched wide.

Alice turned and made her way down the hall, her figure vanishing into the darkness once more. Wormpus scampered at her heels, his high-pitched giggles echoing in the cramped space. Izzy's heart hammered against her chest as she watched, horror-struck, as her soulmate was forced to follow along behind them.

CHAPTER TWENTY

WORMPUS AND HIS WITCH

No, no, no. This can't be happening. Tears streamed down Izzy's face, the salty drops slipping into the corners of her mouth. They should have been on their way to see Marlo, but instead Dax had been captured by the dark witch. How did she even see Dax? Frances hadn't warned them that Alice had the Sight. They should have been safe.

Izzy's knees buckled, and she collapsed to the ground, her spirit weapon dissipating before it could touch the floor. A sob shook her petite frame, and she pulled her knees to her chest, hugging herself tightly. The image of her soulmate frozen in mid-run, bobbing along the hall like a child's balloon, flashed through Izzy's mind.

I need to go after him. Using the cuff of her sweater, she wiped her face and stood up. She had no idea how to free him from whatever spell Alice had cast, but she had to try. "Where you go, I go," she whispered, stepping into the hall.

The corridor was dark, lined with portraits of what had to be Alice's ancestors, their faces stern, some eyes twinkling maliciously. Doors to different rooms dotted the wall. At each, Izzy peeked through, searching for Dax. After the fourth door, she succeeded and found herself looking into the kitchen.

Alice stood with her back to the entrance, hunched over her cane. Across the room, Charlotte, the younger witch, clutched a dishtowel at the sink. Her face was pale, sweat glistening on her forehead. Her eyes darted between Alice and Wormpus, who clung tightly to his mistress' skirt, his mouth twisted into a cruel grin.

Izzy slipped quietly into the room and crept toward the kitchen table before swiftly ducking under the tablecloth. Charlotte's grandmother,

Brenda, remained seated, her feet unknowingly close to Izzy's body. Holding the X-ray Shade to her eye again, Izzy peered through the fabric.

"Is it ready?" Alice asked, fixing Charlotte with a hard stare.

"N-Nearly, Aunt Alice." The dishcloth slipped from Charlotte's grip, falling to the floor with a soft thud.

"Nearly?" Alice's smirked as her great-niece shrank back from her. Black magic crackled around the dark witch's twisted fingers. "*Afflicto!*" The black mist shot toward Charlotte, narrowly missed her head, and shattered a jar on a nearby shelf. Shards of glass and goops of frog embryos splashed into the young girl's brown hair. Beads of bright red blood rose from her skin, dripping down onto the white collar of her blouse.

Charlotte's brown eyes welled up with tears, and she bit down on her lip, glancing toward her grandmother. Brenda shook her head slightly.

"Was that necessary, Alice?"

"Your granddaughter is a right disappointment. I expected more from my own kin." Turning toward Charlotte, Alice continued, "That potion had best be ready within five minutes' time, lass. You've no wish to be the weak link in our bloodline, trust me." Her lips gave a cruel twitch as her gaze shifted back toward Brenda. "Have a word with your grandma. She'll tell you what becomes of those who don't measure up in our line."

Brenda inhaled sharply, her head jerking back. "Do not dare speak of my Megan," she responded, her voice trembling.

"My mum? You said she passed in childbirth." Charlotte whispered, confused eyes darting from her grandmother to Alice and back again. "Did she do something to my mother, Gran?"

"No, dear," Brenda said sharply.

"But she just said—"

"Attend to the dishes, Charlotte." Brenda's tone left no room for argument. Charlotte cast one last probing glance at her grandmother before turning back to the pan she had been tending to.

Alice looked down at her familiar. "Wormpus, my dear, would you be so kind as to fetch the bloodstone? It's time."

The brownie's face lit up, his mouth stretching into a broad grin. "Oh yes, yes, mistress. Wormpus would be most honoured, indeed," he chirped, shuffling his way back into the hallway.

As the little man scurried out of the room, Izzy couldn't help but smile. At least she had been successful in ruining Alice's potion. Without the bloodstone, the immortality brew would be incomplete. Izzy imagined the brownie frantically scouring the room, overturning furniture in his haste, perhaps even ripping apart the eerie doll perched on the rocking chair. *You won't find anything*, she thought gleefully. *Now, all that's left is to free Dax and escape this place!*

Her gaze drifted to her soulmate, who floated awkwardly in the far corner. *How can I free him? Maybe if I touch him, I could channel enough energy to break the spell.* And if that didn't work, she could try knocking the dark witch out. Her eyes swept the room, searching for something heavy. They settled on a cast iron pan dangling behind Charlotte. *Perfect.*

Can I actually lift it? She remembered struggling with a stone just twenty minutes earlier, failing to move it. But failure wasn't an option now. Too much depended on it.

I should do it now before her familiar returns . . . The other two witches couldn't see her, though they would notice the pan flying off the wall. But it would be too late by then. *I just need to get the dark witch to look away from Charlotte, and then—*

A piercing scream rang down the hall, making Izzy flinch. She watched Wormpus crash through the kitchen door, his eyes bulging wider as he collapsed at Alice's feet.

"It's gone, mistress!" He pointed a spindly finger at Dax. "Sneaky soul stole it, he did!"

"It's gone?" Alice spun around with astonishing speed, her cane sweeping out to point at Dax. With a flick of her fingers, he crumpled to the floor. "Where is it, boy?"

Dax staggered to his feet, his legs trembling as he struggled to maintain his balance.

"Where is the bloodstone?" Alice demanded, taking a threatening step toward Dax, dark magic curling around her fingertips.

"The bloodstone?"

"Don't you play daft with me, lad. You've got it. I know you have."

"I have no clue what you're going on about."

Wormpus edged closer to Dax, his hands eagerly rubbing together. "Mistress, please, torture his wee soul," he said, turning his pleading gaze toward Alice. "Use the spell you devised for our Dark Lord, mistress!"

"You're right, my pet. Torture will get the lad's tongue wagging." Raising her hand outward, she whispered, "*Excrucador.*"

The air thickened as Alice's fingers twirled, the black mist spiralling toward Dax, slowly covering him in a dark, suffocating blanket. He fell again, his screams resounding around the room as he writhed about on the ground.

Tears sprang to Izzy's eyes as she watched her soulmate. His body arched at wild angles as the screaming increased in pitch, tearing at her heart. Twice, she almost revealed herself before thinking better of it. *Alice can't get the bloodstone*, she thought, clamping her hands around her ears. *He's going to be okay. He can just shut off the pain. He doesn't have to feel it.*

But he wasn't okay. The torture lasted for another minute before finally the last wisp of magic floated away, leaving Dax gasping for air.

"The bloodstone, boy. Hand it over."

"I . . . don't . . . have it," he said, his voice strained.

"*Excrucador.*"

Dax flopped over onto his back, his limbs spasming and bending unnaturally. A strange gurgling sound came from his mouth, and Izzy's chest seized up. *He can't shut the pain off*, she thought. It was impossible, spirits were supposed to be able to control what they felt. But clearly, Dax had no control at all.

The realization had Izzy shooting up from her spot, her body coming out in the middle of Brenda's teacup. "I have it!" she shouted. "I have the bloodstone! Please, stop it! You're hurting him!"

Dax stilled on the floor as Alice turned toward Izzy, her eyebrows raised. Wormpus launched himself at Izzy. "Stinking soul! My mistress will have your head, she will! Curse her! Make her body curl into a ball!" He flew through her body, knocking over Brenda's tea and spilling it all over the older witch.

"Alice, what in the world is going on?" Brenda stumbled back from the table, bumping into Charlotte, who had rushed to her aid.

"Spirits," Alice replied, narrowing her eyes at Izzy. "Nothing I can't handle." Black magic pooled around her body. "My bloodstone, girl. I want it NOW!"

"You can take it. Just please, let him go." Izzy fumbled in her pocket, her fingers searching out the talisman. Her hand wrapped around the cool chain, and she yanked it from her sweater.

"Izzy, don't," Dax said, wheezing.

"I have to, Dax. She's going to kill you!" Izzy said, her voice cracking. She knew she was being selfish. But she couldn't live in a world without him.

"Souls can't die."

Alice moved to snatch the bloodstone from Izzy's outstretched hand. "Don't be so sure, boy," she said, lowering the necklace over her head.

Izzy brushed past her, rushing across the room toward her soulmate. As she fell to her knees before him, tingles crept up her torso and then a chilling sensation. *No!* Adrenaline surged throughout Izzy's veins as she struggled to move. She was immobilized, once again a prisoner.

Dax stared back at her, unblinking, frozen in place with her. She longed to reach out and wrap her hand in his, but her limbs remained rigid, and all she could do was stare at him. *I'm sorry. I had to. I love you.*

She had sacrificed everything—the fate of the world, of her best friend—for him, and she would do it again. It was wrong to put one person over the millions of others. But he was her soulmate—her other half. She couldn't lose him. And even though he couldn't say it, she knew he would have done the same thing. No matter the cost, Dax would always come first.

Gazing into his green eyes, she knew she could live with her choice. She might have damned her soul, but she had saved his. Her chest tightened with emotion as they remained facing each other for a moment longer. And then she was tugged away.

CHAPTER TWENTY-ONE

THE BLOODSTONE TALISMAN

"Come, Wormpus. The alter has yet to be assembled." Alice turned to Brenda, who was staring at her as if she had lost her mind. "Don't be late," she said sharply.

"Yes, sister."

Alice held her gaze cooly for a moment and then slowly made her way across the kitchen toward the backdoor. As Wormpus passed by Charlotte, he poked at her leg with his long nails, leaving a bloody scratch behind. The young witch winced, a tear catching in her eyelash, but she didn't respond.

Izzy floated along behind the dark witch as she stepped out onto the rickety old back porch. A wind chime made of shrunken heads moaned in the breeze. Their black hair brushed against Izzy's arm as she followed Alice down the back steps. An eye flickered open on one of the heads, and it stared through Izzy, locking its dark eyes on Alice.

She's kept them alive! Nausea rolled through Izzy's body at the realization. To keep someone alive, trapped in their own rotting head—Alice was truly evil.

The witch continued her slow crawl across the yard, following a trampled path in the snow. She soon reached the back of the property and paused before the towering, snow-covered hedge. It parted, the leaves twisting into an archway. Alice passed through, her breaths haggard and loud as she leaned heavily on her cane.

"Are you okay, mistress?" The brownie's bushy grey eyebrows drew together as he looked up at Alice.

"Just a bit worn out. Not for much longer though." Alice's eyes were unusually bright as she hobbled into a large clearing beyond the hedge.

They were met with blackened earth—no snow. What little plant life remained in the area was crushed and wilted. In the middle of the field lay the carcass of a giant dragon. Jagged slashes covered its torso, and a vast, gaping hole existed where its heart should have been. Its large eyes were open and glossy, staring lifelessly at the clear blue sky.

A man stood near its jaw, yanking out its teeth, while others collected the dragon's blood and pried off its red scales. The coven was making quick work of harvesting the remains.

"We're done, Alice," one of the witches called out. She stood atop the beast's back, sweat collecting on her forehead.

"Right then. Dispose of the meat in the Channel once you've finished, would you?" Alice then caught the arm of a young boy, yanking him to a stop. "Clear out the dragon bate," she said briskly, gesturing toward a pile of gutted sheep rotting in the morning sun. The sickly-sweet scent of decay rolled off the dead animals. Death seemed to be everywhere.

Izzy's skin prickled with a clammy chill. *They're using the dragon for parts!* She stared at the majestic creature, wanting to cry for it but unable to. Surely dragons were rare. They had to be or else the human world would know of their existence. How could Alice act so casual about its death? Izzy glared at the witch, wishing she could do something to stop her.

Oblivious to the thoughts stewing in Izzy's head, Alice continued past the dragon. Near the edge of the clearing was a small, fenced-in area. A pure white unicorn stood, leaning against its pen. The light within its eyes was dim, and it stared bleakly at Alice as she approached.

Wormpus cackled, his rough voice echoing across the yard. He sprinted toward the pen, slipping through the thick muck surrounding it. Bending down, the brownie grabbed a handful of the sludge and hurled it at the unicorn. The muck splattered onto its white flank. Unable to move away, the unicorn turned its head to gaze out at the forest.

The little man continued throwing muck at the unicorn until Alice finally caught up to him. Growing tired, he moved toward his mistress and curled against her leg. She patted his head, giving him a loving smile that made Izzy's stomach turn. *She approves of his behaviour.* Her eyes grew hot as she gazed at the mud-covered unicorn. *How can she be okay with this?*

"Now, Wormpus," Alice crooned, "you stay put and watch over these two. I'll see to them once we're through with the ceremony."

"Yes, mistress," he said, reaching up to kiss her finger.

He stood beside Dax, watching Alice leave. Then he abruptly wheeled on Dax, attempting to stab his leg. A growl escaped him as his fingers met nothing but air, passing through Dax as if he were made of mist. With a petulant stomp, he flung his foot against the ground before tossing handfuls of the sodden earth at the unicorn again.

"Wondering how Wormpus caught you trickly little souls?" he asked, aiming a mudball at the unicorn's horn. "Wormpus and mistress have the Sight. The Dark Lord has gifted us, he has. His most loyal servants. My mistress will be rewarded for all her hard work, she will!" He laughed hysterically as he caught the unicorn in the back of the head with the mud.

A loud thud, followed by a shrill cry, rang out. Wormpus whirled around, a disturbingly gleeful glint in his eyes. The sheep remains had been cleared away, and a large stone slab stood in its place. A small brownie was howling on the ground next to it, clutching at her crushed foot. Blood stained her leather boot, soaking into the dark earth as another brownie dragged her away. More little people gathered by the stone, their shoulders slumped as they rested against it. A golden chalice stood on a nearby table, gleaming in the sunlight.

The brownies scattered out of the way as Charlotte approached. The bubbling cauldron floated ahead of her as she neared the altar, her ceremonial robe dragging across the ground. With a snap of her fingers, the cauldron landed on the table beside the chalice. She took her place next to the stone slab, and her grandmother, who was also dressed in a scarlet robe, soon joined her.

More witches gathered around the altar, forming rows in front of it. As soon as the entire coven was present, they settled into silence. Alice emerged again through the hedge, wearing a robe that resembled the other witches' but was made of richer material.

Behind her floated a young man, no more than fifteen years old. Like Izzy and Dax, he was immobile, his strange grey eyes wide and glistening with unshed tears. *A warlock!* Izzy remembered Rhylynn speaking of the witch community's hatred of warlocks. *Alice must have chosen him on purpose!*

"My mistress is brilliant, isn't she? The Dark Lord is most impressed with how she tweaked the binding spell—something to use on nasty little sneaky souls," Wormpus said, glaring darkly at Dax.

As he spoke, the coven parted, creating a pathway for Alice. She slowly walked up to the altar and floated the warlock down onto the stone slab. The black candles flickered to life around him, their long flames dancing and brushing against his bare skin.

He's just a kid! Izzy struggled against the invisible bindings holding her in place. A steady pounding filled her ears as she tried mentally breaking the spell. It was a fruitless effort. Weariness crept up on her, and a hollowness settled in her stomach. She couldn't move, couldn't even cry out for help. She was powerless. The boy was going to die, and there was nothing she could do to stop it.

Alice cast the warlock a disdainful look, and then turned to face her coven. "The Dark Lord has granted me the ingredients for the gift of immortality. With this new power, I shall be able to continue the Dark Lord's work for many years to come." Alice paused to cough before continuing. "We have much to accomplish, and now, I have the time to see it through. We will dismantle the World Council of Supernatural Beings and obliterate the warlock community once and for all!"

A cheer rose from the coven, except from Brenda and a few elder witches, who exchanged wary glances as Alice turned to her brownie.

"Wormpus," Alice called out, gesturing for her familiar.

The little brownie rushed across the ground, kicking up rocks and sludge as he scurried over to Alice. He knelt down on one knee and beamed up at her. "My mistress, how might Wormpus serve you best?"

"Wormpus, my familiar, my most trusted servant. Be a love and fetch the Chalice of Midas and gather the lad's blood as it flows."

A wide grin stretched across the brownie's face, exposing several decayed teeth. He stumbled slightly under the weight of the chalice as Alice handed it to him and then climbed up onto the altar. Positioning himself near the boy's head, he waited for Alice to make the next move.

She approached, and her hand vanished into her robe, returning a moment later with a small dagger. Moving to stoop over the teenager, she entwined her fingers in his blond hair, yanking his head back to expose his slender neck. The blade danced across his flesh, grazing the edge of his larynx. Pulling hard on the dagger, Alice carved through his throat, severing his arteries.

Blood sprayed out into the chalice, splashing over the rim and soaking into Wormpus's clothes. The air was heavy with the metallic scent of it.

Alice took the chalice from Wormpus and walked back to the table. The brownie hopped down from the altar and scurried after her, his tiny feet sliding on the wet ground. The coven continued to watch in silence. Any revulsion over the sacrifice was well hidden—fear likely keeping any heroics at bay.

A lump formed in Izzy's throat. *At least he's free now*, she thought as white smoke wafted from the body. It gradually shaped itself into the likeness of a teenager. The boy turned to look at the dead body, tears streaming down his pale cheeks.

An emerald light flashed behind the boy's head as a portal materialized. A moment later, a hand belonging to a small, freckled figure rested on the spirit's shoulder, turning him around. The spirit guide gazed at him with weary eyes, a pained smile on her face.

Izzy's chest was suddenly struck with a jolt of recognition. *Priscilla!* Her spirit guide was actually here. And for once, Izzy was happy to see her. She stared hard at the shorter woman, willing the guide to notice her. *Look over here, Priscilla! Please, just look over here.* It no longer mattered that her guide would erase her memories—not if it meant rescuing them from whatever Alice had planned.

But Priscilla didn't look. Instead, she slipped her hand into the boy's and led him through the portal. The green light dimmed and then disappeared, leaving Izzy and Dax alone once more.

A sea of grey engulfed Izzy, dulling everything around her. *No one is coming for us.*

She wished she could see Dax. If she could just look into his eyes, she knew she'd find some semblance of comfort. But she couldn't turn her head, let alone blink.

We're never going to escape, she thought, her chest tightening. *I won't even get to say goodbye.*

Consumed by dark thoughts, Izzy almost missed Alice pouring the chalice into the cauldron. Thick plumes of red smoke puffed into the air, staining the blue sky. The green fire beneath the pot intensified, its flames shooting upward, hiding the cauldron from view.

"You," Alice said, pointing to a younger witch. "The unicorn's mane, now!"

The boy's eyes lit up at being assigned such an important task. He hurried toward the pen, leaning through Dax to reach the unicorn's head. The animal didn't even fight back. It just stared numbly at him as he used his small dagger to slash off its mane, leaving behind short tufts of white hair.

Alice took the mane and dropped it into the cauldron. Sparks shot up from the potion. Alice glanced over at her great-niece, a pleased smile curling her lips. "Remarkable, Charlotte, you've actually managed to follow instructions for once. There might be some use for you yet."

Alice turned back to the potion. Reaching into her robes, she retrieved a small glass vial. "Now, for the drop of hellfire, which our Dark Lord has graciously provided me." An ominous red flame flickered inside the vial, casting an eerie glow upon her face. Without hesitation, she tossed the whole thing into the cauldron, producing a thunderous explosion that shook the ground and caused some of the coven members to stumble.

"The last piece now," Alice continued, lifting her necklace over her head. She clutched the heart-shaped black stone in her hand, letting the silver chain dangle between her fingers. "This once belonged to Sarah Goode. If that daft girl had known what power lay within, she might not have met her end." A wry smile creased Alice's features as she caressed the stone. "Drenched in the lifeblood of one thousand men, women, and children, this necklace holds a darkness that should be feared across the globe!"

A thousand humans died for that stone? Fear gripped Izzy's chest. No wonder Marlo wanted it so badly. It was the most powerful item on the planet, possibly even in the spirit world. And now Alice Dame was going to use it. Judging from what Izzy had seen Alice do so far, her intentions with the ring weren't good. *I can't do anything to stop her. If I'd just listened to Dax, I—*

A haunting scream pierced the air, dropping many of the witches to their knees. As the bloodstone dissolved into the potion, Alice began chanting two words in a low voice: "*Potere Immortale.*" The rest of the coven joined in, their voices blending together in a powerful incantation that caused the air to vibrate with energy.

When the final echo of the chant faded away, and silence fell over the coven, Alice picked up the chalice and carefully dipped it into the cauldron. Golden droplets of the potion dripped over the brim as she raised it to her lips. Alice tilted her head back and drank greedily, then slammed the cup onto the table with a thud.

For a moment, nothing happened. Alice whipped around to glare at her niece. "You botched it deliberately, girl."

"I didn't, Aunt Alice. I-I swear it!"

"Lies!"

The dark witch advanced toward Charlotte, the air around her thrumming with the power of her black magic. And then she stopped, clutching at her chest. She blinked rapidly, her gaze sliding over to meet her sister's. Slowly, her appearance began to transform. Alice's skin smoothed and tightened, erasing years in moments. Her greying hair grew darker and longer, and her body became curvy and firm. Her back straightened out, giving her several more inches of height. When the transformation was complete, Alice Dame looked entirely different, except for her pale grey eyes, which still held a cruel glint.

Wormpus had also transformed, growing younger and less revolting. However, his attitude remained as unpleasant as ever. He danced about the altar, taunting the other brownies peering out from behind the dragon's carcass.

Charlotte's expression grew darker as she watched him. "Aunt Alice," she said, breaking away from her grandmother's firm grip.

Alice turned to her, levelling her with a cold stare. Her dark hair curled around her shoulders, framing her now wrinkle-free face.

Undeterred, Charlotte took another step toward her aunt. She licked her lips and then tried again. "Aunt Alice, surely there is enough potion to spare for the elder witches. My grandmo—"

"No."

"But she's your sister."

Brenda reached out, trying to pull her granddaughter back. "Charlotte, don't," she pleaded.

Charlotte pulled away from her and moved closer to the potion. "Please, Aunt Alice. One sip to grant her a decade more."

"I said no!" Alice strode over to the table and upended it. The cauldron flew to the ground, spilling golden liquid onto the dark earth. Her mouth twisted into an ugly smile as she locked eyes with Charlotte.

"Alice, don't," Brenda said, dropping to her knees in the muck. "She's young—foolish. She meant no harm."

Ignoring her sister, Alice continued to stare intensely at Charlotte. The younger woman shrunk back, her shoulders hunching over as she gazed at the dark witch with wide eyes.

"Insolent child, how foolish do you take me to be? You dare ask that I share my powers? Do you harbour some secret desire for your grandmother to challenge me for coven leadership?"

"N-No. I—"

"*Immbolisi.*"

A dark ball of energy hit Charlotte in the chest, causing her arms and legs to snap violently to her sides.

She's attacking her own niece? Catching sight of Brenda's face, Izzy felt a wave of sorrow wash over her. Sobs shook the older woman's frail frame, and another witch moved to embrace her. She held Brenda back as she struggled to reach for her granddaughter.

A cackle spilled from Alice's lips. She flung her arms out, and Charlotte rose along with the movement, floating above the coven members. Black energy misted around Alice as she laughed manically. "*Quasso!*" she said cruelly, directing the mist at Charlotte. It shot toward the younger woman, curling around her limbs before disappearing into her open mouth. A second later, her body exploded, knocking several brownies off the dragon. Izzy's stomach lurched as a mist of bone and brain fragments rained down on the coven, soaking their robes in gore.

CHAPTER TWENTY-TWO

THE CRIMSON WASTELAND

Alice straightened her back, tilting her chin upward as she addressed the other witches. "Let this serve as a lesson for any blighter who fancies questioning or defying my command." Glancing down at Brenda, she added, "Cry not, dear sister. She is with her mum now."

Brenda fell against the other witch, hugging her tightly as tears streamed down her face, mingling with her granddaughter's blood.

Turning away from them, Alice called out to her familiar, "Come Wormpus, there's a great deal to attend to."

The little man jumped off the altar into the mud, splattering Brenda's robes. "I am most eager to see what my mistress does to the sneaky, snoopy, wee souls," he said gleefully, following along behind Alice.

The dark witch stopped before Izzy and Dax, a cold, calculating look on her face. She tilted her head and pursed her lips. "What to do with you?"

The brownie wiped his sweaty hands on his vest, his face lighting up as he looked up at Alice.

"Oh, mistress, I have the darkest of ideas. Rip their souls apart! Yes, Wormpus would love to see that. Or electrocute them! Sizzle and fry them. Let the air fill with their rotten stench."

"All splendid ideas, Wormpus. Alas, there is no time for such pleasantries."

"Then kill them, mistress. Strike them dead—forever dead!"

"I do not know of such a spell, pet."

"Perhaps, mistress, the Dark Lord knows of a spell—"

"The Dark Lord, should he possess knowledge of such an enchantment, has not deemed to entrust me with it. And I'm not one to pester him, Wormpus. Now, let's see what they were doing here, shall we?"

The binding spell broke with a snap of her fingers, sending the soulmates tumbling to the ground.

"You're a monster!" Izzy said, hurling herself at Alice. She passed through the dark witch, falling next to the unicorn pen.

"Mind your tongue, child. I've little patience for insolence, particularly from impudent children."

Dax edged closer and moved to stand in front of Izzy. His hand came to rest on her arm, and he squeezed it once—a subtle warning. "The demon you're helping will eventually turn on you, Ms. Dame. You realize that, don't you? Continue on this path, and your soul will darken. When you die—"

"I don't plan on dying, lad."

"You drank an immortality potion. That doesn't make you invincible. You will die. But it's not too late. You can still fix things. Just let us go, and—"

"Enough! Explain yourself! Who sent you?"

"No one. We were lost."

"A lost soul . . . how coincidental," Alice said. "And you just happened to come across my bloodstone? No, I'm not convinced. This is the last time I'll be asking, lad—who sent you?"

"He already told you," Izzy said, pushing past Dax, "we're lost. We were looking for a map."

"Of course you were," Alice remarked, her gaze shifting to her familiar. "Wormpus, love, did you catch that? They're adrift and can't seem to navigate their path. Such a pity. We ought to guide them on their journey away from these parts, don't you think?"

With a high-pitched, grating cackle, Wormpus began to dance, his movements as erratic as the sounds escaping him. Izzy's gaze, however, remained locked on Alice, whose eyes had transformed into deep, black chasms. A dark, electric energy sparked along her fingers. With a deliberate motion, she pointed at the empty space behind Izzy and Dax. "*Croesi!*"

Izzy leaped out of the way of the spell. It narrowly missed her shoulder, and the air around her began to warp and twist, like colours on a canvas mixing together. A line appeared down the middle of the swirls, pushing the tangle of colours to either side. As the parting grew wider, it revealed a red landscape. The barren and lifeless terrain seemed to stretch on endlessly before them.

"Now you'll truly be lost. Search all you want, but you'll never find your way home," Alice said, flicking her wrist. The air stirred, a sudden wind rising. It swept Izzy and Dax off the ground and hurled them through the portal.

They fell in a heap on the red earth, their limbs entangled. As the portal closed up, the last thing Izzy saw was Wormpus dancing happily behind Alice as she returned to her house. The little brownie caught her eye and paused to stick his tongue out at her, spittle spraying from his mouth. And then he was gone, replaced by an endless horizon of deep crimson.

"No," Izzy said, scrambling to her feet and dashing to where the portal had been. Only empty air greeted her. Alice's home had vanished. *Where did she send us?* Tears welled in her eyes, and she clutched a handful of her blond hair. She took in the desolate expanse around her—cracked earth, dying plants, and barren trees wasting away in the distance. A deep wrongness settled over her. This couldn't be Earth, or at least not a part she had ever seen. *How are we going to get home?*

She sank her teeth into her lip and lifted her gaze to meet Dax's. The realization struck like a physical blow—they had failed their mission. *Oh my god, what did I do?*

She had given up the bloodstone. She had chosen Dax over everything and everyone else.

The guilt of her decision gnawed at her. She hadn't been thinking clearly. All she'd been able to see was her soulmate crumpled and writhing in pain. Even now, Izzy could not bear the thought of it. With a deep, aching pang, Izzy now understood the agony her mother must have felt losing her husband.

I could have waited a bit longer though, Izzy thought. Even if Alice could have killed Dax, she wouldn't have acted until she had the bloodstone in hand. There would have been a chance to save him at some point . . . if only Izzy hadn't been so impulsive.

Now Rhylynn was in danger. Alice had been so cruel to her sister and niece—so callous speaking to them. And the way she had killed Charlotte . . . If that was how she treated her own family, her enemies were in for even worse.

And Dax was going to return to Marlo empty-handed. She didn't know how the god would react, and the thought made her heart still. As tears continued to stream down her face, Dax pulled her into his arms.

"I messed up big, Dax. Rhylynn, you, everyone I care about . . . you're all in danger now—all because of me."

She sobbed harder into his chest. She felt as if she'd lost a battle.

But she couldn't give up yet. Shaking her head, Izzy stepped back from Dax. "I need to get to Rhylynn," she said. "I have to warn her—and Mrs. Rivers. The entire witch community is at risk. And the warlocks . . ."

"She'll start a war," Dax said sombrely. He glanced around at the dying planet and added, "This is what will become of Earth if she's not stopped. Humans have too much technology. They won't allow themselves to be enslaved. The war will destroy the world for everyone."

"She needs to be stopped."

"I have to get back to Marlo. He needs to know what has happened," Dax said, rubbing his face wearily.

"You can't go back to him. He might smite you!"

"Smite me?"

"Kill you. He's a god, Dax. We screwed up the mission. Marlo is going to be furious."

"Yeah, he will be. But Izzy, he's not going to kill me. Remember, souls can't die. Besides, he's a god of light. He wouldn't hurt anyone."

"You don't know that for sure. Don't go back."

"I have to. This is bigger than us, Iz. Medusa created a spell to torture souls! The gods need to know."

"Medusa? Alice was the one who created the spell."

"She created it for her dark lord—I'm assuming that's Medusa, or someone that she's working with. Alice used hellfire in the immortality spell. It's only found in the Kingdom of Hellfire!" Dax rummaged frantically through his pockets, then cursed under his breath.

"What's wrong?"

"I can't find my Meli coin. I had one left."

"Are you sure?"

"Yes. It must have dropped out of my pocket when we tumbled from the bottle earlier." He ran his hands through his hair, scanning their surroundings. "We need to find a village—any place with people. Sooner or later, we'll come across a spirit guide. That's our ticket out."

CHAPTER TWENTY-THREE

THE WARTMONGER

The sun cast a weak light over the ground as they set forward over the crumbly dirt at a quick pace. The occasional breeze blew swirls of dust around like mini-twisters, and the only sign of life was the odd cockroach scurrying about the large boulders and dying plants. *Humans couldn't exist on this planet*, Izzy thought, her mouth going dry.

As if reading her mind, Dax spoke up. "We're on Katswyn. It's a dying planet. The sun started to burn out years ago. Witches and mages still live on it though."

"How would Alice even know about this planet?"

"All witches on Earth are descendants of Katswyn. That portal spell Alice used is an ancient spell. I doubt many witches know of it—only the descendants of the coven leaders who first came to Earth."

They came up to a desiccated lake that was nothing more than a sunken depression in the earth. The scattered remains of fish and other aquatic animals lay strewn about, surrounded by small pools of stagnant water. Dax's pace slowed, and he paused. His lips turned downward, and his eyes seemed to lose focus.

"This was once the most beautiful planet to incarnate onto."

"We've lived here in a past life, right? You mentioned it before."

A sweet smile lit up Dax's face. "It was one of the best lives we've had together. It took us years to save enough tokens to incarnate here, but it was worth it."

"It takes a lot of tokens to incarnate as a witch, right?"

Dax nodded. "Yes, it does. But we weren't witches on this planet . . . just humans."

"How many tokens does it cost to incarnate onto Earth as a human?"

"Not too many."

"I wish I had worked a little longer and saved up more then. It would have been cool to be born as a witch," Izzy said, glancing down at her body.

A shadow fell over Dax's face, and his smile disappeared. He tried to turn away, but Izzy caught his arm and held him back.

"What is it?"

"What do you mean?"

"Something I just said . . . it upset you."

"No . . . I just had dirt in my eye. I'm fine."

"You're a soul Dax. You *can't* get dirt in your eye!"

"I'm tired then. Iz, seriously, don't worry—"

A loud croaking noise carried through the air. Izzy glanced over at the muddy remnants of what remained of the lake. Nothing moved. No sounds came from that direction at all. *Maybe it was the wind?*

"Dax, is there something you're not telling—"

The noise sounded again, loud and drawn out. *Okay, that wasn't the wind.* Izzy walked closer toward the lake's edge and peered into the murky puddle. It sounded like a toad. But how could that be? There didn't seem to be any life left in the water.

"We need to get going, Izzy. It's probably nothing."

Izzy nodded slowly, turning toward Dax. The darkening of his expression was the only warning that she had. A moment later, a heavy weight crashed down on her, slamming her to the ground. Whatever it was crouched on her back and wrapped something slimy around her waist.

Craning her neck, she glimpsed the bulbous body of a monstrous toad. It was covered in rough, warty skin, and when it opened its mouth to let out another croak, Izzy caught sight of its jagged teeth. She screeched and clawed at its tongue, her efforts only rewarding her with slime-coated hands.

The toad slid off her, then drew her in closer, turning her to face its body. It pushed off the ground, sending them several yards forward. They landed with a thump, clouds of dust billowing around them. A second later, it jumped again, propelling itself further away from Dax.

It's hopping off with me, Izzy thought, a panicked giggle slipping out of her mouth. This had to be the most bizarre thing that had ever happened to her. Kidnapped by a toad. Her laughter slipped away as the toad looked down at her, its bright yellow eyes flaring red along the edges like flickering flames.

Demon! Izzy yelped and began to claw harder at the creature, trying to release its hold on her. Her bracelet banged against her wrist as she slammed her hand into the rough tongue. *Why isn't it working? It's supposed to protect me from harm!*

"Dax!"

"I'm here!"

"It's a demon!"

"I know. It's a wartmonger—one of Mara's pets."

Mara! Izzy's body broke out into fierce trembles. She fought to erase them by squeezing her eyes shut. Mara had found her again. She really did want Izzy dead. But why? She couldn't have been the only one to expel one of her creatures. Dizziness washed over her, black spots clouding her vision. *If she kills me, she'll keep my soul in the Realm of Nightmares, torturing me forever!*

"Get this thing off me!" Izzy yelled, clawing at the demon.

"I'm trying to! It keeps hopping away from my boomerang. Izzy, can you . . . oh crap!"

"What?" The shrillness in Dax's voice was far from reassuring. Izzy wasn't sure how things could possibly get worse, but apparently, they had.

"There's a portal up ahead," Dax called out, his voice sounding further away. "It must lead to Mara's kingdom. Izzy, use your spirit weapon!"

Her spirit weapon. Of course! She mentally slapped herself. How could she have not thought of that? Her hands were free! Closing her eyes, she pictured her sword and whispered the incantation. Her hand wrapped around the familiar leather hilt, and when she opened her eyes, her sword was there, gleaming in the dying sunlight.

She held it awkwardly over her head, stretching her body out to give herself more room to swing it. The wartmonger launched itself closer to the portal, the pulsating green light illuminating the demon's body. It was almost there. One more good leap and she was done for.

Adrenaline coursed through Izzy's veins, and she brought the sword down on the wartmonger's tongue, severing it from her waist. She fell to the ground, landing hard on her back as the demon burst into a shower of purple sparks above her. They blew away as if caught in the wind, and seconds later, the portal closed.

"Izzy!"

"I'm okay," Izzy said. She allowed Dax to help her to her feet. He wrapped her in a tight hug, nestling his face in her hair.

"I thought I was going to lose you."

"I can't believe I didn't think of using my own spirit weapon," Izzy replied, her cheeks heating up. "Why didn't my bracelet work?"

"It wasn't trying to hurt you. The bracelet only works when there's an intent to harm. That's why it didn't work on Alice either. She wasn't technically hurting us."

"It was bringing me to Mara!"

"Yes. And had she tried to hurt you, it would have reacted—although I don't know how effective it would be against a god . . ."

Izzy pulled away, her face taunt. "What am I going to do? If Mara found me here—of all places—she can probably find me anywhere!"

"Marlo will know what to do."

"And if he doesn't?"

"Then I'll take it to the Orbistian gods." Dax pulled her back into his arms, hugging her tight against his body. "I'm not going to let anything happen to you!" he whispered into her ear. Despite everything, Izzy believed him.

CHAPTER TWENTY-FOUR

VILLAGE UNDER FIRE

Time seemed to stretch on as they continued across the barren landscape, searching for signs of life. Although the need to return to Earth was never far from Izzy's mind, she couldn't help but appreciate the downtime with Dax. As they walked, Izzy bombarded him with questions, eager to learn more about him. She found out that he occasionally worked for the Bureau of Magical Entertainment and Athletics, helping to organize the Skyscuttle games. He was really creative, actually, and had even been a famous author in one of his past lives on Earth.

Eventually they came across a road leading into a village. It was an ancient one, with a surface worn smooth by centuries of use. The air was thick with the scent of scorched earth, and the plants along the roadside were wilted, their leaves curling inward.

"Is there a lot of wildlife on this planet?" Izzy asked.

"There was. Most are gone now," Dax replied. "As the planet cools, much of the life here struggles to adapt."

"What about brownies?" She spat out the word.

"Where there are witches, there are brownies. So, yeah, they'll be here too."

"Great," Izzy said bitterly.

"They're not all bad, Iz. Wormpus has just been tainted with Alice's darkness. Rhylynn probably has a familiar too. Ask her when you wake up."

"I will," she said, her mind drifting to her best friend. Was there such a creature attached to Rhylynn? She hoped not. Despite what Dax said, she couldn't imagine a brownie being anything but evil. She hadn't seen any brownies around her friend, but that meant nothing. Emily's wasn't always with her either. She had assumed a familiar was just a witch's pet.

It made sense that they would have lives beyond their witches. *I wonder if they have families.* The image of a baby Wormpus flashed before her, and she shuddered. *He'd be the type to eat his own mother. Breastfeeding must have been awful.* She snorted at the thought, catching a raised eyebrow from Dax.

Before long, they arrived at the village gates, where iron bars cast intricate shadows on the ground. Beyond, Izzy could see the outlines of square mud-brick homes, some in ruins. There should have been signs of life—animals roaming, children playing. Instead, silence enveloped the area. It was as if the town had been deserted, stripped of all its inhabitants.

"Do you feel that?" Dax asked, his hand hovering just above the ground.

"Feel what?"

"Look," he said, gesturing downward.

Izzy knelt beside him, her gaze fixed on the dirt.

Sand grains danced against one another, as a distant rumbling filled the air. Something was approaching.

A cloud of dust billowed up from the road they had just travelled. Moment's later, a horse appeared, halting abruptly before the gates. The rider dismounted and shoved the gate open with a clang. He then returned to his horse, seizing the reins to lead it through. Secured to its back was a petite woman. Her vibrant red curls lay matted against pallid skin marred by a dirty gag. Tears welled up and spilled over her cheeks as she let out muffled screams against the cloth stuffed in her mouth.

"Quiet, witch!" the man barked, leading the horse past Izzy and Dax, his black robes rustling against the dusty ground.

Izzy glared at the man. She balled her hand into a fist and stepped forward.

"I know you want to help her," Dax said, pulling her to a stop, "but we can't."

"Doesn't it ever frustrate you, being unable to help?"

"Of course it does," Dax replied, his jaw clenching. "But it's against Orbistian law for us to help carnies. Unless it involves demonic activities, like with Beau, or a dark artifact, like the bloodstone, we can't get involved. The only ones allowed to warn carnies are spirit guides, and even they have their limitations on how much they can do."

"But you interfered when you tried to warn me about the Christmas elf, and then again with Sydney."

"I wasn't supposed to. If the Orbistian Council knew, I'd be in trouble. Besides, it used up a lot of my energy."

"I still don't like it. I hate not being able to help."

"No one likes it. That is probably why you don't see many spirits wandering around like us. It is what it is though. Free will is important. People are responsible for the decisions they make."

"Yeah, but free will should have its limits when it infringes on someone else's rights."

"There are billions of carnies spread across this universe, and just a handful of gods and demigods who can intervene. They're already overwhelmed with managing the demons and overseeing the spirit world."

"I hate feeling so powerless," Izzy murmured.

Dax intertwined his fingers with hers. "I know," he said gently, squeezing her hand.

They trailed behind as the man hastened toward the village square. The town centre unfolded before them—a weary, dust-coated clearing ringed with deserted vendor stalls and dominated by a large iron bell suspended from a weathered post. The man let go of the reins and strode toward it. He seized the rope and yanked on it, ringing the bell violently.

Townspeople began to trickle into the square: gaunt men, hollow-eyed women, and children whose coughs tore through the silence. Whatever was about to happen felt ominous and unsettling.

An elder with stained robes and a wild, grey beard shuffled forward. His deep-set eyes were shadowed with fatigue. "What's going on here?" he asked.

The horseman returned to his steed and released the bindings that held the woman in place. He watched, detached, as she crumpled to the earth. Izzy ground her teeth together, her eyes narrowing to slits. She wished, not for the first time, that she was in her physical form so she could intervene.

The man stooped and roughly hauled the woman to her feet. She flinched away, but he kept a hand around her neck, holding her in place. "This, my fellows, is the witch that has brought the dragon fever upon us. I have traced the origins of the fever back to an encounter involving this *thing*."

As murmurs spread through the crowd, Izzy leaned closer to Dax and whispered, "What's dragon fever?"

A shadow flickered across his face. "It feels like you're boiling alive under your skin—one of the deadliest illnesses around. It's especially lethal for children."

They watched as the horse rider dragged the woman over to an iron post set firmly in the ground. Her eyes widened, and she dug her bare feet into the hard-packed earth. Struggling against her restraints, she tried to extend her fingers, but the man seized her hand, crushing it beneath his. A grimace flickered across her face, tears gathering on her lashes.

"Your magic is of no use to you now, witch. You will find those bindings impossible to remove," he spat out, delivering a backhand strike to her face. Blood spurted from her nose and dripped down her chin. Her eyes hardened into a silent challenge as she returned the man's gaze.

The man continued dragging her forward. Within minutes, she was bound tightly to the stake, and he was issuing commands to the unafflicted townspeople. They scattered, returning quickly with arms full of dry wood. A pyre rose around the witch, the kindling stacked high, almost reaching her hips.

The villagers drew closer to the pyre, their faces stretching taunt as they sneered at the witch. Negative energy poured off them in waves, thickening the air with their hatred. Izzy shivered, instinctively moving closer to Dax. He wrapped his arms around her, drawing her tightly against him.

"This is . . . disgusting. I don't understand. How can they allow this to happen?"

"I know," Dax said quietly. "There's an ongoing war between mages and witches. No one here will intervene. She could be innocent of everything he accuses her of, and they would still let her burn."

"Why do they hate each other so much?"

"Once, they coexisted in peace. But as the sun began to die, so did that harmony. Each blames the other for the planet's decline."

"That's ridiculous!"

"It's not like Earth, Iz. Carnies here know nothing about science and technology. They've always relied on magic to ease their way of life. That's what once made this planet so appealing—no wars, no stress from materialism—but now, the golden era has ended." He sighed heavily, the sound swallowed by the clamour of the crowd's angry shouts.

The horse rider yanked the gag from the witch's mouth. "Last words, witch?"

"Disgusting little mage," she said, spitting in his face.

The gob of mucus oozed down his reddening cheeks, mingling with the strands of his beard. With a guttural shout, he drew back a fist and drove it into her abdomen, expelling the air from her lungs. "Do you confess to your crimes, witch?"

"I-I confess," she gasped, struggling for breath.

The man reeled backward, widening his eyes. "You . . . you confess?"

"Yesss," she drawled, a twisted smile distorting her features.

"Dozens are dead—good men, women, and children!"

"And I pray to my Dark Lord that more will follow." The witch's cold and merciless laughter cut through the square's silence, leaving the crowd shivering with its echo.

A young girl stepped forward, her face pale and streaked with tears. Her voice trembled as she clasped her arms tightly around herself. "What did we ever do to you?"

The witch snarled, spittle flying from her twisted mouth. "Your very existence is an abomination, an insult to my kind."

"Enough!" The horse rider jammed the soiled cloth back into her mouth, firmly securing the gag. "You have confessed, and you shall burn for your crimes!" Flames sprang to life in his hands, coiling around his fingertips. "Burn in hell, witch!"

Fire erupted from his palms, engulfing the kindling. In moments, it was ablaze, sending plumes of thick, black smoke skyward. The hem of the witch's dress succumbed first, the fire greedily climbing her form.

Her gaze never wavered from the crowd, her expression a mask of spiteful triumph. Only when the flames began to caress her skin did a flicker of awareness cross her face. She glanced down at the whispers of fire kissing at her fingertips and then back at the crowd. Smoke swirled around her, obscuring her form from view, while her screams cut sharply through the air.

Izzy cringed, trying to suppress the bile that threatened to spill up from her stomach. She covered her ears with her hands, desperately attempting to block out the noise. As she looked on, a group of mages stepped forward, their palms ablaze with fire. They directed it toward the pyre, engulfing it in flames. Before long, the screaming faded away, leaving only the sound of the fire crackling as it devoured the wood.

Gradually, the villagers dispersed, a scant few remaining as the flames dwindled to embers. In another context, it might have been inviting—a bonfire beneath the darkening sky—except someone had died. Izzy inhaled the earthy scent of charred wood, exhaling slowly. *Smells like my grandparents' house up in Madoc*, she thought, her eyelids fluttering shut. But then, abruptly, her eyes snapped open. Where was the scent of burnt flesh? Shouldn't the smell of roasting skin have overpowered everything else?

"What's wrong?" Dax asked.

"I don't smell her . . . burning."

Dax edged forward, taking in a deep breath. "You're right. It's just the wood."

"And where is her soul? Or her spirit guide? We should have seen them by now, right?"

"Yeah . . . we should have." He walked closer to the embers, searching the pyre before returning to Izzy. "She's not dead," he said.

"What?"

"Think about it. She didn't start screaming until the fire touched her skin, and even then, it was almost like she had to remind herself to do it."

"Well, I believed it. That scream . . ."

Dax scratched his head, his eyebrows drawing together. "She's a good actress," he said thoughtfully. "I wonder how she did it?"

"But her hands were bound, Dax. She couldn't have used magic."

Dax shrugged. "If she was a powerful enough witch, she could have. Some can call forth their magic with just a single thought. It's a secret that the mages aren't aware of, or else they would have killed her on the spot."

"Where do you think she went?"

"Somewhere far from here," he replied, his eyes fixed on the distance. "We should get moving. We won't find any help here."

As they made their way across the yard, they had to carefully navigate around a mage who had stepped forward to extinguish the fire. Her hands emitted a gentle mist that shimmered in the light, and as it fell upon the hot coals, it produced a soft hissing sound.

The village grew silent once again as they continued down the narrow streets. Dax weaved in and out of the homes, disappearing for a moment before popping back out to walk alongside Izzy. Pausing, she rubbed the base of her neck, where a nagging ache blossomed into a dull headache. *Can spirits even get headaches?* Dismissing the thought, she quickened her pace to catch up with Dax, who was already at the next house.

"What are you doing?" she asked.

"I'm looking for a spirit guide. There has to be one somewhere in this village. We need to search all the buildings, especially ones that look like children live in them . . ."

"For that witch to bring that fever here . . . she's evil."

"Don't worry. Her soul will be imprisoned as soon as she passes over. There's no coming back from what she's done."

"Good."

"There's so much hate here," Dax murmured, peeking through another wall.

"I don't understand it," Izzy said. "What is the difference between mages and witches anyway? They both wield magic."

"Mages can only control an element, but they can manifest that element better than any witch ever could."

"It reminds me of the warlocks and witches back on Earth. Rhylynn said they don't get along either."

"Hate is universal," Dax said as he approached a house on the town's outskirts. "People hate what they fear. It takes a strong person not to let their fear rule them."

"You would think they would put their differences aside when their planet is dying."

"You would think." Dax stepped closer to the mud hut, peering inside.

While she waited, the prickling at her neck grew sharper, pulling taut like an invisible thread. She stumbled, her hand flying to the base of her skull. A sudden lurch sent her swaying, and she grasped Dax's jacket to steady herself. He withdrew from the wall, his smile fading.

"What's wrong, Iz?"

"I-I think my body's waking up."

"Are you sure?"

"Yes! It's like last time, but it hurts." Izzy winced as another sharp tug pulled her from Dax's arms. "Why is it hurting?" she asked, fighting to move back to his side. An unseen force seemed to drag her away again. Each step she took against it drained her strength.

Dax reached for her, pulling her into his arms. "It's going to be okay," he murmured into her hair.

Tears streaked her face as she gazed up at him. "I don't want to leave you here!"

"We'll be together again. Besides, I just found my ticket out of here."

"A guide?"

"No. It's—"

A final force yanked Izzy skyward, the air whipping around her, snatching his words away. "I love you," came his distant cry, fading in the rush of wind. He diminished to a speck in the distance, soon vanishing entirely as the pull of her waking body swept her into space. Below her, the planet shrank to a dim, red sphere, its sparse oceans mere speckles across its expanse.

Spots began to dance in her vision, and she started shaking. *Maybe I'm dying?* It was possible, but Dax hadn't seemed overly concerned—just sad. He had mentioned before that returning to her body from such a distance would be uncomfortable. Now, she was beginning to understand why. Groaning, she pulled her knees up to her chest and wrapped her arms tightly around herself.

As a slight pressure grew in her head, she felt a sudden, sharp pop. When she opened her eyes, she found herself hurtling through the Astral Plains. Far below, she could see the soft, glowing Astral Highway stretching out into the distance, winding its way through a landscape of white sand.

Soon the highway vanished, replaced by the dunes. The mounds of sand sparkled like diamonds under the starry sky, casting a dazzling glow across the landscape. A group of demonic bats hovered near the ground, their red eyes glowing as they saw her. She flew past them, disappearing from their view as she popped into another realm.

As Izzy soared through space, her eyes suddenly came to rest on a giant blue sphere. Its surface was mixed with vibrant greens and different shades of browns, and she immediately recognized it as Earth. A lightness washed over her, and the tension in her shoulders dissolved. She was home.

The brief moment of tranquility was short-lived as she neared the planet and was pulled down toward it. Overwhelmed, she closed her eyes, feeling her stomach churn and dizziness wash over her.

Her descent slowed, and she opened her eyes once more to find the town of Belleville sprawled out beneath her. The Bay of Quinte twinkled in the morning light, its surface glistening with snow. As she drew nearer, the farmland and small clusters of trees vanished from view, replaced by the distinct rooftops of urban townhouses that grew larger with every passing second.

Rhylynn's two-storey house came into view. The small, square backyard was covered in a thick blanket of snow, and the hedges lining the perimeter were barely visible. Without warning, Izzy plunged through the roof of the house, fell through the small crawl space that served as an attic, and finally landed in her friend's room.

Rhylynn was still sound asleep, with only the top of her curly brown hair poking out above the comforter. Across the room from her friend, Izzy's physical form stretched out as her eyelids fluttered, signalling the first stirrings of awakening. A gentle tug drew her toward her sleeping body, and within seconds, she was merging back with it. As a comforting warmth spread through Izzy, the world around her dimmed into darkness.

CHAPTER TWENTY-FIVE

BREAKFAST WITH BROWNIES

"Wakey wakey, eggs and bakey, give your little leg a shakey!"

Izzy groaned and rolled away, tugging her pillow over her head. "Wakey wakey, eggs and bakey, give your little leg a shakey!" the voice shrieked louder. The scent of frying bacon wafted over, and Izzy's mouth watered.

"Eggs and bacon, eggs and bacon, get your little butt a shakin'!"

"I'm awake," Izzy grumbled, pushing herself into a seated position. Across the room, Rhylynn rubbed sleep from her crusty eyes.

"Eggs and bakey, eggs and bakey," the voice continued, accompanied by the patter of tiny feet. Beside Izzy's nightstand, a miniature bacon figure danced, its slender arms flailing theatrically. In its grip, it held a plastic frying pan, a little egg nestled within.

"Wakey, wakey—"

"Jeepers! I'm awake, okay," Rhylynn mumbled, her voice muffled by the pillow. The little bacon figure nodded and trotted back into the small house perched on the nightstand's edge. Cheerful whistling floated from within as it shut the door behind itself.

"Now I am hankering for some bacon and eggs," Izzy said, swinging her legs over the bed's edge.

"Well, lucky for you, I can make that happen."

"You can magic me up some breakfast?"

Rhylynn laughed. "No, I can't do that, although that would be super convenient." She opened the door and stepped into the hall. "Come on." She beckoned to Izzy. "Mom might already have breakfast on the go."

Izzy's feet sank into the warm carpet as she stood. She followed Rhylynn, pausing at the animated photos on the stairway. Each frame played a scene from the past—Rhylynn's tentative first steps, her sister's ballet recital, their parents swaying at their wedding.

Descending, Izzy saw a snapshot of two girls decked in frilly princess attire, giggling as they painted their father's face with makeup. One of the little girls—Rhylynn—began twirling around the bed, sending a palette of eyeshadow clattering to the ground.

"Dad was always a good sport. We used to love 'making him beautiful.'" Rhylynn said, coming to stand next to Izzy.

"Is this a digital picture frame?" Izzy reached out to touch it.

"No, it's one of my mom's memories. She magicked it into the picture frame."

"Seriously?" Izzy asked, her fingers tracing the edges of the enchanted image.

"Yeah. Mom's sentimental like that. The whole house is covered in her memories." Rhylynn moved through the room but stopped to look back at Izzy. "Maybe don't go into the upstairs washroom. Some pictures are embarrassing."

"Oh, I'm totally checking it out now," Izzy replied impishly.

In the kitchen, Kalan Rivers stood by the stove, spatula in hand, while three miniature black marbles orbited her head like hyperactive satellites. "Butter for the rolls!" chirped one, zipping close to her ear.

"Of course," she sighed, pressing a hand to her forehead. "I knew I was forgetting something!"

"Morning, Mom," Rhylynn said, slipping into a chair at the kitchen table.

"Morning, sweetie," Kalan replied, setting down a plate heaped with bacon. She leaned over to peck Rhylynn's cheek. "And who's this?"

"This is Izzy, Mum," Rhylynn replied, batting away a marble as it knocked against her head. "Do you have to use these stupid things? They're annoying!"

Kalan returned to the stove, her hand sweeping protectively over the marbles. "They've come in handy on more than one occasion," she said defensively.

"They're called Lost-Ur-Marblers," Rhylynn said in a low voice to Izzy. "Mom's a bit forgetful. They're supposed to remind you about things you're forgetting to do."

"Wait until you've had children, Rhylynn. You'll use them too!"

"Doubt it," Rhylynn mumbled, biting into a strip of bacon.

Placing a plate before Izzy, Kalan offered a warm smile. "Nice to meet you," she said, tucking a strand of brown hair behind her ear. "What's your family name, dear?"

"She's not a witch, Mom."

"Oh?" Kalan said, her eyes going wide.

"It's okay, Mom. She's cool. Gran's approved."

"Lila's met her?"

"Yup. Gran's friends with Izzy's aunt."

"Well, if Lila's okay with it," Kalan said, gently squeezing Izzy's shoulder.

Thudding footsteps echoed through the hallway, punctuated by heavy grunts. The kitchen door creaked open, and a small man walked in. He struggled to carry a massive turkey that looked almost comically oversized in his thin arms. Dressed in crisp jeans and a striped t-shirt neatly tucked at the waist, he moved through the room toward Kalan. As he craned his neck past the turkey to glance at her, beads of sweat made their way down his pointed nose. Struggling to keep hold, his nails—long and sharp—sank into the bird's frozen body.

At the sight of the brownie, Izzy's muscles stiffened, and she quickly clasped her hands under the table to hide her trembling. Even though Dax had told her that not all brownies were nasty, Izzy couldn't help the unease spreading through her. After all, she had had too many negative experiences with these little creatures, and the bitterness they had left behind was hard to ignore.

The brownie also brought with it the reminder of her failure to stop Alice from using the bloodstone. Izzy pushed her plate away, her appetite lost. She felt like a fraud, sharing a meal with Rhylynn, eating her mother's food, while harbouring a secret that had put them all at risk—not just the Rivers family, but the entire world. A hollow feeling settled within her. She knew she needed to confess to her friend.

"You didn't take the turkey out to unthaw," the brownie's high-pitched voice squeaked.

Kalan groaned, taking the bird from the brownie. "Of all the things to forget! Thank you, Balmbee."

Balmbee beamed a yellow-toothed grin at her as he said, "*The Price is Right* is on, but if you need help . . ."

"I'll manage. Go watch your show," Kalan said, waving him away. As Balmbee scampered out of the room, she sighed and looked down at the turkey, her mouth curving downward. One of the marbles bounced against her head, and she swatted at it. "Stupid thing," she muttered, "why didn't you remind me about this!"

"Try a warming spell, Mom."

"I can't. It would start cooking in some spots . . ."

"Do you want me to call Gran? I bet she would know what to do."

Kalan's eyebrows knit together as she looked up at Rhylynn. "Absolutely not! And don't you go mentioning this to her either, Rhy Rhy." Clutching the turkey, she left the room, grumbling about defrosting it in the bathtub.

"Mom's a bit proud," Rhylynn commented, taking a big bite of bacon. "She married into a strong line of witches, so she's probably embarrassed about not knowing a simple defrosting spell."

"Is Lila her mother?"

"No, Gran is dad's mom. We are having a late Christmas dinner with Mom's family tonight—hence the turkey. Dad's already left to pick up my grandmother from the airport."

Rhylynn deftly speared some fluffy pancakes from the centre of the table and placed them carefully on her plate. The sweet aroma of maple syrup filled the air as she poured it on her food.

In contrast, a sourness filled Izzy's mouth. She remained quiet for a moment, watching Rhylynn eat. With Kalan gone from the room, this was the time to tell Rhylynn about Alice Dame. But where to start? "So, Balmbee is your mother's brownie, then?" Izzy asked. "He seemed . . . nice. Where's yours?"

"Oh, Grizzel is on vacation in Florida right now. She hates winter, so she usually goes for a couple of weeks each year. Does wonders for her attitude, I think." She paused, syrup dripping from her fork as she looked at Izzy. "You know about brownies too?"

"I've seen Emily's before, and last night I met some more . . ."

"You met some more last night?" Rhylynn's fork clattered against her plate as she dropped it. She leaned forward, almost tipping over her glass of orange juice. "You astral projected again, didn't you?"

Reluctantly, Izzy recounted everything that transpired overnight. Once she finished, her gaze remained fixed on the ground, unable to meet Rhylynn's eyes.

"I'm so, so sorry, Rhy Rhy," she said, her voice coming out thick.

"For what?"

"I handed the bloodstone over to Alice. I'm the reason you're in danger now."

"Izzy, that prediction is so vague . . . and honestly, this Marlo character sounds pretty shady. I wouldn't be surprised if he made it all up to pressure you to get the talisman. What kind of god goes around collecting dark artifacts anyway?"

"Dax is sure that Marlo is a god of light."

"Maybe . . . It's just a prediction though. Half of them never come true. The future is unpredictable."

"Even if you're right, I still allowed a dark witch access to a powerful object. She's unstoppable now."

"She's not unstoppable. Just because she can live forever doesn't mean she's invincible."

"So . . . you're not worried?"

Rhylynn pushed her glasses up on her nose. "Oh, I'm worried! Alice Dame is well known in the witch community. She's bat crap crazy! I need to tell my Gran right away so she can update the World Council of Supernatural Beings."

With a groan, Izzy let her head fall onto the table. "So, it is a huge deal then!"

"It's a huge deal. But Izzy, don't underestimate the value of saving someone you love. You faced a difficult choice, and most people would have made the same one. I mean, as annoying as my little sister is, I would have given Alice the talisman too, to save her life."

Izzy raised her head to meet Rhylynn's gaze. "I need to make things right, Rhy. I have to help stop Alice."

"*You* aren't doing anything. This is a witch problem. Alice was already dangerous before she drank that potion. You need to stay away from her. Let the council take care of it."

"I'm not weak. I can help."

"I'm not saying that you are. This just isn't your problem. You already have enough to deal with from the sounds of it. The Queen of Nightmares wants you dead, remember?"

"Dax is—"

"Looking into it on his end. You told me. But until he gets help, you need to watch your back. You can't do that if you're hunting down Alice Dame."

"I guess you're right."

"I am right," Rhylynn said, getting up to clear the table. She placed the dishes in the sink, where the sponge sprang to life and coated them in a generous lather of soap from the dispenser.

"I need to head to Gran's for training. You're welcome to stay here if you like. Dinner should be interesting. Mom does not get along with her mother."

I can relate, Izzy thought, thinking of her own mom. She fiddled with the ring on her finger, her thumb rubbing over the smooth surface of the gem. Her chest felt heavy, weighed down by the guilt of having not returned her mother's call.

Her adventures with Dax—almost losing him—had given her a better understanding of Michelle Adams. Her mother had lived through her dad's death. It made sense that she'd been left with a profound fear of loss, a fear that now extended to her three children.

I need to call Mom. She's probably worried something happened to me. She stood and ran a hand through her tangled hair. "Thanks for the invite, but I can't stay. I need to go back to Toronto."

Rhylynn raised an eyebrow. "Toronto? You literally just came from there."

"I know . . . but it's my mom. I need to talk to her in person. It's important."

"Everything okay?"

"Yup."

"You need to talk about it?"

"Maybe later. It's a heavy topic."

"I can make time."

Izzy smiled at her friend. "I know you can. But honestly, it's okay, Rhy Rhy. I'm fine. You should go talk to your grandma. She needs to know about Alice Dame. We'll catch up later this week."

An hour later, Rhylynn pulled up to the apartment complex, where Izzy's car sat, just as she had left it the night before. They sat in silence for a moment. Finally, Izzy reached for the door handle. She paused as Rhylynn's hand settled on her shoulder. "It's going to be all right, Iz," her friend said, hugging her.

"I know. I get it. It's stupid for me to go after a dark witch. It's better to leave it up to your council."

Pulling back, Rhylynn's lips curled into a half-smile. "Yeah. But I was talking about your mom. Whatever's going on, she'll forgive you. Mothers always do."

Izzy rolled her eyes. "You don't know my mom."

"You're right. She raised you. She must be just awful."

"You're hilarious, you know that?"

"I have my moments," Rhylynn said, pushing her glasses back up her nose. "Seriously, Iz. If you need to, call me. I'm a good listener."

"Thanks, Rhy Rhy, for everything. I would be totally lost without you."

"You're a part of the supernatural community now, Iz," Rhylynn replied, gazing at Izzy with a sombre expression. "I'll always have your back."

"And I'll always have yours," Izzy said, stepping out of the car.

She was immediately greeted by a gust of frigid wind biting her cheeks and nose. Wincing, she squinted as she watched Rhylynn pull out of the parking lot.

Izzy continued to wave as Rhylynn's truck squealed around the corner and out of sight. Her teeth chattering, she made her way to her own vehicle and settled into the cold leather seat. Despite turning the heat to its maximum, the warmth blowing from the vents did little to dispel the icy feeling building inside her.

It would be a long drive to Toronto, and there would be no warm reception when she arrived. Rhylynn didn't know her mother. Michelle didn't handle change well, and her need for control had intensified over the past year. She would never forgive Izzy for going against her carefully laid-out plans.

CHAPTER TWENTY-SIX

THAWING HEARTS

Izzy needed to make a pitstop before returning to Toronto. She wanted to shower and freshen up before seeing her mother again. The side streets were still snowy, and her Honda Civic almost got trapped twice in the drifts on her way back to Loyalist College. Izzy's shoulders sagged when she finally caught sight of the residence building beyond the treeline. As she pulled into the parking lot, her car skidded on a patch of ice, narrowly missing Arlo's car. She wrestled for control of her vehicle and managed to slide it into the spot next to his.

Closing her eyes, Izzy rested her head against the steering wheel, willing her pulse to slow down. That had been too close. *Arlo would have killed me!* She glanced up at her friend's car and immediately wished she hadn't. Melanie strolled past on her way to her own vehicle, and their eyes met.

Melanie paused, her face lightening up as she recognized Izzy. And then her smile fell, curving downward as a blush spread along her cheeks. Izzy's gaze turned icy as Melanie scurried to her car, skidding across the slick pavement.

Izzy held her breath, silently hoping her roommate would fall, then turned away, her face burning. She knew that wasn't a nice thought.

She waited until Melanie had left before slowly entering the residence building. The hallway reeked of wet shoes, the carpet damp with slush from outside. Wrinkling her nose, Izzy hurried down the hall to her apartment door and pulled hard on the handle.

The door swung open, hitting the wall with a loud clang. *Someone must have oiled it over the holidays*, Izzy thought. She walked into the kitchen, sighing at seeing dirty dishes stacked in the sink. *At least it's not a spaghetti mess this time.*

Arlo and Vishvesh sat in the alcove, cards spread before them. They looked up as she entered the room. Arlo grinned at her, his freckles standing out against his pale face.

"Hey, Izzy-bo-bizzy. You just getting back now?" he asked, setting his cards aside.

"Hey, guys," she replied, collapsing into a chair beside Vishvesh. "I got in last night, actually. I stayed over at Rhylynn's place. What about you?"

"Vishvesh ditched me for his girlfriend, so I hung out here," Arlo said, grumbling.

Vishvesh rolled his eyes and gave Arlo a playful kick under the table. "Stop acting like I deserted you." Turning to Izzy, he added, "He was here all night with Melanie."

Arlo shifted position, suddenly interested in a nearby plant. Izzy sighed. "Arlo, it's okay. I don't care if you hang out with her. She's your friend too."

His green eyes brightened, and he straightened up in his seat. "Oh, good. So, does that mean that you're going to come back to the MonkeyShiners?" he asked, referring to their group of pranksters.

"You're the only one who calls it that."

"It's a good name," Arlo said, shrugging. "So, are you?"

Izzy glanced over at Emily's closed door, her thoughts drifting back to the prank she had pulled on her roommate last term. She hadn't meant for it to be cruel, but it hadn't gone the way she'd planned, and now Emily hated her even more. *My roommate is a witch!* She shivered, pulling her coat tighter around her. No, she was done with pranks and told Arlo as much.

"Are you sure," he said, his smile faltering. "It's not the same without you."

"I'm sure . . . I need to focus on school anyway. Get my grades up so I can get into university."

Vishvesh's eyes lit up. "You applied? Good for you! Does your mom know?" Vishvesh knew all about her family troubles. One afternoon, he had found her in tears, sitting in her car, and she'd spilled everything. He'd listened—truly listened—because he understood. He faced similar pressures from his own family back in India.

"Yeah, she knows. It didn't go over so well," Izzy said, shrugging. Vishvesh's eyes softened, his fingers pressing gently on her arm.

Arlo cleared his throat loudly and leaned back in his chair. A weak smile played on his lips as he stared at Izzy. "Speaking of your mother . . . she's here. In your room."

"What?" Izzy bolted to her feet. "She's here?" She turned to stare at her door, the blood rushing to her face. *Mom's here? Why?*

"She got here last night," Alro continued. "She spent the night when she realized you had gone out."

"You couldn't have told me that when I first came in?"

"I didn't think about it. She's really cool, actually. Ordered in pizza for Mel and I."

"She bought you pizza?"

Arlo slumped down in his seat. "I think she might have felt bad for us . . . it being New Year's Eve and us without anywhere to go." He glared at Vishvesh as he said the last part.

"Arlo, you knew I had plans with Tabby! Quit—"

"I should go see why she's here," Izzy said, turning away from them. Leaving her roommates to their bickering, she approached her bedroom slowly. The knob was cool to the touch as she turned it and stepped inside.

Michelle Adams lay curled on Izzy's bed, the quilt pulled to her chin. Her face was pale, and dark circles stood out starkly under her eyes. Izzy paused for a moment, listening to her mother's soft breathing. Michelle appeared fragile, a characteristic Izzy had never associated with her.

Her throat tightened as she gazed at her mom. *Why is she here?* Michelle had made the journey from Toronto on New Year's Eve, treated Izzy's roommates to pizza, and spent the night in her dorm room. It was entirely out of character for her, leaving Izzy uneasy.

She clutched the doorframe, her knees weakening as different scenarios flooded her mind, each more unsettling than the last. *Oh god, what if something happened to Eddie or Kate?* She shook her head, tossing away that idea. No, her phone had been silent all night. If her siblings had been hurt, her mother would have kept calling her—not spent the night waiting for her to come home.

Michelle stirred, her body stretching out on the bed. She yawned, her eyes blinking open. Spotting Izzy, she sat up abruptly, the quilt slipping down to reveal her day clothes—jeans and a sweater—still on from the night before. *Also out of character*, Izzy thought.

"Morning, Mom."

"Isabelle, I—What time is it?"

"Almost noon."

Michelle yawned again, her hands coming up to scrub at her face. Strands of blond hair tumbled over her forehead, matted and oily—an unusual sight.

"Mom . . . are you okay?"

Michelle's eyes lifted, her expression blank. "Am I okay?"

"It's just that, well, it's weird for you to be here . . . You've never come up to visit me before."

Her mother flinched. "Yes. I know. I should have." She exhaled heavily and ran her fingers through her hair. "Your father was much better at this," she mumbled.

"Why are you here, Mom?"

Michelle gestured to the space beside her on the bed. "Please come sit down, Isabelle." She waited until Izzy had settled down next to her and pulled her into a hug.

Izzy tensed, her body stiffening under her mother's touch. Hugging wasn't her mother's thing, and it felt unnatural. But as Michelle held on, Izzy's resistance fell away, and she melted into the rare comfort of her mom's arms.

"Isabelle . . . Izzy, I've had a lot to think about this last week."

"Mom, it's—"

"Shush. Let me finish," Michelle said, loosening her grip on Izzy as she turned to face her. "New Year's Eve was always special for your father and me, particularly as you kids grew up and started doing your own thing. We never went out. Instead, we'd stay home, watch a movie, dance, and drink champagne at midnight."

Izzy nodded, remaining silent. She had never really known how her parents spent New Year's Eve. She had always assumed they had gone out like everyone else. This revelation surprised her. It sounded almost romantic, not something she expected from her mother.

"Last night was difficult for me," Michelle continued, her voice low. "I was home, just like in previous years. But this time, I was alone. I'll always be alone . . . Your father is gone." Izzy watched as Michelle winced at her own words, tears welling up in her eyes. "So, I played a home video. I just wanted to see your father again, even if only on a screen. I even closed my eyes and listened to his voice, imagining him beside me."

"Mom . . ."

They sat silently for a moment, emotion thick in the air. Michelle finally cleared her throat and resumed her story. "It was a home video about you, Izzy."

"Me?"

"Yes, your father was teaching you how to swim. It was at Crowe Lake in Marmora. Do you remember going there?"

"Vaguely."

"It's a lovely town up near Madoc. We had rented a cottage for the week. Your father dragged us to the beach every day. He used to go swimming there with his friends when he was a kid. In the video, he was trying to teach you to float, but you wouldn't take off your life jacket."

A smile flickered across Izzy's lips as the memory came alive again. "He told me to face my fear, or I'd never learn to swim. Something like that, right?"

"Yes, and you listened. You took it off, and soon after, you were floating," Michelle replied, her voice softening. She took a deep breath, reached out, and gently took Izzy's hands.

"Izzy, watching that video made me realize something. You, Kate, and Eddie—I've been trying to be your life preserver."

"What?" Izzy replied, her gaze fixed blankly on her mother.

"I've been holding you and your siblings close, too afraid to let you find your own paths. I-I can't bear the thought of losing you like I lost your father," Michelle said, her voice faltering. She closed her eyes and whispered, "If I lost you too . . . I don't think I could survive it." Her shoulders drooped. "But it's not fair to any of you. I need to let go—to face my fears. For your sake, I need to let you float on your own."

"Mom—"

"I'm not finished," Michelle said, wiping her face. She turned to Izzy again, her eyes red-rimmed. "I'm far from being a perfect mother. I've come to realize that. I've always ensured that you never wanted for anything. But I've never really given you myself."

She paused, reaching over to grab a tissue from the box on the side table near Izzy's bed, then dabbed at her eyes. "I don't know you," she continued. "I don't know your likes or dislikes, your hobbies . . ." She stopped to wipe her face again. "And I should know all those things. I've been so focused on my job, on pushing my career on you. I-I've failed you as a mother."

"Mom, it's okay."

"It's not okay, Izzy. I should've done better. I *will* do better!" Michelle stroked Izzy's hair. "I've been so lost without your father . . . It's not an excuse. I know I've never been a warm mom, but my grief made it worse. I-I'm so sorry."

Warmth radiated throughout Izzy as she stared into her mother's brown eyes. For the first time in a long time, they weren't cold. She leaned into her mother, wrapping her arms tightly around her.

"I love you," her mom finally said, kissing Izzy's head.

"Love you too, Mom."

"I want you to be happy. If going to university is what you want, then I support you."

"Are you sure?"

"Yes. I've already spoken with Kate. She has agreed to take over the Belleville location. Eddie and Lyssa will run the Toronto home once I retire. Lyssa will need additional schooling, of course."

"And Lyssa is okay with that?"

"Yes."

Izzy exhaled deeply, her tension melting away. She thought she had lost another parent—that her mother wouldn't want her around. But she had been wrong about Michelle. It was clear now that they both had much to discover about each other.

She leaned closer to her mom, breathing in the sweet scent of her perfume—jasmine and honey. *I never want this moment to end.* And then Michelle's stomach emitted a comical gurgle.

Her mother pulled back. "Oh, excuse me," she murmured, pressing a hand to her belly with a sheepish smile. "I'm famished."

"That's what happens when you sleep until noon, Mom," Izzy said, laughing. "Shouldn't have been up all night partying with a bunch of college kids."

Michelle's face flushed a deep shade of red. "I wasn't partying with your friends!"

"That's not what they said."

"What?"

"You bought them pizza."

"Well, yes. I showed up unannounced, and they had no plans for New Year's Eve. I felt bad for them."

"Arlo's very taken with you now."

"What!" Michelle flinched, her mouth gaping open. Izzy fought to keep her expression neutral, but her mom must have seen the teasing glint in her eyes. Grabbing the pillow, she playfully thwacked Izzy on the head.

"Not funny," Michelle said, her jaw twitching.

"Kind of funny—and not far from the truth. He thinks you're really nice."

Ignoring Izzy's comment, Michelle stood and stretched, arching her back. Her stomach rumbled again.

"I'm sure there's leftover pizza if you're hungry."

"Cold pizza? I don't think so." Michelle approached Izzy's coat rack and grabbed her jacket. "Isn't there an IHOP near here? Come on. My treat."

As she followed her mom into the bright afternoon sunshine, Izzy tilted her head up, relishing in the warm glow that matched her happiness. Despite the frigid wind whipping around them, her joy remained undiminished.

Her relationship with her mother had taken an unexpected turn, and things were finally starting to look up in her life. Sure, she still had a demonic queen who wanted her dead to contend with, but she had the support of the supernatural community—Rhylynn, Mrs. Rivers, and Lovepreet. Things were changing in both her worlds, but she wasn't alone. With her friends and family on one side and Dax waiting for her on the other, she would never be again.

EPILOGUE

Darkness surrounded Dax, clinging to his skin like an unwelcome embrace. It was so dark, at times, he questioned whether his eyes were even open. Dax shuddered in the cramped space, his arms wrapped tightly around his body. It was so cold.

Squeezing his eyes shut, Dax concentrated on shutting off his senses. It was second nature to him. He should be able to do it. Nothing happened.

How is it not working? I shouldn't feel anything.

But he felt everything—the biting cold that numbed his feet, the cramp in his leg from standing for so long, and the scrape on his face from the stone that pressed against him. It was tortuous.

That was what demons thrived in—torture. And they had found a new way to torture souls. He squatted, which was all the space allowed him to do. The pressure eased a bit—for now. Soon his calves would start burning and he would have to stand again. It was an endless cycle that left his legs weak and trembling.

His thoughts drifted to his soulmate, her blue eyes piercing through the darkness of his mind. Those eyes—they could be warm and playful one moment and transform into an icy stare in the next, making even the bravest person fumble in their steps. They were beautiful. And he would never see them again.

Izzy.

Tears crested Dax's eyelids, frosting over his lashes. He was so grateful that she had been pulled away, and not a moment too soon. *She's safe,* he reassured himself. And then he remembered—Mara was coming for her.

He felt his pulse pounding in his throat and leaned his forehead against the slab of rock trapping him, overcome by a wave of dizziness. There wasn't anything he could do to save his soulmate. No one knew where he was. No one was coming for him.

This is hell.

Shattered By Darkness

After surviving another attack from an enemy, Izzy Adams discovers that her soulmate, Dax, is missing. Joined by his sister, Maddy, she begins a new mission in the spirit realm. Their path leads them through the Kingdom of Nachtmahr, where they encounter demonic assaults, imprisonment, and intense heartbreak. Throughout her journey, Izzy forges unexpected alliances and uncovers deeper secrets of the spirit world that threaten to cost her everything.

About the Author

Jessica Lee Sheppard lives in rural Ontario with her husband and four children. Her debut novel, *The Adventures of Izzy Adams: Descending into Darkness*, draws inspiration from her daughters, Izzy and Rhylynn. Jessica graduated with a degree in psychology from York University, a social services worker diploma from Loyalist College, and a master's degree in social work from Windsor University. Her diverse experiences spanning mental health, child welfare, and education infuse her stories with depth and understanding.

When she's not writing, Jessica enjoys gardening, reading, and serial-watching television shows she puts off to write. Aside from establishing a successful writing career, Jessica dreams of watching her children grow into happy adults and of one day travelling to Greece.

Sign up for Jessica's newsletter for exclusive offers, insider content, and updates on new releases.

Join the Community!

Dive deeper into the "Adventures of Izzy Adams" series. Connect with Jessica on social media for discussions, giveaways, sneak peeks, and more!

- Facebook
- Twitter
- TikTok
- Instagram
- YouTube
- LinkedIn
- Goodreads

For updates and exclusives, visit jessicaleesheppard.com